THE ODYSSEY OF
NATH DRAGON
BOOK 1

Exiled

CRAIG HALLORAN

Exiled
The Odyssey of Nath Dragon Book #1
By Craig Halloran
Copyright © 2017 by Craig Halloran
Print Edition

TWO-TEN BOOK PRESS
P.O. Box 4215, Charleston, WV 25364

ISBN eBook: 978-1-946218-24-7
ISBN Paperback: 978-1-979519-81-6

www.craighalloran.com

Edited by Rachel Hert

Publisher's Note
This book is a work of fiction. Names, characters, places, and incidents either are the product of the author's imagination or are used fictitiously, and any resemblance to actual persons, living or dead, events, or locales is entirely coincidental.

CHAPTER 1

ITH THE COOL AIR OF the higher altitude in his face, Nath let out a joyous howl. "Wooooweeeeeee!" He was flying. Not under his own power, but something vastly bigger and more powerful, with great wings that spanned over a hundred feet. Those wings flapped with mighty strength, propelling them higher and faster. They were dragon wings. The wings of his father. "Go faster, Father! Higher!" Nath's strong voice was almost drowned out against the wind that rushed through his hair.

"If we go too high, you'll get too cold," Balzurth, the dragon beneath him, said. His voice was easily heard, rich, loud, and full of wisdom. "I can't have you freezing to death on your one-hundredth-year celebration."

"I'll be fine!" Nath slapped his father's broad neck. Balzurth's scales were red, some flecked with gold, and shone like newly polished armor. Two grand horns adorned the top of his head. He was huge, magnificent, and most importantly, the king of the dragons. Nath climbed up between the two horns. Standing on the top of Balzurth's skull, he wrapped his arms around one of the horns, which was much taller than him. "Higher, Father! Higher!"

"It's *your* celebration day." Balzurth's long neck bent, turning his face in Nath's direction. His golden eyes were bigger than Nath's own head. "Hold fast, son. I don't want to lose you."

"I will. I promise."

Balzurth gave a nod. His wings pounded the air in slow, monstrous strokes, lifting them higher and faster. He punched through the clouds, plunging them into a sea of mist. Seconds later, they broke through the mist, and the clouds stretched out like a field of cotton below them. He skimmed the top of the clouds then rose even higher.

Nath's flame-red hair whipped like a banner behind him. The wind stung his eyes. His heart raced like a team of horses. Tingling with energy from head to toe, he spread one arm out wide and let out another elated cry at the top of his lungs. "Wooooooo-weeeeeeeeeeee!"

Balzurth continued upward.

Nath's teeth chattered. His nose and ears felt like icicles. He didn't care. He loved flying with his father. Nothing in all the world thrilled him more. But he dreamed of flying on his own one day. To soar through the heavens on his own—nothing could be more wonderful.

"Are you getting cold yet?" Balzurth asked.

With his teeth clacking together, he replied, "No."

"Hah!" Balzurth's huge body shuddered with rumbles from laughter. He turned his head slightly and puffed out a blast of steam.

The gust of hot air warmed Nath up instantly. "Ahhh," he moaned. "That felt so good."

Together, they rode the skies for hours. Balzurth blasted through flocks of birds. He dipped, dived, and barrel-rolled. Nath clung to his father like drying paint. Nothing in the world could wipe the smile from his face.

"Father, will you take me over the cities? I haven't seen them since I was very little," he said.

Balzurth's scales rippled beneath Nath's feet. For a moment, his wings skipped a beat. "You are still little."

"No, I'm not. I'm a hundred years old." Nath pulled a lock of his hair from his mouth with his finger. "That's older than most people live."

"How do you know that?"

"Maefon told me."

"That elf has a big mouth," Balzurth grumbled.

"She said elves, aside from dragons, live the longest, as much as a thousand years or so. The dwarves and gnomes live for centuries, but humans and orcs whittle away long before they are one hundred. She says that is because they are so inferior. She says they live foolishly and lack self-control."

"Maefon says a lot that she should not be saying," Balzurth said. "I need to have a talk with her."

"Why?"

"Well, there are many things that I prefer are not mentioned in Dragon Home. The elves are our guests, and they need to follow the rules of the dragons." Balzurth's head dipped. He scanned the forests and grasslands miles below them. "The world of the races is very complex, Nath, and I don't want the elves telling you about them. The elves that serve us have proven good and trustworthy, but their view of the other races can be jaded. I prefer to teach you myself, when the time comes. Do you understand?"

"Is now the time?"

"Soon."

"But I want to know now. They sound exciting. Maefon says I look like a human. She says I look like a young man or old child, but I'm man size. You know, big."

Balzurth shook his head. "You still have growing to do yet. Be patient."

"Ugh!" Nath rolled his eyes. "But you sleep sometimes five and ten years at a time. Can't you tell me more now? I'm one hundred. That's older than most people ever live. I'm ready to know, Father. You've even said yourself..." Nath imitated Balzurth's deep voice,

"'You're never too young to be ready.' At least you say that in regards to my chores."

"We'll talk about it later," Balzurth said. Beating his wings harder and faster, he picked up speed.

Swept away in the moment, Nath closed his eyes as they dipped down and went higher, and spread out both arms. For several moments, it felt like he was flying on his own. His body spun in the air, and he plummeted toward the earth. He caught a glimpse of his father. Balzurth was going up. Nath was going down. He stretched out his arms and yelled, "Father!"

CHAPTER 2

ACK FACING THE GROUND RUSHING to greet him a few
thousand feet below, Nath looked skyward to his father.
Balzurth's humongous frame had become little more than a
speck. He called out again, shrieking in the wind. "Father! Father!"
He lost sight of his father when he passed through the blanket of
clouds. Spreading his arms and legs out, he twisted in the air, rotating
himself so that he faced downward. The trees seemed so far away at
first, but they were getting larger.

Guzan! This is bad!

His efforts slowed his fall as he cupped his hands while keeping
his chest toward the world. Everything below him that had once
appeared beautiful and peaceful now rushed upward, ready to destroy
him.

"Father!" Nath's cheeks flapped against the gusting air. The wind
roared in his ears. He spun out of control. The green treetops of
the forest no longer appeared like somewhere he could make a soft
landing. The trees spread apart, revealing seams and cavities of sharp
rocks waiting like gnashing teeth that would swallow his broken
corpse whole. "Faaaatherrrrrrrrr!"

Seconds from being dashed on the rocks, four small metallic-blue dragons, half the size of Nath, darted in from nowhere. They latched their talons onto his wrists and ankles. Their claws dug deep into his skin as their wings beat, slowing Nath's death-defying fall.

"Ow!" he said, wincing. "You don't have to wound me, though I am thankful, little brothers." The group of dragons flew Nath upward, making a straight line for Balzurth, who'd just burst through the clouds. The dragon king's golden eyes smoldered like cauldrons of boiling gold. "Uh-oh."

"Take him to the ground, my life-saving blue razors." Flying alongside them, Balzurth glared at Nath. "You and I are going to have a long talk!"

Twenty feet above a clearing in the forest, the blue razors' talons released. "Whulp!" Nath landed hard on his feet and fell down. Eyeing the dragons who'd just saved him, he said, "You could have been a little gentler!"

The blue razors flew in a tight circle, flicked their tongues at him, then darted away with alarming speed. In two seconds, they were out of sight. He dusted off his hands. A tremendous shadow fell over his shoulders. Tree branches popped and snapped beneath Balzurth as he landed right behind him. Unlike most dragons, Balzurth's arms and legs were longer, giving him a more human-like appearance when he stood. "Heh, that was a close one, wasn't it, Father?"

Sitting on his rear legs, with his front arms crossed, Balzurth said, "You could have died!"

"I know I'll never die if you are around." Nath dusted off his knees.

Balzurth's tail swept Nath off his feet. He flipped head over heels, landing hard on his rear end. "I do not command power over life and death. Who will protect you when I am not around? Hmmmm? Would you have pulled off such a stunt if I was not there? Hmmmm?" He snorted out a hot blast of air. "No! Of course not, so why do it at all? You did this the last time, and the time before that. And you wonder why I don't take you flying more. I wouldn't have even considered it today if it wasn't your hundredth year of celebration." Balzurth's tail rose over his head. It hung there for a moment, swaying a little from side to side, then *wham!* It came down like a great cedar. "I thought you would have wised up more by now! I am disappointed!"

Nath shrank beneath his father's heavy stare. The hard scales on Balzurth's heaving chest heated to a brilliant orange color. At any moment, Nath expected flames to explode out of his father's mouth. He'd seen those flames before. The purifying, scalding heat destroyed anything it touched in an instant. With his head down and trembling, he said, "I'm sorry, but I just want to fly like my brothers and sisters."

"You still have a defiant tone, Nath. You lack patience. And you know, Sultans of Sulfur, you know that you cannot fly without wings. Do you see the wingless red rock dragons try to fly?" Balzurth poked him in the chest with a massive talon. "Do you? No, because that would be foolish."

Nath's trembling stopped. He sat up cross-legged. "Well, that's only because all they do is bask in lava. They are the laziest dragons I've ever seen."

"They do more than that. You just don't pay attention."

Nath rolled his eyes. "I know, I know, the red rocks protect the border and enrich the soils." He picked at the grasses, plucking out handful after handful and tossing it aside. "I don't think they are capable of much more."

"They serve their purpose."

"And what is my purpose? I don't even know that. You won't tell me. I know I'm a dragon born a man. The only dragon who talks to me in the Mountain of Doom—"

"Don't call Dragon Home that."

"Fine then." Nath held up a finger. "Let me rephrase. The only dragon that talks to me in the Mountain of Boring is you. All of the other dragons ignore me. Why that is, I don't know, and you won't tell me, but I'm positive that it's because I don't have any scales and they do."

"I've seen you engage with the other dragons plenty of times. You wrestled quite well against them. It makes me smile when you do that."

"They don't like me. None of them do. They treat the elves better."

"Friendships and trust take time to build. Dragons can be very picky and peculiar."

"That's an understatement." Nath hopped up. "When do you see it, when you sleep, one, five, ten years at a time. And look at this." He showed Balzurth his wrists. They were bleeding where the blue razors latched onto him. "They didn't have to dig in to me like I'm some varmint they snatch from the trees."

"That's the thanks they get?" Balzurth shook his head. "That's hardly a scratch. And don't try to deflect this argument away from the subject at hand. You did something foolish, and you will be punished for it."

"I'm sorry… and I'm glad I'm saved, just surprised. I didn't think other dragons really cared." Nath picked up a rock and chucked it high over the trees. "But it's my celebration day."

"Yes, and you need to make the most of it, because tomorrow, you will reap what you have wrought."

"And what will that be?"

Balzurth lowered himself and said, "Get on. You'll find out tomorrow."

With his shoulders slumped, Nath climbed onto his father's back. *Please, please, please don't let this day end.*

CHAPTER 3

WITH SWEAT ON HIS BROW and running down his back, Nath dug the shovel into a pile of coins. They clinked together with a distinctive metallic sound unique to the precious metal. He dumped the hundreds of coins into a half-empty wooden wheelbarrow. This was the twentieth load of the day, and the huge pile of treasure didn't look any smaller now than when he started. He kept digging, dumping in shovelful after shovelful of gold and silver coins, accented by countless precious stones such as diamonds, emeralds, rubies, and pearls. It wasn't all loose coins and gems either, but necklaces, bracelets, tiaras, chalices, silverware, and gilded china plates.

Shirtless, Nath stopped shoveling and dabbed his face on a towel woven from gold-colored cotton. "I hate this punishment. It's boring. I'd rather have the dragon switch taken to me a hundred times than this." His eyes swept the massive chamber. Treasure was stacked almost as high as his chin from one side of the chamber to the other. Back in the corners, it was stacked up even higher. His father once told him that this treasure throne room had more treasure than all of the kingdoms combined times a hundred. Nath never had a hard time believing it. But now, the treasure just seemed to sit there, useless.

He shoveled until the wheelbarrow was filled over the brim, dropped the shovel, lifted up the handles, and started pushing. The front wheel squeaked as he went down the paths between the piles. The sound echoed off the towering arches of the vaulted ceiling. The chamber had to be plenty big for the largest dragon of all, Balzurth, and there was ample room for him in there, even when he was standing. The chamber could hold two dozen dragons the size of Balzurth if needed.

Rolling by Balzurth's throne, Nath came to a stop. It was a huge armless and backless seat made from polished stone. It was more than big enough for Balzurth. Its design was simple, all stone, with some precious stones that twinkled in the ancient engravings. It was the most dominating object in the room, but out of place somehow. It seemed lonely. Balzurth used to sit on the throne and tell Nath stories that lasted for hours. The dragon king was a grand storyteller. They were some of the best times, but as he became older, the stories became old and a little boring. Balzurth, once he started, was very long winded. And the names he spoke of seemed to get longer and take forever.

Nath patted the leg of the throne. "Don't run off anywhere. You might be my seat one day, though I find it hard to believe that I'll be so impossibly big at the rate I'm growing." He eyed the grand murals on the walls behind the throne. The painted images showed dragons of all sorts and kinds—flying through the skies, nestled in caves, or snaking through the willowwacks. All the images seemed to move ever so slightly with life of their own. It wasn't an illusion. He could leave and come back days later, and all of the images would have moved elsewhere completely. This was where he came when he was younger and his father taught him about the dozens of kinds of dragons. Nath learned about their powers, too. The only thing he never learned was how to get them to like him.

He sighed through his nose and resumed his trek to the other side of the throne room. Coming to the end of the path, he dumped out the treasure and sat down. "Twenty loads down, nine hundred and eighty to go. That should do it, anyway." He picked up a coin and flicked it with his fingers. It shot across the room, hitting an adjacent pile. A waterfall of coins skidded down, revealing the edge of a picture frame. There were plenty of paintings in the chamber. The largest ones, even bigger than Nath, were propped against the walls. Some of them hung from the gigantic pylons and pillars that held up spots in the vaulted ceiling.

Nath crossed the path, climbed up the pile of treasure, and wiggled out the painting. It was wider than his shoulders were broad and even longer than he was tall. He held it out. It was a portrait of a lovely woman against the backdrop of a star-filled sky. Her wavy platinum locks framed her fair skin. Her soft, pale lips smiled slightly as her head tilted a little to the side. Her extraordinary eyes sparkled like diamonds. The detail was so realistic Nath found himself trying to find his breath. He'd seen plenty of elves and some pictures of humans, but no woman was anything like this.

"Whoa. She's a gorgeous thing, isn't she?" a playful woman's voice stated.

Nath jumped and dropped the painting. "Maefon, quit sneaking up on me! You aren't even supposed to be here!"

"Oh, it looks like someone is in love with the pretty woman in the painting. Kissy-kissy."

Nath frowned at her.

"Oh, Nath, don't be mad. She's very fetching for what appears to be a human woman. And the work is extraordinary." She squatted down with her dark eyes fastened on the picture. Maefon's flaxen hair was pulled back in a braid. She seemed about Nath's age and had been his closet companion since she arrived a few decades ago. In a way, they had grown up together, though she was more mature. She had a teardrop face, cat-shaped eyes that caught everything, and a dazzling smile that a blind man could see. Her sleeveless shirt was buttoned up to her neck just below the chin, and she wore all black from neck to toe. It was a casual ensemble that fit snugly on her elven frame. She cocked her head. "Do you love her, Nath?"

"Stop being silly. How can I love her? I just saw her." He picked up the picture. "But she certainly is worthy of my attention. If I didn't know better, I'd say that she is almost as striking as me."

Holding her stomach, Maefon erupted with laughter. "Oh, you are so vain. You, good looking—now that's rich. Why, you are the most unhandsome dragon I ever saw."

He tossed his hair. "That's only because I look like a human."

"You are only an average human at best." She climbed to the top of the pile and stuck her face in front of the picture. "Unlike me, who is the prettiest of the elves."

"You always say that, and I know you don't mean it. Your eyes stay glued to me even when you think I don't know you are looking." Eyes narrowing, he said, "I wonder who this is?"

Maefon grabbed the painting. Trying to pull the picture out of his grip, she said, "It's nobody real because no human looks like this. It's inhuman. Something from a dream. Trust me."

"You don't know. I think it's real. It could only be real, even if it is otherworldly. Maybe she lives beyond the murals."

"Maybe she's been dead millennia already. Who cares?" She yanked the frame out of his grasp.

"Careful," Nath said with a smile.

Maefon's eyes grew big. She fought for balance and footing. Coins slid beneath her feet. "Whoa! This is heavy!" She fell backward and slid down the hill of coins all the way to the bottom. An avalanche of coins covered her completely. Only her hands were still stuck out, holding the picture frame. There was a muffled "Help me!" coming from under the pile.

Nath slid down the pile, picked up the picture, and gently set it aside. Kneeling, he dusted treasure from her face. "That picture frame was heavy, wasn't it?"

She spit out a ruby as big as her knuckle. "I hate you."

He reached into the coins, grabbed her hand, and pulled her out. "I know. I hate you too."

They both burst out laughing.

CHAPTER 4

"**N**ATH, ARE YOU FINISHED YET?" Maefon sat at the edge of Balzurth's throne, legs crossed and kicking. "I'm getting bored watching you work."

"You are welcome to help." Nath finished loading up another wheelbarrow and tossed the shovel aside. He wiped off his sweaty face on a towel. "I only have a few dozen more loads to go." He gestured to the treasure that had dwindled down to a manageable pile. "See? You can handle this."

"Oh no. This is your punishment, not mine. Watching you is my punishment." She made a playful smile as her eyes grazed over his muscular body. "Sort of."

If Nath noticed her attention, he didn't show it. Instead, he pushed the wheelbarrow down the path. As he passed her, he said, "If you get caught sitting on my father's throne, you're going to be punished, too."

"Oh, he doesn't care. Balzurth is gentle and wise. We are just children to him. He would forgive me, don't you think?"

"Eh, I suppose." Nath ambled down the path and dumped the treasure on the new pile he'd created. He stretched his aching back and groaned. "Oh, I can't wait to rest. This is awful. Who would think being in a chamber filled with such wonderful treasure could be so miserable."

"It is a burden," Maefon replied. "True treasure comes from simpler things."

Nath made his way back to the pile. "Such as?"

"Well, having friends to share time with. Working in the gardens. Nurturing the young dragons." Her eyes lit up. "Oh, how I enjoy that."

"They try to bite me."

She giggled. "They do not. You exaggerate."

"No, I don't. They hate me. All of them."

Maefon hopped off the throne, landing lightly on her feet. She followed after Nath. "Now, are you feeling sorry for yourself again? Hmmmm? Pouting is not an admirable quality for a king's son."

Nath picked up the shovel and got to work. "How can I be the prince of the dragons when I look like this? If it's absurd to me, then it's absurd to them. You know it." He dumped a shovelful in the wheelbarrow. "And I know it. What if you had to go and live among men? Wouldn't you feel out of place?"

"Oh no, I am certain they would worship me." She untangled her honey-colored hair from the braid. The bouncy locks fell perfectly over her shoulders, somehow further enhancing her natural beauty. "Don't you agree?"

Nath swallowed. He thought *yes*, but said, "I don't know. I haven't been around any humans to know. Maybe they would be frightened to death of you."

"Hah! They would not be frightened. In awe, yes, but not scared like little children."

"You really are a piece of work." Nath refilled the barrel. He enjoyed Maefon and her wit. If it weren't for her, he might go crazy. The other elves who served the dragons were friendly, but more as a matter of courtesy. Maefon was a true friend. She cared for him. "Have you spent any time with the humans?"

"I studied all about the other races in Elome. I know all that I need to know."

"You don't think that gave you a jaded point of view? After all, what you've learned would be from an elven perspective." He grabbed the handles of the wheelbarrow and moved on.

"The elves are the purest of the races," she said, following behind him with her hands behind her back. "What they record is a neutral view of things. Hence, I believe what I read. The orcs are stupid, the dwarves are difficult, humans are unpredictable, gnomes are impolite, halflings are childish, and ogres are smelly. Should I go on?"

"No, no, your research is beyond convincing. So deep, well thought out, and thorough. I am overwhelmed." He laughed. "And what does it say about dragons?"

"Well, there are many kinds, and we are still learning about them. That is what I'm trained for, being one of the Trahaydeen. So far, you are the most interesting."

He dumped the wheelbarrow. "I'm not even a dragon. How can I be interesting?"

"You are. And you are a good, obedient son. Not all dragons heed the dragon king's words. They seek their own purposes elsewhere." She put her hand on his wrist, and her voice lowered to a whisper. "Many wander far from home and become wicked. They serve themselves and not Dragon Home. Many others are lost, never to return home. It troubles Balzurth. We wonder why that is."

"Dragons, like any other race, can make their own choices. Nalzambor's a large world filled with many dangers and delights, the way I understand it. Dragons can make the most of their own lives, but they always have Dragon Home to come home to. Sometimes they just need help finding it. That's what Father says."

"The races fear the dragons. They hunt and kill them. They call

Dragon Home the Mountain of Doom." She plucked an emerald-studded tiara from the treasure pile and placed it on her head. "How does it look?"

"It makes your head look really big."

"Oh, shut it." She slapped his arm then slung the tiara away. "Anyway, the races capture and torture dragons. They turn their scales into clothing. Sell dragon blood for potions. Their teeth, claws, eyes, or horns are used for decoration or jewelry. They are very nasty out there."

"How do you know these things?" He started pushing the wheelbarrow along.

"It's well known in the world, Nath. You are sheltered here. You only know what Balzurth tells you. I'm sure he only tells you what you need to know, and he is wise for it, I'm sure, but you should know more, just in case…" Her voice trailed off.

He stopped and looked down at her. Her head came to the top of his chest. "Just in case what?"

"Oh, nothing. I'm just rambling. Don't pay any attention to me. I've said enough already."

He grabbed her arm. "No, finish your thoughts. Out with it."

"I was just going to say, just in case something ever happens to your father. You'll have to know more about the world of men. What if he leaves to the land beyond the murals and does not return for a very long while? You would be in charge, wouldn't you?"

Nath's brow crinkled. He glanced at the mural behind the throne. It was a place where only dragons could go that his father said he'd learn all about one day. Usually, older dragons went to the land beyond the murals when their work in the world of the races was no longer needed. But only his father could go back and forth. It was something he didn't fully understand.

"No, the dragons have a council. They run things when he's gone. I just do whatever."

"I think you should be in charge of things. After all, you are the prince."

Nath shook his head and started pushing the wheelbarrow down the path. "You really need to temper your imagination before it becomes a dangerous thing. Why don't you run along, Maefon? I'll find you later. I just want to finish this on my own."

"I'm sorry, Nath. Have I offended you?" Her big, dark eyes were sad.

"I said I'll see you later."

CHAPTER 5

A COUPLE OF DAYS PASSED. NATH ran along the rocky ledges of Dragon Home. He hopped over chasms and gullies of the barren mountainside. The mountain was at least a league of walking if he went all the way around the bottom. Its rocky crevices and ledges led to a small flat on the tip-top that hovered just beneath the first layer of clouds in the sky. About halfway up, lava flowed in bright, burning seams of orange, down into the sulfurous springs below. It formed liquid pools at the bottom. One thing could always be said—Dragon Home never got cold.

Nath angled up to a ledge that jutted out several feet like a flat nose. He took a seat on the edge and stared out at the vast land in the distance. For some reason, he was agitated. Maefon's words bothered him deeply. Even though the dragons were nothing short of rude to him, he hated that the races hunted them. It didn't seem right. At the same time, when she suggested that his father might leave for some time, it went right through him.

It was just something about the way she said it that rankled him. And if Balzurth did leave, shouldn't Nath be in charge? Or at least he should be in the conversation. Of course, the dragon council could handle things in Balzurth's absence. They always did, but next time, perhaps, Nath should pay closer attention.

Next time Father goes, I'm going to attend all of the council's meetings. After all, it's my right... but I've been before, and they are so boring. He clenched his teeth. *And so long, not that I have anything better to do, but dragons talking takes forever.*

Nath sat a very long time. The sun hung high in the sky, just beneath the clouds, lowering an inch at a time until the bottom dipped behind the trees. The sky became a light purple, a little gloomy, but promising in an uncanny sort of way.

"I do love the sunset."

Tired of being out of place, Nath often considered leaving. His father told him that he could leave when he was ready but not before. What Balzurth didn't say was whether or not he would leave as a dragon or a man. Nath waited for the change to happen. He wanted wings and scales like his father, but they had yet to come. He wanted to see the world with his own eyes and find out what it had to offer.

I guess I'll just have to wait... forever.

A small winged dragon flew right in front of him. Its scales were orange, and it was little longer than the length of his arm. Its wings beat quickly as it chirped out words in dragonese.

"Training? Now?" Nath sighed. "Fine. I'll be there, little brother." The dragon snorted at him, narrowed its eyes, and flew away. "Nice talking to you too, you little winged rodent."

Inside the mountain, Nath walked down the main tunnel that spiraled and weaved through the mountain. It was a vast, hollowed-out channel, more than large enough for Balzurth to walk through, with smaller tunnels that broke off from it, creating an intricate network. Nath had walked them all.

Walking up the slope, a huge bull dragon headed his way. It was powerfully built with brick-red scales, somewhat reminiscent of Father's, but not nearly as big. Still, it was a huge dragon, and Nath marveled. A smaller group of dragons, all bulls, trailed behind it. "Hello, mighty one," Nath said, moving aside as it passed. He didn't often see the larger dragons in Dragon Home. They liked the lands outside, which were more suited for them. "What brings you home? Taking the family for a visit?"

The bull dragon moved on without a look Nath's way. The pack behind him were the same.

Nath waved and said sarcastically, "Yes, very nice talking to you too, fat scaly lummox."

The bull dragon halted. Slowly, it turned toward Nath. The bull dragon's eyes had a deadly intent. "Did you say something, little dragon prince? Say it louder. I did not hear you. Something about a lummox?"

Nath touched his chest. "My, the lummox can talk. Why, that's almost as impressive as those horns on your head. And I didn't think bull dragons could talk. Something I read about them being very slow to speak. No, that's not it. That would be a compliment. No, bull dragons, those marvelous in size, are known to be dumb, or stupid, rather."

The bull dragon's chest swelled. Hot breath came from his mouth. Flames flickered behind his teeth.

"Only jesting, grand one," Nath said, lifting his hands up as he backed away. "I've always heard that bull dragons were known for their expansive sense of humor."

With the pack of smaller dragons behind him, the bull dragon approached. He stopped when he was face to face with Nath. The bull dragon's head was as high as Nath was tall. His orange eyes glared into Nath's. "No respect given, no respect received. No wonder you are thought so ill of."

"I offered courtesy. You didn't reply."

"Because you are not a dragon! You are a menace to our kind."

Nath blanched. The words stung. "I am not." The bull dragon

turned and walked away. As he did so, the tip of his tail lashed out, knocking Nath's feet out from under him. He hit hard, lying on his side, gaping. "If anyone is a menace, you are!" The bull dragon and his family vanished around the next bend in the tunnel. "I am not a menace!" His words echoed back. "You are a menace."

CHAPTER 6

T HE TRAINING LAIR GREETED NATH with sweltering heat. Torches and urns blessed with the everlasting dragon fire illuminated the large chamber-like cavern. Veins of lava flowed through the walls, giving it an eerie illumination. On the floor were racks of weapons such as swords, halberds, battle-axes, and spears. The cave floor was open, jagged rock formations spread out in random places. On the back wall, a lone dragon sat like a dog on a flat slab of stone. She was the size of a horse, and her scales were forest green all over, but her breastplate was a much lighter green. Her eyes, unlike male dragons', had long lashes. The horns were like the sharpened antlers of a deer.

Nath walked on his hands across the training floor. He climbed over the rock obstacles one at a time, leaving a trail of sweat as he did so. "Even if I didn't have my legs, I don't think I would walk this way, Dragon Master Elween."

The forest dragon's voice was sharp. "The purpose of this exercise isn't about walking on your hands. It's about discipline. Something you can never—"

"'Have enough of,' I know. But I do think I have this mastered. How about some sword play?"

"No," she said flatly. Her eyes slid over to the racks of weapons.

Nath followed her line of sight. It had been a while since he'd trained with steel. He hungered for it. It took his mind off things.

From out of nowhere, someone slammed into him. Nath dropped his shoulder and rolled. Before he could get to his feet, a shirtless elven warrior tangled up his legs. The slender man was a knot of well-defined muscle, with many braids in his hair. His size almost matched Nath's. Nath reached for the man. As he did so, a second elf caught him in a headlock. The elf cranked up the pressure. Nath's eyes bulged. He lost his breath.

"What's the matter, Nath? Having trouble speaking?" the elf who had Nath in a headlock said.

"I believe he's confounded." The other elf fought against Nath's kicking legs. "Choke him out, brother. Choke him out!"

Nath wedged his fingers between his neck and the arm of the elf on his back. He pushed through, breaking the elf's grip. The elf kicked away. "No you don't, Pevly!" Nath snatched the elf's quick feet. With a yank, he pulled Pevly to the ground. Hand over hand, he dragged Pevly toward him. "I've got you now!"

Pevly kicked him in the face. "That's going to leave a mark... I hope."

Nath glared at the elf. "You shouldn't have done that."

"What? This?" The elf executed another perfect kick to Nath's face. "Now that looked like it hurt. Did it?"

Nath's cheeks warmed. "Now you've asked for it!" He twisted Pevly's foot.

The elf cried out in pain.

"Yield!" Nath said.

"Never!" Pevly's face became a grimace of pain. "You won't break it! You won't break it!"

"I don't have to," Nath said, applying more pressure.

"Eeeoow! I yield! I yield."

Nath let go. He turned his attention to the elf fastened to his legs. He wrapped his arms around Tevlin's waist. In a tangle of limbs, the pair wrestled across the floor.

"Beat him, Tevlin! Destroy him!" Pevly shouted as he rubbed his ankle. "Avenge your brother!"

Tevlin executed move after move. His quick hands and feet battled to take Nath down. He landed short kicks to the ankles and stiff punches to the ribs. Elbows and knees pumped like an ironsmith's hammers.

Nath blocked, punched, and countered. The grapplers rolled over the floor. Finally, Nath shoved Tevlin onto his belly, drove a knee into his back, and pulled both of his arms backward. "Yield, Tevlin!"

Defiant, Tevlin shook his head.

Pulling harder, Nath said, "I'll yank your arms out of their sockets. I swear I will!"

Tevlin shook his head again.

"Pevly, talk some sense into your brother, will you? You remember what happened last time."

"Yes, I remember, but my brother is very stubborn and highly resistant to pain, as you know. So I don't think I'll be able to talk him into anything." Pevly pulled his knees to his chest. "I guess you'll have to call it a draw then. Tevlin, do you agree to a draw?"

With his nose on the ground, Tevlin nodded.

"What says you, Nath?" Pevly asked. "A draw then?"

Tevlin still wriggled against him. The elf was strong. Very strong. Nath was stronger. "We never had a draw before today. There won't be one now, either. Last chance, Tevlin. Yield or no yield?"

Again, Tevlin shook his head.

Nath tugged harder. Tevlin's shoulders gave. *Pop! Pop!*

Pevly jumped to his feet. "Nath, how could you do that?"

"It's been a bad day, and he should have yielded." He let go of

Tevlin's arms. They flopped at the elf's sides. "Master Elween, is this match over?"

"You've incapacitated your opponent. Hence, it's over. But your training is not yet done."

"Of course not."

"Why?" Pevly moaned. "Why? You have crippled my brother, Nath! He's useless now! Just look at him."

With help from his brother, Tevlin sat up. His arms drooped heavily at the shoulder in unnatural positions. Tevlin's head was down. His long brown braids hung over his eyes.

Pevly pointed a stiff finger at Nath. Dramatically, he said, "You are cruel! Cowardly! Shameless, Nath! How can you live with yourself?"

"I guess because I can't live without myself," Nath replied. "And what is eating at you? This isn't the first time... Oh, I see what's going on. The Trahaydeen are preparing for the Showings, aren't they?"

Pevly crossed his arms and stuck his bottom lip out. "Possibly."

"And as always, your performance is incredible, Pevly. Very convincing. The dragons will like it. As for you, Tevlin, would you like me to help put your shoulders back in their sockets?"

Tevlin nodded.

"Permission to repair, Master Elween?"

"Yes, of course."

With the assistance of Pevly, Nath shoved both of Tevlin's shoulders back into their natural spots. Nath rubbed the mute elf's head. "All better?"

Tevlin gave him a stern look and a quick nod. The elf brothers were twins, each half a head shorter than Nath. Tevlin was expressionless, while Pevly's face always expressed a wide range of emotion. For elves, they appeared to be young adults and had been a part of the Trahaydeen for the last few decades. Like Maefon, they were some of Nath's best companions, even though he didn't see them all the time. The Trahaydeen rotated in their duties caring for the dragons.

The dragons didn't need care, so to speak, but they enjoyed the attention. The elves massaged the dragons' scales, polished and filed their talons, rubbed the grit from their horns. They even grew special food in their gardens that helped clean the dragons' teeth. It was pampering, and the dragons delighted in it.

"So, Pevly, what are the Showings about this time?" Nath asked.

Pevly brightened. "It's called the Trap. It's about a young dragon, surrounded by enemies, but he doesn't even know about it. Danger lurks in every crevice and corner, waiting to strike until—" He smacked his hands together. "Whazmo!"

"Well, go on," Nath said, excited.

"I can't spoil it for you. Oh, and Nath, watch out behind you."

"I'm not falling for that. Seriously, what is—*ulp*!"

A serpent's tail coiled around Nath's neck. With a fierce yank, he was jerked from his feet.

CHAPTER 7

NATH FOUND HIMSELF TANGLED UP with a dragon. It was a gray scaler, little bigger than him, serpentine and nasty looking. The dragon's claws were pitch black. Its front paws locked around Nath's wrists. It eyed Nath, opened its mouth filled with rows of sharp teeth, and hissed.

Choking, Nath pulled the dragon in closer. He head-butted the dragon on the top of its snout. The dragon's tail and grip slackened. Nath twisted free. He slipped behind the dazed dragon, grabbed it, and body-slammed it to the ground. He put the dragon's serpentine neck in a headlock and squeezed with all his might. Entwined, they rolled and thrashed over the floor. The dragon twisted and jerked. Nath held on for dear life. Their bodies collided against the stones jutting from the floor.

"I'm not letting go!" Nath said. Muscles bulged in his arms. Veins popped up in his neck. "Yield!"

The gray scaler's tail tapped on the ground.

Nath released it. Panting, he said, "Thank goodness that's over."

Without a glance, the gray scaler slunk away with its head low and black wings folded behind its back. It vanished into a smaller tunnel in the rock.

Nath's eyes swept the room. Only Master Elween, Pevly, and Tevlin were there. "How did I do, Master Elween?"

"Horrible. You may have defeated your opponents, but you were surprised both times. If they wanted to kill you, they could have… easily."

"I suppose," Nath said, rising to his feet, "but this is only training, not the real thing. If it was, I would be ready."

Master Elween hopped from her rocky perch. Standing like a man, front arms up and tail on the ground, she walked on her hind legs to Nath. Fully upright, the forest dragon stood eight feet tall. Though dragons typically walked on all fours, some of the kinds were much like a man that could walk upright on its legs. Her probing stare seemed to size up everything there was to know about Nath with a look. She smacked Nath on both sides of his cheeks. "No one is ever ready for the opponent they have never seen. That is the one you must look out for."

Nath started to say, "I know," but he checked his tongue. Master Elween was one of the few dragons that did speak to him, thanks to the training. The Dragon Master had never been kind, but at least she conversed with Nath.

Looking into Nath's eyes, Master Elween said, "What is on your mind, Nath? Questions lurk in your eyes. Out with it."

"You speak as if I have an enemy that I don't know about already. You always have, to some degree, but lately, you've brought it up in all of my training. Is there something I should know that you are not telling me about?"

The elven brothers looked at each other briefly before turning their attention to Master Elween.

"I'm not teaching you any differently than any other."

"If that's the case, then why do I train with swords, knives, axes, and hammers?" Nath pointed to the weapons racks. "The other dragons don't train with them." Master Elween frowned at him. "Do they?"

"You are not here all of the time." Master Elween moved to the weapons racks. She lifted a longsword off its post and tossed it to Nath. She grabbed another one with a clawed hand much like a man's. "Let me show you what a dragon can do with a blade." She whipped the sword through the air, cutting with masterful strokes and precision.

Nath found the moves awkward, quick, but fluid. He'd never imagined seeing a dragon fighting with a sword before. Why would they? Dragons had claws as sharp as swords and other powers of their own. Eyes following the quick movements of Master Elween's steel, he said, "You are amazing."

"I've studied the weapons of the races for centuries. I should be." Master Elween held the sword up. The tip of her taloned finger tapped the blade. "Understanding your enemies' weapons helps you understand your enemies. Do you understand?"

"I never thought about that before."

"That's because you do little thinking at all, based off what I've seen," Master Elween replied.

Pevly giggled.

"Silence."

Pevly clammed up.

Master Elween continued, "Always have a plan of action in mind, Nath. Be ready." She set her feet in a fighter's stance. "On guard!"

Without hesitation, Nath attacked. He chopped at Master Elween. The dragon master parried the blow aside, countering with a slash of her own. Nath jumped backward. The tip of the dragon's sword missed his chest by an inch. "You are fast, Master Elween, but I am faster." Nath launched a flurry of strikes. He jabbed, stabbed, slashed, thrust, and cut. Steel collided with steel.

Clang! Bang! Clang!

Swordplay had been Nath's favorite training since he began. Over the past few decades, he'd trained on a regular basis. He'd mastered all the weapons, at least the best that his trainers knew how. They taught him different fighting styles. He'd learned to fight with two hand axes but swung them like a dragon attacking with claws. He spun a bo stick like a dragon's tail, sweeping enemies from their feet. It was the sword that he was the most fond of. Now, his skills were put to the test.

Master Elween's tail swept over the ground at Nath's feet. He jumped it. "Hah! I was ready for that, wasn't I?"

The dragon unleashed a hard swing. The metal striking metal jarred Nath's arms up to the elbow. Master Elween struck faster and faster. It took everything Nath had to parry. His arms ached. The muscles in his shoulders burned. Master Elween did not relent. She beat down Nath's sword. The blade fell from Nath's grip. He'd never been disarmed before. Now, the point of a sword pressed to his throat. He swallowed.

"My body was not created to fight with a sword. The body you have was. Yet here you are, defeated." Master Elween put her snout in Nath's face. "You have very much to learn, Nath. Very much. You are never as good as you think."

"I would be if you started training me like this twenty years ago," Nath said, not hiding his defiance. No matter what he did, it was never enough for Master Elween.

"So it's my fault?" Master Elween shook her head and put her sword back on the rack. "No, it's your fault. If I was not here, could you not have taught yourself? Ask yourself this—how did the first master master anything? Hmm? A shame. You've had a hundred years, and not once have you shown initiative in anything."

CHAPTER 8

"Nath! Nath!" Maefon hollered. She was dressed in her sleeveless all-black garb. Her honey-colored hair had been braided. Gold hoop earrings hung from the lobes of her pointed ears. Her sweet voice echoed down the corridor. "Wait up!"

Nath's stride didn't slow. He moved with determination into the lower levels of the mountain. His jaw was set. A lit torch was in hand.

Maefon ran in front of him and tried to bar his path, but he went around her. "Where are you going?"

"To the forges. And I'm going alone."

"The forges?" she said, catching up to him. "Why would you go there? And I don't even know where they are."

"I do. See you later." He left her standing alone with her mouth hanging open. He didn't want to be around anyone.

"Well, that was rude, and I am coming." She caught up with him again. "I don't know what you are pouting about this time, but if you talked about it, you wouldn't feel so mad."

"Not talking about it." Nath continued his descent, turning out of one of the main tunnels into a smaller one that split from it. The Mountain of Doom was like the inside of an anthill, twisting and turning into many paths. Every route he took had been paved with stones. The larger ones had light from urns and torches that ran along the sides, burning with the everlasting dragon fire. The side tunnels and narrow passages were often dark. The dragons didn't need light as much as men. Their keen senses more than compensated for it. When Nath was younger, he'd traveled the tunnels in total darkness, exploring, alone, and honing his one superior sense. It was at least one thing he did have in common with the dragons.

"Your stride is too long, Nath. Slow down. And what is your hurry? Whatever it is you are looking for isn't going anywhere."

"I suggest that you keep up if you don't want to get lost."

"Are you being overbearing because Master Elween thrashed you at the Training Lair?"

"Who told you—never mind. Pevly can't keep silent about anything. If I didn't know better, I'd guess you were his sister."

"What are you implying, that I talk too much?"

"You haven't stopped talking since you arrived. And I told you that I didn't want to talk about it." He angled into another corridor. "And I didn't want you to come either. I want to be alone."

"Now Nath, you don't want to be alone. You complain about it too much, so I know better. And you shouldn't take a thwarting from Master Elween personally. She's supposed to do that." She wrapped her arms around his elbow. "That's why she's a master."

He tried to pull away, but she held him fast. "I know that. She's walloped me plenty over the years for this or that. She said I didn't have initiative."

"So you are going to the furnace to find initiative?" Her nose crinkled. "That doesn't make any sense. Care to explain?"

"No."

"Ugh!" She let go of him. "You are so hardheaded!"

Using only torchlight, he continued down the black corridors.

After an hour of walking, with Maefon clinging at his side, he turned in to a chamber with a vast opening.

"Hello?" Maefon squinted toward the darkness. Her voice echoed for a moment and faded.

Nath lifted his torch toward another torch that hung on the wall. Flames spurted from it, leaping across the room, and jumped from one torch to another until all were lit. More balls of flame dropped from their perches into the stone urns below them. In seconds, the massive chamber was illuminated with a warm orange glow.

Maefon's dark eyes became giant pearls. "This is the biggest forge I've ever seen. Of course, I haven't seen many, but still… it's so vast." She scratched her head. "Nath, being a young Trahaydeen, and still learning your ways, I haven't devoted time to finding out why dragons would need a forge. Do you know?"

"Yes." Nath started down the stone staircase, which was as wide as the chamber's opening. Centered in the middle of the room were a dozen forges—every station fully equipped and ready to use. There were bellows to pump the fires, tongs, anvils mounted on stone stands, hammers, and cooling tanks of water. The coals in the mouth of the forge were cold and black. Nath stuck his fingers in one of the beds of coals. "They are warm still but don't burn."

"How can they be warm? Is there magic in them?" she asked.

"I suppose. They have always been warm since I remember. Father brought me here once and told me all about it. The forges were used by elves and dwarves to make metal to use in the wars against the orcs when they lost their lands to the brutes. That was millennia ago." On a nearby table, he looked at a mold made for a sword. He ran his finger through the groove. "The dragons, seeing the danger, came to an agreement with the elves and dwarves. They would aid them, so long as they kept the secrets of Dragon Home to themselves. But in their lust for greater knowledge, they stole the secret of Dragon Steel from the dragons. The elves blamed the dwarves, and the dwarves blamed the elves. Both races were banished. All of this happened before my father was king. Dragon Home has been a quieter place ever since."

Traipsing through the smithy, fingers touching everything she passed, Maefon said, "Have you ever seen Dragon Steel?"

"No." Nath picked up a pair of hammers. He banged on an anvil with them. "But it can only be made from metal of the mountain that flows in the veins of the lava. Father says the elves or the dwarves, possibly both, stole some of that metal along with the secret of how to shape it." He imitated his father's voice. "*That's why the races can never be fully trusted.* The forges have been cold ever since."

"But your father allows the Trahaydeen?"

Nath shrugged. "Again, it was a long time ago." He walked over to the bellows and started pumping it with his foot. The coals in the forge caught fire. Smoke wavered up into the hood.

"I don't think you should be doing that." Her slender arms were crossed over her chest. "Why are you doing that?"

"Master Elween says that I don't have any initiative. Well, she's right, but I'm taking initiative now. If I want to understand a sword, then I'm going to build one on my own."

CHAPTER 9

FOR DAYS, NATH WORKED IN the smithy, laboring away with long strips of metal, trying to shape them into any weapon he could. His hair was tied back behind his head. Sweat coated his face and dripped from his chin onto a heavy leather apron. His trousers were soaked, and his feet inside his boots burned from all of the standing.

"I'm getting better at this. I swear I'm getting better at this!" He pounded on a strip of metal that glowed orange on one end. He didn't know what was taking a worse beating, the anvil or him. With his arms throbbing, he struck blow after blow, flattening the end of the metal. A long edge began to form the more he battered at it. "Come on, metal. You are a sword, and you know it. Now be it!"

He wore heavy gloves on his hands. One hand swung the hammer, the other held a pair of iron tongs that fastened on the tang or grip of the sword. It took him days to master holding the tang by the tongs, and he wasn't even sure if that was the right way to go about it, but it worked for him.

The sword he made was long, edged on one side, with a curve on the tip. It wasn't going to be anything fancy. The only thing that mattered was whether or not it would hold up for cutting or striking.

Hammering away, he noticed a bend in the main body of the metal. Cooling on the anvil, it started to bow. "No!" He pounded on it a few more times. The bow popped back into shape. "Great Guzan! Warped again!"

Nath took the blade and stuck it back in the hot coals. From there, he moved to a workbench where several earlier sword versions rested. He picked them up one at a time, inspected them, and said as he set each and every one back down, "Bent. Bent. Bent. Cracked. Cracked. What in the world happened to this one? It's curvy. I've seen sidewinders that are straighter." He picked up a hammer. "Perhaps I should try something simpler, like this, or an axe, perhaps." He thumbed the perspiration from his eyes. "I don't know. Just when I think I'm getting better, it looks like I go backward."

"I think you are getting better," Maefon said. Nath whipped around. She'd snuck into the smithy and sat cross-legged on a table behind him. "After all, it would be impossible to do worse with all of this practice."

"Will you quit sneaking up on me? It's only proper that you announce yourself." He dropped the hammer on the table. "You could end up getting hurt."

"I keep my distance, and I'm always wary of your temper tantrums."

"That would be wise," he said. "Case in point." He poked his finger at a nearby wall. A sharp flange of steel protruded from the rock. "I wasn't looking when I threw it earlier."

She wiggled her shoulders from side to side. "Lucky for you, I'm an excellent dodger. And why so edgy, Nath? You make it sound like I'm an assassin creeping up behind your back."

"I know how those tickling little fingers of yours work. You've dug them into my ribs on countless occasions. You make me jumpy."

"You're never jumpy. Just flat footed. You are so absorbed in what you are doing that you make it easy. You're a deep thinker, Nath. If you aren't careful, you'll miss what is going on around you."

"Listen, I just want to build a nice sword. Are you here to help or drone on like my father or Master Elween?"

She untied the braid in her hair and combed it out with her fingers. "I was hoping you were going to give up on this experiment. There are more exciting things that you could do."

Nath walked over to a bin that sat on the floor with a variety of metal shafts stuck inside. Rummaging through them, he said, "What could be more exciting?"

"We could go for a walk. I'll even let you hold my hand like you used to. It's been a while since we walked. I miss it."

Nath wasn't about to admit that he missed it too. He liked Maefon, more than he cared to admit. There was no one he was closer with than her. She was beautiful, smart, witty, and understanding. It was easy to talk to her, and she got him to talk even when he didn't want to. She had a special soothing and pleasant way and a smile that could melt his heart. "You know that I would love to, but I'm focused on this right now. I'm making progress." He pinched his fingers together. "I'm this close. I can feel it. I just need to find the right metal to work with."

Maefon frowned as she picked up a metal file that lay on the table where she sat. With ginger fingers, she touched up her nails. "Nath, you are more prepared for things than you realize. Master Elween will never stop pushing you. And no one can be prepared for everything. She tries to convince you that you can be. Nath, in the world of men, you would be nothing short of extraordinary, with or without a shiny sword."

"I don't know about that."

"You underestimate yourself." She slid off the table, walked over to him, took the metal shaft out of his grip, and set it aside. She grabbed his hands. "You are special, and as ready to handle anything as anybody. You can defeat many of Elome's finest elves in hand-to-hand combat. Your knowledge of language and the texts is as good or better than any of the Trahaydeen. Believe me, only the finest of the elves are sent here, and that's after decades of training. You are unlike any man I have ever seen. I just wish you were elven."

Nath pulled back his shoulders. A charming smile crossed his face. "Well, when you put it like that, I suppose that I am a bit of a marvel."

She looked into his eyes, rose on tiptoe and said, "You are beyond marvelous, Nath. You are perfect."

Nath's heart pounded. He put his arms around her waist, drew her in, and kissed her. Maefon's soft lips eagerly engaged. Her body melted in his arms. She moaned with passion.

NATH.

He broke the kiss off. Heart racing, he turned his eyes down the hall.

"What is it, Nath?" she said with dreamy eyes. Her lips started to pucker.

NATH.

Gently, Nath pushed her back by the shoulders. "Did you hear that?"

"No. All I hear is my heart fluttering like hummingbird wings."

"It's my father. I can hear him." Eyes searching, he said, "Yes, Father."

COME TO THE THRONE ROOM.

"Er, right away!" He peeled his hands from Maefon's sticky fingers. "See what you've done. Father saw us."

"You kissed me. I didn't kiss you, but I would have."

"I have to go." He dashed out of the chamber. *Oh Gads, I hope he doesn't banish her.*

CHAPTER 10

NATH STOOD OUTSIDE THE THRESHOLD of the doors that led into the throne room. The split doors were massive things, each standing over thirty feet tall and half as wide. The wood doors were framed with polished brass. The hinges were as long as Nath's forearm. Head down, he sighed. It wasn't the first time he'd been called to the throne room through a calling in his mind. It had been a while, though, and the last time it happened, it shook him. He'd drawn the anger of his father.

I never should have kissed her. I never should have kissed her. I knew I shouldn't have crossed that line. Why did I do that? Father's going to either kill me or have me shovel treasure from one side of the throne room to the other. He put his hands on the door. *Just suck it up and get it over with.* He pushed.

The door quietly swung inward. Nath stepped through a gap just wide enough for him and closed it. Straight ahead, his father sat on the throne, same as a man, great wings folded behind his back. His clawed hands were on his knees, and his eyes were closed. Behind him, his long tail coiled around the legs of the throne. Everything in the room seemed insignificant in his presence.

Nath walked forward. His feet scuffled over the loose treasure covering the floor. Metal clinked against metal, making it difficult for him to move in his preferred silence. He chose to abandon any subtlety and announced himself. "Father, I am here."

"I know," Balzurth responded in a low, canyon-deep voice. "I understand that you have been spending your time in the forges. You and Maefon."

"I can explain that." Nath rolled his thumbs behind his back. "It just happened. It won't happen again. I swear."

Balzurth's right eye popped open. The big orb had a golden flare to it. His chin, covered with short horns on the bottom, tilted. "Why would you stop?"

"Uh, it's forbidden."

Balzurth scratched his chin. "I don't recall making weapons being forbidden. Of course, it's been some time since the forges were used, but when I heard the news that you were hammering steel on your own, I admit, I was excited."

He doesn't know! Yes!

"Well, that's a relief," Nath said, rubbing the back of his neck.

Balzurth leaned toward him. "Unless, you were talking about something else? Were you?"

"Well, uh..."

"Out with it, Nath. Now is no time for secrets." Balzurth pressed him. "You are a hundred years old. You must be honest, forthcoming, and trustworthy if I am to rely on you. The bond between father and son should be like iron. Will it be, or won't it be?"

The last thing Nath wanted to do was get himself or Maefon in trouble. What he did was egregious. His father's eyes seemed to bore into him. *I think he knows. He has to know. He's toying with me.*

"Nath, look me in the eye. What happened?"

He avoided Balzurth's gaze for moments and finally, without looking at him, confessed. "I kissed Maefon, Father. I'm sorry. I... I just couldn't help it." Then Nath looked at his father. He wasn't certain, but Balzurth's thin lips seemed to be bent up in a smile at the corners. The smoldering eyes of judgment seemed almost approving. "Please don't punish Maefon. It was my doing. I swear it. She is innocent."

"So that was your first kiss?" Balzurth asked.

"Well, yes. And the last. I promise. I know it's forbidden."

Balzurth leaned back. He patted the side of his throne. "Climb up here, son."

Nath did as he was told and plopped down beside his father. Balzurth put his hand behind his back in support. *Oh, he's going to crush me.*

"Relax, son. You aren't in trouble, and you haven't done anything wrong, but we do need to talk about it. Even though that isn't what I brought you here for. But it's the perfect time to address this *unique* situation." Balzurth's finger patted him on the back. "To be clear, it is forbidden for dragons to be intimate with the races. For example, a dragon couldn't marry a human. They are of a different kind. But your circumstances are different, being a dragon born a man. You will have feelings like a man, and you will experience like a man and be tempted like a man. But what you must remember is that you are a dragon, and one day you will meet a dragon that is meant just for you."

"So it's fine that I spend time with Maefon?" he said, hopeful.

"She is Trahaydeen, Nath, and their relationships with dragons are limited. A more intimate relationship with her is not something that she should pursue. That is forbidden. They are caretakers, given much trust to live among the dragons. They should not break their word."

"What will happen if she does?"

"She will have to leave."

CHAPTER 11

NATH JUMPED UP. "No, I don't want her to leave. It was my fault!"

"Easy son. Sit."

Nath complied.

"We'll let this one incident pass. I don't see a point in mentioning it. But you should be mindful of the consequences, and now you are. Do you understand?"

Head down, Nath nodded. "Yes, I understand." His heart twisted inside his chest. Now that he couldn't have her, he wanted her more, but he didn't want to lose her. "This won't be easy. She's my closest friend."

Balzurth nodded. "Yes, I know. It's good that you have one. We all need a friend we can rely on, and the Trahaydeen are here in part to make life easier for you, but even they can become infatuated with the dragons. If they are overcome by it, they are banished."

"Father, it might not be so bad if I wasn't shunned by the dragons. I just don't understand it. I'm your son. Why don't they like me?"

Sadly, Balzurth shook his head. He let out a sigh filled with his warm breath. Some smoke rolled from his nostrils. "It's not because of anything that you've done. I think it's because of something that happened long ago."

"What happened?"

"I wish I could share it, but we vowed to never speak of it in the mountain. However, it has to do with a betrayal from a man the dragons trusted."

Nath's back straightened. "It's not fair to judge me for someone else's works, is it?"

"Of course not. Listen, as I've told you, in time, you will earn their respect, but you are young. You just need to remain on the path you are on. The right one. The higher road must be sought when you deal with the world of the races. Some days, it's a delight, and others, it's a tightrope."

"I'm good on a tightrope." Nath looked to Balzurth. "So I'm going to deal with the races at some point? What do you mean?"

"Well, that's part of the reason that I brought you here. It's time for a talk, because soon I must go."

Nath made a puzzled look. "Go? Go where? You sleep most of the time."

"I don't," Balzurth said, stretching out his speech. "It's mostly meditating."

"No, it's sleeping. I've never seen a dragon snore when they are meditating." Nath punched his father in the thigh. "But if you want to call it meditating, that's fine. After all, you are the king. So where are you going?"

"To the land beyond the murals." Balzurth turned his head toward the massive mural behind him, filled with painted images of dragons in different parts of the lands. "It's something I do, part of my charge as the dragon king. I won't be gone long, a few years perhaps, depending on my duties."

"Is Mother there?" Nath asked. He never knew who his mother was, and Balzurth never talked about her. He saw the narrowing in

Balzurth's eyes. He'd asked often, and it seemed to irritate Balzurth as if a deep pain reflected in his eyes.

"No," Balzurth replied, showing a frown.

"Father, if she is dead, then you can tell me. I can understand it."

"I've never asked this, but I'm going to ask now. Don't ever ask me about her again. When the time comes, you will know. You must trust me on this matter."

Nath's shoulders slumped. "You say that about everything. Just wait. Just wait. Just wait. I'm tired of waiting. I'm ready for anything."

"No, you are not!" Balzurth's outburst shook the throne room. Coins slid down their piles. In a stern voice, he continued, "You must learn patience, Nath. You have a long life to live; don't rush into it. If you do, you might find yourself on a path that you cannot recover from, one filled with malice, haste, regret, turmoil, lies, and deceit. That is the world out there, and that is the world I brought you here to speak about. Do I have your attention?"

"Yes, Father," Nath said, nodding. The temperature in the room went up. He was sweating again. "I understand."

"Your understanding is youthful. My understanding is ancient. There is a difference. That is what you need to understand. Time and experience bring wisdom. The dragons live long and have learned and experienced much. That is why you must learn from them. Don't be so eager to venture out with a full head of steam. It can be dangerous, and you are important."

"Father, I just, I just want to... live."

"And you will." Balzurth's voice lowered. "The time will come when you will be ready to leave Dragon Home. You need to be best prepared."

"I'll be leaving?" Nath said, feeling a tingling sensation running through his body. "Does that mean that I'll be a dragon soon? I'll get my scales?" He stood up, inspecting his arms with his eyes. "My wings?"

"No, you will be going just as you are, Nath. A man. It is out there that you will have to earn your scales, and it won't be easy. You'll be surrounded by the races. They are full of folly."

"How soon? I'm ready... er, I mean, I'll be ready when the time comes."

"In another century, on your two-hundredth celebration day, you should be fully ready."

"Two hundred!" Nath plopped down. His face sank into his hands, and he shook his head. "That's forever!"

"A hundred years is not even a drop in the pond when compared to forever. In time, you'll look back, and it will seem little more than nothing."

Nath groaned. He didn't think he could put up with another hundred years of being shunned by the dragons. And he certainly couldn't resist Maefon another hundred years. That would be impossible. "I'm sorry, Father, but I'm about to burst out of my skin. I won't gain my scales, and I guess I can't do anything different. It will all be the same day over and over again. I need a challenge. I want adventure."

"You have the forge. Mastering steel can take many years, even decades. Focus on that."

Nath hopped out of the chair. His feet hit the ground hard. He started walking away. "Suddenly, I've lost interest."

CHAPTER 12

"NATH, YOU AREN'T DISMISSED." BALZURTH's tail slid out from underneath the throne and blocked Nath's path. "I haven't even told you everything that I brought you to hear. And you should know better than to walk away from me like that. It's disrespectful."

Throwing his arms up in the air, Nath said, "I don't know what could be so important now that you just can't share it with me later. After all, we have at least a hundred more years, assuming that I don't have to wait another hundred on top of that. I'll probably have a beard down to my toes by then. And what if my hair turns gray? Did you even think about that?"

"Your hair won't turn gray for a very long time, trust me." Balzurth lifted his head toward the ceiling and puffed out the armor-like scales on his chest. "Look at my scales—they are still as red as ever. Even the gold keeps its luster. Now sit and listen."

"I'll sit, but I might not listen." Nath took his seat on Balzurth's tail. He knew he was being disrespectful, but he couldn't help it—he was mad. His cheeks were hot from it. "Go ahead, and if you will, try to keep it short, seeing how I have to get back to nothing to do for the next century."

"If you keep it up, Nath, then I might not give you your present for your one-hundred-year celebration." Balzurth's clawed hand scratched at his chin. "It would be a shame to keep it all to myself, considering it was made specifically for you."

Nath leaned forward, his eyes wide. "You made me a present?"

"Yes, one that has been decades in the making. It took a little longer than I'd planned, but it's finally ready."

Nath's rigid demeanor shifted. His frown turned upward into a smile. Inching upward from his seat, he said, "Where is it?"

"Well, there's no fun in that, now is there? You know how we play this game. Your present could be anywhere in the throne room."

Nath's smile stretched all the way across his face. He took off running. Ever since he was young, he had come to the throne room and searched for his present among the treasure. It happened every ten years, but this year, he'd forgotten about it completely. He couldn't believe he was so distracted that he forgot about his celebration-day present. Running up and sliding down piles of treasure, he scanned for anything new. "Hot or cold, Father? Hot or cold?" He dug elbow deep in the piles. "Hot or cold?"

"Cold, but remember, I'm only giving you a fair amount of hints."

"Yes, yes, I know." Nath jumped from one pile to another. He had many unique treasures his father gave to him, but this was the first one that had been made by his father. "Is it buried?" he said, not hiding his excitement. "The last time you buried it. It was hard to find."

"Perhaps a little. Maybe half in, maybe half out."

Nath came across the painting of the radiant platinum-haired woman. He picked it up and said, "It's not this, is it?"

"No."

"Is this Mother?"

"No," Balzurth said, slowly shaking his head.

"Do you know who it is then? She's incredibly fetching. Even

Maefon says she thinks she's beautiful, and you know Maefon doesn't think anyone is prettier than her."

"Yes, I know the unforgettable face, but the name is slippery in my mind. Trinity, Minos... Ah, it's been so long, but like any treasure, there is a story behind it."

Nath tossed the painting aside and kept searching. "Hot or cold? Hot or cold?"

"You are getting warmer."

Rummaging through every pile, Nath's eyes swept over the stacks. He was plenty familiar with the objects in the throne room. He'd played here often as a boy. And even though he hadn't seen everything, he certainly had a feel for most of it. Coins and gems sliding under his feet, he jumped the piles like a frog on a lily pad. He landed on the object he had his eye on. "Hot or cold, Father? Hot or—"

"Hot."

Nath's eyes seized on the sword handle protruding out of a treasure pile. The pommel was fashioned with the face of a dragon. A handle that could be gripped with two hands was a rich brown with the distressed look of dragon horn. The crossguard of the sword was two metal dragon heads plated with gold. Each had gemstone eyes, one with emeralds and the other rubies. Nath had never seen such intricate work on a sword. For a moment, he wondered if it was only part of one. He looked back at his father and said, "Is this it?"

Balzurth nodded.

Using both hands, Nath pulled the sword free. Coins chimed against the edge of the blade. The lighting in the room flickered. *Shing!* The double-edged blade looked as sharp and straight as any he'd ever seen. The metal was bright with a blue shine shimmering within the steel. "It's magnificent!" Nath said with awe.

"Thank you," Balzurth replied.

Nath cut the blade through the air using short strokes at first that became longer. He spun the blade with his wrist then fancifully behind his back. "The balance is perfect! It has heft without being heavy. Yet it's so big."

"It's dragon steel blessed by magic, son. It cannot break. It will cut anything. That sword does not have an equal, I assure you."

"Whoa! And you spent decades on it?" Nath said, flipping it from side to side between both hands. "Just for me?"

"Yes, and I enjoyed every hour and every day making it. Dragon steel is very hard work, and I had to be patient. If I had not been, the work would not be what it is today. It would be incomplete. With patience comes perfection."

Nath was only half listening. The sword was nothing short of an extension of his own arm. He was one with it. He chopped, thrust, parried, and sliced with lightning-quick movements. The shining steel whistled when it cut the air.

"How could you make this when you are so... vast?"

"I have my ways. Like Master Elween, I'm built differently than most dragons. But I'll teach you more about that—"

"I know, later." The blade handle shocked Nath. He dropped the sword. "Ow!"

CHAPTER 13

BEFORE THE SWORD LANDED, HE caught it on the toe of his boot and kicked it back up. He snatched it with his other hand. "It stung me. Why did it sting me?"

Balzurth shrugged his wings. "Perhaps he thought you were being disrespectful."

"He? The sword is a *he*, like a person?"

"Yes, he has his own thoughts and enchantments and will keep your best intentions in mind. He will be a friend that you can count on."

"Well, I can see that already." Nath's eyes were still glued to the blade. "I can't thank you enough, Father. Do you have a name for him?"

"No, I left that honor for you."

"Hmmm... What is a good name?" He rubbed the palm of his reddening hand. "Sting might be a fine name. Do you like that?"

Balzurth shrugged. "Perhaps if it was a much smaller blade, but that is a great one."

"Ah, true." Nath glanced between the sword and his father. That was when he noticed his father's teeth jutting out over the side of his mouth. The name hit him like a hammer. "Fang!"

Balzurth gave an approving nod. "I like it."

"I think he does too," Nath said. "The handle is warm, like a living thing."

"I'm sure you and Fang will have much to learn in your journeys when the time comes, but for now, Fang must remain in the throne room."

All of the excitement in Nath's body deflated. The boundless energy within him leaked out of his toes. "Huh? I can't take my present with me? We will only be in Dragon Home. And I want to share with Master Elween. I know she can't beat me if I have Fang. I need to train with him."

"There are a few more enchantments I have left to do before I turn you both loose in the world."

"Turn us loose?" Nath rested Fang against his shoulder. "What do you mean?"

"That is the second reason that I brought you here, though I'd wanted to do it in another order." Balzurth put his hands on his lap and cleared his throat. A puff of smoke came out. "We've talked about the races over the years and our relationships with them. You've studied in the Trahaydeen libraries about them. But the time will come when you will have to move out into the world of men, and it is there that you must earn your scales."

Nath returned to his seat on his father's tail. Balzurth had his full attention now. "So I will become a dragon then?"

"Of course. But you will face many trials in order to do so. Unlike dragons, you are born a man, and being such, the path you will take will be much harder. That is why I want you fully prepared for the journey. It won't be easy. Trust me."

"Well, what am I supposed to do?"

"You have many lost brothers and sisters who are suffering. The races trap them, hunt them, sell them. You will be charged with rescuing them. Protecting them. But you cannot get too close to the races. They have different ambitions than dragons. I'm not saying there isn't much good in them—there is plenty—but the bad in them is much worse. Time among them brings much temptation. You are too young. With time, you develop wisdom."

"But I want to save the dragons now." Nath shot to his feet and started pacing. "I mean, if they are in danger now, shouldn't I go and help them? They need me. And if I help them, they will like me. Yes?"

Balzurth shook his head. "Don't ever expect a thank you for your good works. Your works should come from your heart. That is all that matters. Do you understand?"

"No, not really."

"That's because you are still young. You might look like a grown man, but you are very youthful inside. You must pay attention and observe the actions of others. That is how you will learn." Balzurth's massive mouth opened like a cave full of teeth as he yawned. "Listen, I promise to talk to you more about all of this when I return. In the meantime, the High Dragon Council will be in charge. Don't give them any trouble. I want a good report when I return. Until then, keep yourself busy. I think Fang will need a scabbard. That would be a fine project for you. And take your lessons seriously. You still have much preparation to do."

"You're leaving now?" Nath said, watching his father ease out of his chair. The end of his father's tail brushed past Nath's leg. "You just can't leave me on the edge like this. Not now. I have so many questions."

"Son, there are affairs that I must attend to in the land beyond the murals. Duty requires my presence every few decades or so. Now, the time has come again. You will understand one day." Heading toward the mural, Balzurth looked at him. "Son, make the most of the mountain, and do not depart from it no matter what. You are not ready. Also, spend more time with your older brother, Slivver. He should be returning soon. And most importantly, remember, I love you, no matter what."

"I-I love you too." Nath's voice trailed off as he watched his father walk into the mural behind the throne. Balzurth became a part of one of the painted images in the mural, flying among the other dragons but clearly the greatest one of all. "Goodbye."

With his father gone, the throne room felt like a tomb. Nath instantly missed him. He stared at the mural for the longest time, the images moving with very slow and subtle changes. His father flew farther away until, hours later, his image was gone.

One of Nath's knees sagged. It stirred up his blood, waking him from a trance. There was so much running through his mind. He had Fang. Eventually, he would have scales. He wanted to do it all now. Traipsing through the treasure while swinging Fang from side to side, he said, "I can't wait one hundred more years. That's forever, Fang. Don't you think?"

Fang's blade shone in the light.

"I don't really think that any more work needs to be done to you, either," he said to the blade. "You look perfect to me."

"And you look perfect to me," Maefon said, peeking inside the throne room door. "I see you have a new friend."

"Yes, and I see that you have invaded my father's throne room without permission. You can't do that, Maefon."

Easing her way inside, she made a pouty frown. "I was worried about you. I've been waiting outside in case I needed to come to your defense. After all, none can resist me."

Nath marched toward her. "Yes, keep telling yourself that."

Peeking past him, she said, "So King Balzurth is gone now, right?"

"Yes." He halted her from going farther inside with his arm.

"I knew he was gone. There was a stir in the air. A chill. It was as if a great warmth had left the mountain." She clung to his arm. "I've never felt anything like that before, but with you here, I know that all will be right. What did your father say about us? Are you in trouble?"

"No," Nath said, forcing himself to look in her eyes. "But I'm sorry to say that it's best that we don't spend as much time together as before. You're Trahaydeen. You understand, don't you?"

Her eyes watered. She turned and ran away.

CHAPTER 14

NATH SPENT THE NEXT FEW weeks in the smithy. Even though he had Fang to look forward to using, he still needed to keep his mind off of things. He labored in front of the forge and hammered metal on the anvil, making small hammers, axes, and knives. He'd started off too big before, and now focused on mastering the smaller items first. At the same time, he was able to avoid Maefon. At least, it kept his thoughts occupied. It hurt seeing her storm out of the throne room, and he hadn't seen her since.

He pounded the sharp edge of a one-bladed battle-axe. Sparks flew from the hammer. *Bang! Bang! Bang!* He lifted it from the anvil. "Looking better. Much better. I think I'll be able to put a nice shine on it." He set it aside on the table where many handleless weapons lay. A lot of them were warped and cracked, but some were usable.

Nath rinsed his sweat-smeared face off with water from a bucket that sat on the floor. Flinging the water from his fingers, he made his way over to where the scabbard hung on a cold forge. He'd made it for Fang. He smiled at his handiwork. Fang was longer than a normal sword—too long to carry from his hip. So he'd made a sword belt that he could strap over his shoulders. As for the scabbard itself, that was a different animal altogether. Fang's blade was sharp enough to split hair. Sliding the blade in and out of the scabbard would damage it if it wasn't designed precisely. He shaped the scabbard out of hard wood he'd stained black. He made sure the neck opening was firmly made to guide the blade straight inside. Fang would snap in snugly to the lock at the top. Then to soften the exterior, he wrapped the scabbard in dyed leather. He took it to the throne room, tested it once, and seeing it worked perfectly, he brought it back to the smithy to add the finishing touches.

It might not be a sword, but knowing how to care for a sword is a big step.

Nath's stomach let out a growl. He'd become so consumed that he'd forgotten to eat for days. Deciding to call it a day, he shut down the forge, tidied up his work, grabbed the scabbard, and left. On his way to eat, he figured he'd put Fang in his new sheath. As he traversed the corridors, his mind started to wander. Images of Maefon came to mind. He missed her and hated the fact that he'd hurt her.

I should check on her. I'm sure she is well, but I have to see her.

Even though Nath had avoided crossing her path, he had a pretty good idea where she would be. If she wasn't with him, she spent her time in the Trahaydeen's inner sanctum. If she wasn't there, she would be in the dragon nursery. Maefon loved the nursery, and she was as happy there as anywhere.

Nath changed direction and headed to the nursery. Even though the scabbard wouldn't be something that interested Maefon too much, at least he could show her what he'd been working on.

A natural archway made with seams of pure gold let into the nursery. Inside the archway was another large, well-illuminated cavern. The stone walls were smooth and slick. Rocks made a trough at the bottom filled with water that ran along the edge of the cave. A natural spring ran over the high rocks, making waterfalls of clear water. It was a very peaceful place. Small dragons, newly born, scattered behind the rocks in the room the moment they saw Nath.

Kneeling down, Nath said, "Come now, there is no need to be afraid of me. You'll dislike me enough when you're older, I'm sure. I see no reason why we can't have a truce now."

The fledglings were an assortment of breeds. There were husky bronze and slender copper dragons. Green lilies with very long tails, and baby red rocks with no wings at all on their backs. A very cute crimson dynamo crawled toward Nath with its head low. "Hello, little one," Nath said, letting the dragon sniff his finger. "See, there is nothing to fear from—" The dragon bit him. "Ow! You little brat!"

The Trahaydeen in the cavern started laughing. There were five of them, men and women, each holding a dragon to their chest and petting them. One of the five remained still, her back to him. Her hair was bound up on top of her head. She dipped a hand in the pool of water surrounding her where baby dragons swam.

Nath waved to the Trahaydeen. "Greetings."

"Be well," they replied, each with a warming smile. The elves were gentle and kind, all dressed in similar fashion—dark robes with light-blue flower patterns sewn at the sleeves and bottom of their robes. For a change, Maefon was dressed in the same modest manner.

Nath sat down beside her. "Hello, Maefon."

Her eyes remained fixed on the dragons swimming in the pool of water. The water bubbled and swirled beneath them. Steam rose from the water. Finally, she said, "Hello, Nath. Did you come here to break my heart again?"

"Come now, Maefon. You know that I would never ever hurt you. And it's not as if this isn't hurting me too. You know I adore you. How couldn't I?" He rubbed her shoulder. She scooted out of reach.

"If you *adore* me and *care* for me, then why haven't I seen you in weeks? Hmmm?" Bitterness filled her voice. "That doesn't sound like an *adoring* and *caring* person to me. You are just fooling yourself."

Rubbing his neck, he replied, "I've been working on my

blacksmithing skills, and time got away from me. Look, I made this... for Fang."

Her gaze drifted to the scabbard. "What is that, a stick wrapped up in leather? How delightful."

"Listen, I worked hard on this. There's no need to be insulting. I would never do that to you."

Maefon put her face in her hands and started crying. Her body trembled with every sob. "Oh, Nath, I am so sorry. I don't mean to be so spiteful, but it hurts so much knowing that I cannot be with you." She clutched her chest. "My heart aches."

Nath's eyes watered. He wiped them. His own heart turned in his chest. Maefon was always so strong and confident. He found himself stunned that she'd come undone all on account of him. Heart pounding, he swallowed the lump in his throat. "You know I would do anything for you, Maefon. Anything, not to hurt you. But I can't risk getting you banished from here. Then I would never see you."

With tears dripping from her pretty eyes, she said, "I love you, Nath, and if I can't be with you the way a woman should be with a man, then I can't live like this."

"What are you saying?"

Barely able to control herself, she stood up. "I'm leaving the Trahaydeen." Without another word, she departed, leaving Nath with his heart breaking.

CHAPTER 15

I NSTEAD OF SITTING IN THE nursery with his jaw hanging, Nath got up and chased after Maefon. She was nowhere to be seen, and there were so many paths through the mountain she could have taken. Nath's nostrils flared. He caught the sweet fragrance of perfume lingering in the air. It was Maefon's, mild and pleasant. With his senses in full swing, Nath ran after her.

Maefon's bare feet slapped on the stones, echoing in the corridor. She was fast, as most elves were, but no match for Nath. He caught up with her and grabbed her by the wrist. "Maefon, stop. Please," he pleaded. "We have to talk about this. And you can't leave. You just can't. It's your dream to be among the dragons. You love it more than anything."

"Apparently not," she said with her chin down. "Just go, Nath. Leave me. It's all for the better." She jerked away and started walking from him with her fists balled up at her sides. "And don't chase after me anymore!"

Nath ignored it, catching up to her but keeping a little bit of distance. "I read in the Tomes of Alvareen that women like to be chased after and they get mad when you don't."

"Alvareen is a fool. And clearly he writes from a man's point of view."

"He's an elven sage. The great romancer. Certainly, in his thousands of years, he couldn't have been that far off base." He stepped in front of her and smiled. "Come now, you don't doubt the wisdom of such a grand philosopher, do you? You've read his words with your own lips to me, trying to woo me."

She pushed through him. "Don't joke about this."

Nath recited one of his favorite poems. Short but fluid, the elven words spun from his lips like silk from a spider's web. She stopped in her tracks.

There's flourish in the meadows where the cattle chew the hay,
The grasshoppers' legs sing the dance,
With moist lips, the young maiden serenades the moon,
And the stars in the sky delight,
On the sweet breath of the wind, the fairies spin a woven song,
Where the honey of the bees flows like gold.
Never tarry for love that waits from the reeds to the chasms on high.
Nothing fades, all comes aflutter, when the troubadours of mirth
march on.

She turned with a glowering look. "That was not Alvareen. It was horrible."

"Horrible. I wrote that one. You said you loved it."

"Yes, and I suppose I lied. I shouldn't have, but I did because I didn't want to hurt your feelings." A ray of a smile started on her lips. "Did you steal it from an orc?"

"Now, that is unfair. I know you like it, or you wouldn't be smiling."

As the color returned to her cheeks, she said, "I'm only smiling because it's laughable. '*Never tarry for love that waits from the reeds to the chasms on high.*' What does that even mean?"

"It's poetry. It doesn't really mean anything. You just write what you feel, and it comes out a jumble. I don't know."

"Please, just don't say it again, at least in elven."

Playfully, Nath crept toward her with his fingers needling the air. "Someone needs a tickle."

"Don't you dare!" She ran. Nath pounced on her, tackling her to the ground. His fingers dug at her ribs. "Stop it, Nath! Top it!" She giggled so hard she couldn't get the words out. "Top it!"

"Are you saying *stop it*? Because I am hearing *top it*, and I don't know what that means. Top what?"

She elbowed him hard in the ribs. "Stop it!"

"Ow." Nath winced as he rolled away from her body. "I'm topping it. Gads, you didn't have to bust a rib. I was about to yield."

Catching her breath, she let out a long sigh with a bit of laughter contained within. "At least you can still make me laugh. It's another one of your irresistible gifts. You are growing into a fine man, or dragon. I guess that's why this is so hard for me. I'm drawn to you more than ever."

He reached over and held her hand. "I feel the same. Perhaps on my next century of celebration, when I leave, then you can come with me."

She looked at him with her brows lifted. "What? Another hundred years you must stay? That's a long time, and I'm only slated to be here another fifty years. But you are ready for the world out there now. I know this." She squeezed his hand. "You are ready for anything. I just think your father is very overprotective."

"Father is wise."

"Yes, I know, but you are wise too." She put her arms around his waist, snuggling up to him as she placed her cheek on his shoulder. "You know, I told you I didn't want you to chase me, but I did. You are very wise for a young man."

"Alvareen said some women like pursuit and few shun it. They want a man to work for it—"

She put her finger on his lips. "Sssh. I don't care what Alvareen says. Those are just books we read from some lonely old hermit that lived in a tower all of his life. He never married. How wise could he really be about women? But his poetry is quite splendid. No, Nath, you figured it out. You know my heart. I just wish I could give it to you. And thanks for pursuing me. Normally, I would shun that, but I know that you care deeply. You truly are a prince, and every woman in the land, whether they admit it or not, is looking for a prince, even me, and now I've found one that I can't have."

He kissed her hair. "Let's take it a day at a time and see what happens." A trio of silver dragons, sleek in build and stunning in color, moseyed down the corridor without giving them so much as a look. "And to think that I am prince. Hah, an outsider would never know it."

"Well, I do." She kissed his chin. "Oh, prince."

CHAPTER 16

AEFON CASUALLY MADE HER WAY back to Covelum, the home of the Trahaydeen. She had a small spring in her step, and her long curls bounced on her shoulders after she let her hair down. Covelum was a mill of quiet activity. The elves who weren't busy tending to the dragons took care of the elven village built into the rocks. There were fountains in the plaza and a small outdoor theater for entertainment. Hutches for quarters had been dug out above storefronts. It was all carved out of the mineral-rich mountain rocks in the likeness of the homes in the elven city of Elome. The rock had been shaped and chiseled to look like trees. The branches and leaves had been painted, giving it all the strong illusion of reality.

"Hello," she said, waving as she passed by her friends. There were two hundred elves in all, living in quiet and humble service to the dragons. They required little but slept in facilities much like home. They ate fish that swam in the streams that coursed through the mountain. There was rich soil within the rock that the elves enchanted to harness the sun's light. Almost everything an elf would need was provided for through their cooperation with the dragons.

Hurrying up the steps, she slipped onto the terrace of her hutch.

Covelum had been her home for a long time, and she was more than fond of it. She tousled her hair and arched her back, watching the elves steadily fulfill their duties. Not a single thing was ever out of place, it seemed. They moved in harmony, setting tables, preparing food, and cleaning up after one another. Every day was devoted to making things better, not worse. They sought perfection. Order.

A soft whistle caught her ear. She turned. A heavy, deep-blue curtain was drawn in the back. She pushed the curtain back. An elf with wavy black hair and long sideburns that came to a point lay on her bedding. Dressed in attire like hers, he'd propped himself up against a pile of colorful pillows of all shapes and sizes as he chewed on a lime-colored apple.

"What a surprise to find you here, Chazzan," she said, offering a welcoming smile. She crawled onto the bed with him and took a bite out of his apple. "You aren't supposed to be eating in bed. It's awful manners."

"I was sleepy, hungry, and tired of waiting, Maefon. You have been missed. And even though it's mostly my idea, I have to admit, I'm a bit jealous of the time you spend with the dragon man." Chazzan spoke with the slyness of a serpent. A cunning intelligence lurked behind his dark eyes. His elven features, sharp and distinct, seemed even more so than a typical elf, leaving him with an air of rigidness about him. "So how goes the seduction, my priceless treasure?"

She batted her eyes at him then made a sad face, allowing tears to stream down her face. "I turned on my geysers, and he ate it all up. I'm certain he would do almost anything for me at this point. He is strong but naïve, though I tell him otherwise." She palmed his chest with her hand, rubbing it back and forth. "It's not nearly like you and me, of course." She took the apple out of his hand and tossed it away. Crawling on top of him, she kissed him fully. "All of this deception increases my longing for you. It's hard to focus on him when I'm thinking about you."

"I can't say I blame you. Perhaps it would be the same for me, if I were in a like situation. Ho-hum, I was beginning to think that Balzurth would never leave, but now, the moment has arrived." Wrapping her up in his arms, he pulled her against his chest. "Decades of planning will finally be executed."

"I'm surprised the Trahaydeen have been deceived. There is no doubt among them. They, like Nath, trust us fully, as do the dragons."

Chazzan smelled her hair. "We are Caligin. Deception is what we are born to do. We are elves, the elves with ebony hearts in our chests. No one sees us coming until it is too late. Think about it, Maefon—we have infiltrated not only the Trahaydeen, but Dragon Home. The world is ours to master as the Lord Dark Day says. Once we execute his plans, we shall be united with him and rule at his side forever."

"I can taste victory on my lips."

"And I on mine, but I like the taste of yours better." He kissed her again, long and fully. "You ignite me."

"Chazzan, are you certain this is safe? We stand little chance against the dragons if caught. Actually, none at all. We'll be turned to ash."

"Nay, we'll be long gone. And with Balzurth gone, there won't be any pursuit. The Dragon High Council cannot depart from Dragon Home in his absence. The dragons will stay put and mete out justice later. They are patient, more so than elves. Only Balzurth can unleash them. Besides, they won't be prepared for what is coming. The chaos and misdirection we spread will be in place. They won't know what to do."

"And all of this is because of Nath?"

Chazzan shrugged. "Lord Dark Day wants him separated from the flock. That is all. It seems absurdly simple but at the same time brilliant. Sometimes, I think I must have thought of it myself."

"No doubt you could have, love," she said, toying with his sideburns. "Do you suppose he'll kill Nath?"

"I don't think he needs him dead. He just needs him out of Dragon Home. Lord Dark Day says the rest will take care of itself."

"He believes the world will consume Nath, doesn't he?"

"Don't you?"

Maefon nodded. "Yes, he won't stand a chance against the races." There was a dark flicker in her eyes. "And the races don't have a prayer against the Caligin."

CHAPTER 17

NATH SPENT THE NEXT FEW days working the metal in the smithy and training with Master Elween. Even though he couldn't show Master Elween Fang, he still took the scabbard he made. Master Elween gave a nod but said very little, as always. Instead, she had Nath do pushups and sit-ups until his arms and belly burned like fires. Then she sent him on a run, carrying a rucksack loaded with rocks. For whatever reason, the tormenting training didn't faze Nath so much as before. His outlook had brightened.

Drenched in sweat and panting after the laden run, he said to Master Elween, "Will you come to the throne room and at least let me show you Fang?"

Perched on her rock as if she were a part of the stone herself, Master Elween said, "No."

Hands on his knees, Nath replied, "Don't say I didn't invite you to anything. Oh, and you could come to the forge. My skill bending metal is improving. I've made knives shaped like dragon claws, and if I don't mind saying so myself, the handles are quite fetching."

Stone faced as a dragon could be with eyelids that never blinked, Master Elween said, "I'll summon you for the next lesson. You are dismissed." The forest dragon slunk off her rock and out of the Training Lair.

Dropping the bag of rocks from his shoulders, Nath said, "So much for impressing her." He shrugged. "Oh well, at least I can look forward to spending time with Maefon in Covelum tonight." He sniffed the air. "Whew! Either I smell as rotten as an onion, or it's this cave. Come to think of it, it's been a while since I bathed. I can't show up to Maefon like this."

Quickly, Nath tidied up the Training Lair and departed. He headed to one of the many hot springs in Dragon Home. The dragons were notorious for lounging in the hot waters. He headed to the spas in the rocks, thick in steamy vapors. Inside were several pools of burbling water. In the largest pool, an orange blaze dragon was stretched out from one end to the other. The long lashes of her eyes were closed as two elves waded in the waters, massaging her scales and filing her nails. She was a beautiful dragon with a body twice as long as Nath was tall and a long tail swishing slowly over the floor by the edge of her pool.

Nath crept in, grabbed a towel, undressed, and slipped into a small bubbling spring all to himself. "Ah," he moaned as he sank neck deep into the water. The bubbling mineral-rich waters massaged his skin and muscles. "Why don't I spend more time in here?" An image of Maefon came to mind. She was splendid in his imagination. "I wish I could be spending more time here with Mae."

When they were younger, they would play for hours in the springs together, but now, that innocence had become something that seemed inappropriate. Still, he wished she were there.

Thinking out loud, he said, "Oh well, I'll see her soon enough. I'm certain we'll figure things out. At least she's speaking to me and we have time carved out for tonight."

A slosh of water caught his ear. He opened his eyes. The orange blaze was leaving. She didn't hide the displeasure on her face either.

"Oh, come now, I can't even spend time in the springs with my brethren without them rudely abandoning me?" Nath grabbed his towel and got out of the water. "Just stay. I'll go. For the love of Balzurth, I've never done a thing to any single one of you."

Storming through the corridors, he headed to his personal cove. The stone staircase he took led into a cave made of smooth walls and floors. There were pillows and folded blankets on the floor, some leather-bound tomes, and a cupboard of dried fruit and meat. Nath didn't sleep much and had little need for things, but he did have some chests and a small wardrobe. They were things the elves of Covelum gave to him. He put on a pair of navy-blue trousers and an old gold cotton shirt. A long rectangular mirror leaned against the wall. Staring at the mirror, he combed his fingers through his hair a few times. He took a brush and comb to his flame-red mane. "Perhaps it's my glorious hair the dragons are so jealous of. After all, they might as well be bald, given they only have scales, and my flowing locks are nothing short of perfect."

He grabbed some dried spice fruit from a cupboard to freshen his breath and hurried out of his room and down the steps to meet Maefon. Jogging, he made it to Covelum a few minutes later. It appeared the majority of the Trahaydeen were present, dressed in the dark elven robes trimmed with blue lace. The light posts that always glowed with lantern light were decorated with colorful wreaths and streamers. Picnic tables had food stacked up high. Fountains of rose-colored elven wine flowed from their cisterns. A small group of elves milled through their brethren, playing flutes and string instruments in perfect harmony. Dragons surrounded the stands, sitting where they could comfortably see the stage.

"Hello, Nath." Maefon slipped in behind him and tickled his ribs. "I was beginning to wonder if you were going to make it. I thought you might have forgotten our budding romance."

"Hah! I'd never forget you, Mae," he said. "You should know better than to doubt that."

"I don't know, I see your eyes caressing the steel. You are obsessed with it." She held his hand with hers and walked him toward the stage. "But I forgive your boyish silliness. For now is the time of the Festival of Change. The celebration of the new elven spring begins, and I'm glad you are here for it."

"Your people are my people," Nath said, holding her hand tighter. "If it wasn't for the elves, it would have been a lonely childhood. When you like to talk, there is nothing worse than not having anyone to talk to. The elves have always been here for me, and I for them."

Maefon led him to a seat in the front, and they sat down together. Sitting hip to hip with him, she said, "I wish you had come early. I would have fed you. The dragon soil has been so rich this season, and the fruit tastes as if it was from Elome's very soil. Oh..." She sighed. "I do miss the sun so, Nath. The change of seasons, the breeze through the branches. I hope to take you to Elome someday."

"I would love that. Perhaps we should take more walks on the mountainside. We haven't done that for years. We can always watch the seasons change from there."

"A walk? Don't you think I can run with you?"

Showing a clever smile, he replied, "We both know you could not keep up with me."

"Hah! We shall see soon then, assuming you don't hide in the hot little dungeon, talking to your forges and irons."

He put his arm on the back of her chair. His fingers rested on her slender shoulder. "I'd never hide from you."

She locked her fingers with his. "You couldn't anyway." She giggled. "Oh look, there on stage. Chazzan—you remember Chazzan, don't you? He is the orchestrator of the shows."

"Of course. I know all the elves. Just because I don't see you often doesn't mean I forget."

Chazzan stood out among the elves. He was the tallest, oldest, and least talkative of them. He was on the stage, helping the actors with their costumes. Along with Maefon, Nath waved. Chazzan turned away. "He doesn't smile so much, does he?"

"He takes his charges very seriously. Just ask him, and he'll tell you. He's very devoted to our discipline. Perhaps too devoted. I think he wants to *be* a dragon. He talks about them as if they were his own people. It's almost offensive."

"Well, he's clearly an elf. Look at his prominent features. Though he's like no other Trahaydeen," Nath said as he caught Maefon's questioning stare. "Aside from you, naturally."

"Good recovery, Nath. And yes, he boasts he is of the purest elven bloodline and that most elves should look more like him. He says many of our features are too rounded." She gave a quick approving nod. "I'm not so certain I believe it because he reminds us so much."

"Come now, I'm sure he is proud of his heritage, as we all are. But if I were to guess, I'd say that you are a perfect example of everything an elf should be."

"Oh, Nath, you flatter me." She leaned on his shoulder. "Don't stop. Go on. Your words are like a soft summer breeze in my hair."

"Softer, I'd hope. So what is this play about?" He caught the brothers, Pevly and Tevlin, on stage and waved. They were dressed like jesters with golden star-shaped hats. They juggled knives and axes hand to hand. Nath gave a puzzled look. "Or is it a play?"

"No, this is a show of talents. Many participate with dance, song, and daring stunts. Chazzan made the change. Not all agreed with it, but it is in line with elven tradition. In Elome, they have plays, musicals, orchestras, and shows of skill and daring. Though I will miss the drama of the old plays, I admit, I'm looking forward to this."

Nath settled back into his chair. "Me too."

Chazzan appeared on the center stage. He lifted his arms. The elves fell silent, the lantern light dimmed. With a bow, he said, "Let the show begin."

CHAPTER 18

FOR HOURS, NATH WAS DELIGHTED with some of the most outstanding elfin showmanship that he'd ever seen. A female Trahaydeen started off by singing a ballad with words so sweet they would make a cave troll cry. And she was just one of many singers with voices that lifted hearts with sheer joy. But there were sad songs too, about lost loves from war, disease, and famine, and what seemed to be the worst of all, broken hearts.

Pevly and Tevlin each climbed their own length of pole twenty feet in the air. Loaded with a scabbard of knives and hatchets, they stood on one foot on poles narrower than their legs. With another twenty feet between them, they juggled razor-edged objects in full circles on their own. They did three blades one handed, and in harmony with one another, they switched to the other. With eight blades, they faced each other, passing them back and forth between them. Their arms and wrists pumped back and forth in a blur.

The elves in the audience roared.

On the edge of his seat, Nath watched a scene like he'd never seen before. The elves, normally calm and pleasant, had stepped out of their skins and gotten a little crazy this year. They swilled their wine.

Shoulder to shoulder, they howled gleeful jollies. They were having fun.

"I'm not used to seeing your people so worked up," Nath said to Maefon.

Behind her, an elf bumped her chair. She frowned. "This does seem a bit zealous, even for the Festival of Change. I never imagined the Showing would invoke so much passion among my kindred. I assure you, though, they are harmless."

"No, I have no fear. I just feel like a bit of a prude sitting here. I feel out of place not partaking in their reveling."

"Perhaps you would feel better with some elven wine to freshen your palate." She patted his thigh. "I think I could use some myself."

"Uh." Nath swept the happy faces in the seats behind him. "I suppose I could join in. But hurry. The next act is about to begin."

Getting up, she winked at him. "I'll be back before you can recite the entirety of your own name."

"The show will be over by then," he said as she went. Hands on his knees, he focused on the stage. There were so many surprises, he didn't know what to expect. A troupe of dancers came out in clothing sewn like bright dragon scales, horns, and claws. Somehow, they came together in a strange contortion the shape of a dragon. A mouth opened in the front, made from arms and hands, and flames erupted. Nath applauded and whistled. "Fantastic!"

Maefon returned with two goblets of wine. "Looks like I missed something."

"No, they are still going," Nath said, not containing his excitement. Absentmindedly, he took the goblet and drank. The elven wine was a sweet juice with a little burn to it. He swallowed it down. "Watch, Maefon, watch this!"

"I'm watching, Nath. I'm watching. But I'm not sure what I enjoy more, the show or watching your excitement." She took his empty goblet and handed him her own. "Here, take mine before you go hoarse from all of the shouting."

The show went through a few more acts, with one just as titillating as the next. Nath couldn't remember the last time he had so much fun. Finally, Chazzan appeared on the stage. His face was painted with dragon-like features. He stood two feet taller and wore pitch-black robes, and his shoulders were unnaturally broad. His hands and feet were covered in oversized dragon-like talons and claws.

Leaning forward, Nath said with a slur in his speech, "What is this? He looks terrifying."

"Chazzan has been telling us about singing an opera song he wrote. I never imagined it would be so showy." Maefon's legs were crossed. One foot was kicking. She bit into her bottom lip. "I think he wants to show off."

"I think you are right," Nath said with awe. "He does want to be a dragon. A scary elven one. No offense—*hic*—but he looks a bit abominable." His eyes were heavy as he stared at the elf. The dragon costume wasn't so complicated. He could tell the elf wore shoulder pads underneath his robes, and he stood on a short pair of stilts. All in all, however, it was a clever costume. "So he's going to sing?"

Maefon shushed him. The rest of the cajoling elves quieted.

Chazzan sang. His voice filled Covelum with a perfect pitch that became louder and more powerful the longer he went.

Goose bumps rose on Nath's arms. "I never would have imagined something so loud could come out of such a small head," he whispered and partly slurred to Maefon. "Is that magic?"

"Hush, Nath. You are being rude." Her eyes were fastened on Chazzan, almost as if she were spellbound.

Nath eased back into his chair and listened. Chazzan sang in old elven with lyrics that flowed like the wind whistling through the trees. Up and down his voice went, accenting the highs and lows of a dangerous journey. He sang of a world where the dragons abandoned men, and a dark life took over. Nath's hazy mind tried to keep up with the story. Sitting up, he said, "What is he singing about?"

"Nath, don't be rude. I am listening."

Chazzan's words darkened. His voice became a thunderstorm and heavy rains. He seemed to control the very elements around him as the lighting changed with his mood. There he stood, arms wide, a menacing terror, with a voice that swallowed all other sound from the room. Nath's goose bumps moved up his arms to the hairs on the back of his neck. With blurry eyes, he looked around at the audience. All of them sat on the edge of their seats with spellbound eyes and mouths half-gaping open.

There was a sound of thunder. Nath noticed Pevly and Tevlin bending a thin sheet of metal from behind the stage. The sound had such a realistic effect. Nath watched Chazzan sing. The elf's lips moved more slowly than the words that came out. Nath's stomach turned inside his belly. He wanted to look away but couldn't.

Chazzan held his arms high, mouth open toward the ceiling. In one hand, he held a clear crystal orb. He let out the last lyric. "There was only doom without the dragons. The days will be dark forever." His high note cracked. The crystal in his hand shattered. His voice halted, and he bowed. There was a long, quiet moment, then the audience was on their feet, erupting in laughter. Maefon clapped heartily. Tears came from the corners of her eyes.

Nath applauded with heavy hands. Something wasn't right. Watching Chazzan walk from the stage, hunched over, with the shifting appearance of some sort of demon, Nath said, "I think I'm going to be sick." He plopped back into his chair. Maefon was in his face, features twisting and saying words he did not fully understand. All he could do was repeat the words, "There was only doom without the dragons." Looking at Maefon, he said to her, "Why would he say that?"

"It's a tragedy. Life is full of tragedy. Come on, Nath," she said with words that finally became clearer. "I'll take you home."

"Why can't I feel my fingers or taste my tongue?"

"I suppose you have a low tolerance for elven wine. Either that, or you drank too much of it." She stood before him, holding him by the waist and keeping him steady. The elves were celebrating in Covelum in a swarm of excited activity. She wasn't smiling when she said her next words. "Nath, you should be more careful."

He scratched his head. "I suppose. I don't understand Chazzan's song. Did you?"

"It's a tragedy."

"It was beautiful but awful at the same time. I'm sleepy."

"Yes, I know." With Nath leaning on her, she led him out of Covelum, away from all of the noise and celebration. She took him to his home and led him up the steps and into bed.

"I love you, Maefon," he said, curling up in his bed and falling into a deep sleep.

"Yes, Nath, I know," she said, brushing his hair behind his ears. "But I love Chazzan."

CHAPTER 19

"MAAAAAAH-ROOOOOOO!"

Nath woke with his face buried in his pillow. His bloodshot eyes cracked open.

"MAAAAAAH-ROOOOOOO!"

He pushed his pounding head up and sat up, wiping the drool from his mouth. Dragons were crying out. Their wailings filled the tunnels. Nath's body quavered. "What in the mountain is going on?" he said, covering his ears.

"MAAAAAAH-ROOOOOOO!"

With his heart racing, he forced himself to his feet and staggered out of his room. Never in his life had he heard the sounds of dragons mourning. Numerous roars from different dragons echoed like thunder through the corridors. There was hurt, disbelief, confusion, and rage.

Nath picked up his pace. With a head that felt like it was filled with cotton, he tried to sort out the last thing he had done. He was at the Festival of Change with Maefon, having as good a time as ever. Chazzan performed a very dark ballad that haunted Nath's dreams. Maefon was there, leading him home. He'd become sleepy, and he rarely slept. He didn't remember anything after that.

I must have overindulged in that elven wine, but it's never affected me so before.

"MAAAAAAH-ROOOOOOO!"

What has happened while I slept?

He stumbled, bumped against the wall, and regained his balance. His legs were still numb. He pressed on, tracking after the harrowing dragon calls. The sound came from the direction of the dragon nursery. Taking a split in the corridors, Nath passed a train of dragons of all sorts and sizes lined up in the channel. They moaned, grumbled, and growled as he passed them. Nath didn't bother asking what had happened. None of them would even look at him. He swore he heard the word *traitor*.

He entered the archway into the nursery where the dragons' lamenting was the loudest. He covered his ears. Inside, dragons were huddled over the fledgling dragons. The baby dragons' bodies were broken and slashed. All of them, once so spry and lively, were dead. Nath's heart sank to his toes as he dropped to his knees. "No," he whispered. "How can this be?"

Dragon blood smeared the floor, wet and drying. It was nothing short of a cruel, inhuman massacre. Dozens of the fledglings had been killed. There were dead Trahaydeen too. They lay on the ground, in their own blood, unattended. Knives had fallen from their hands.

Nath tried to sort out whether or not the elves defended the fledglings or if they were responsible. His nostrils widened. With his dulled senses clearing, the foul odor of charred flesh caught his attention. Near the back of the cavern, a pile of flesh had become a smoking stack of bones. There was no doubt it was elven. Nath's eyes swept the room, looking for others. He didn't see any more bodies, but some of the weapons he'd forged himself were scattered on the floor.

No, it can't be.

Dragon blood was on the blades and handles. His stomach

sickened. He lifted his hands toward his face. Caked blood covered his fingers. Dragon blood.

This is madness. It cannot be.

The dragons in the room surrounded Nath. Towering over him with teeth and claws bared, they crowded him. With narrowed eyes, they said, "Liar. Traitor. Murderer."

A twenty-foot-tall gold dragon pushed through the ranks. "Seize him."

"But I didn't do it," Nath said, trying to address them all at once. "I swear I didn't! I could not have—ever!"

A tail blindsided him. The blow knocked him flat on the floor.

Nath fought to get up. The tail's hard blows pounded him into submission.

Chapter 20

TWO GRAY SCALERS WITH BLACK wings bound Nath's ankles with their long tails. They were as big as he was but sulked on the ground on all fours. Nath rubbed his aching ribs. The dragons throttled him with their tails, but he was thankful he hadn't been burned to a crisp. The intent to kill him was certainly there.

Nath had been brought to the chamber of the High Dragon Council. It was a place of decision-making and judgment. He'd been to several sessions in his lifetime, and the meetings were renowned for taking days, even years. At the moment, the voluminous chamber was empty aside from him and his guards. There were seven flat boulders that circled the chamber. Each was big enough to seat a large dragon. Above, balconies overlooked the chamber. No dragons were there.

Nath sighed. He'd been under heavy guard for several days, isolated from the dragons in a cave. Aside from his guards, he hadn't seen anyone else. No Trahaydeen. No Maefon. He hoped she was safe. He knew that he couldn't have hurt the dragons, and even if he didn't remember anything from while he slept, he must have been set up. It could only have been the elves who'd done it, and if he had to guess one, it would be Chazzan. There was something sinister about the elf the night of the Showings.

Nath's temper rose every time he thought about the innocent fledglings being slaughtered. Even though Nath and the dragons didn't get along, they were his kin, and it hurt him as much as it hurt the dragons. He would find whoever committed the atrocious act and make them pay.

I'll avenge you, little ones. I swear it.

The High Dragon Council entered the chamber. All of the dragons were golden flares, with radiant gold scales that showed brilliantly when they moved. Their horns varied, curling like a ram's horns or flowing toward their backs in twisted spikes. On the left side, three females with long eyelashes and alabaster-colored bellies sat on their rocks. Across from them were three males with heavier-plated, darker, golden-brown chests. The last golden flare took his seat on the mound of rock in the middle. It was the same dragon as at the nursery. Karnax was his name. He nodded to the others. All together, the golden flares reared up on their hind legs and crossed their arms over their chests. All eyes were on Nath.

Karnax spoke dragonese with a pleasant yet stern voice. "Nath, you stand accused of slaughtering twenty-two fledglings. What is your plea?"

"My plea?" he said. "I should not be accused of anything. I would never hurt a dragon, ever. This is insanity!"

Karnax's tail picked up a round stone and banged it on a rock beside his pedestal. "Order! Order!" The other dragons growled in their throats. "I will ask again, Nath, what is your plea?"

"I don't even know what that means. Karnax, you know I did not do this. The real murderers must still be out there." Nath tried to move forward, but the gray scalers' tails were like steel coils around his ankles. "They should be on trial. Not me!"

"Lower your voice, Nath," Karnax's voice boomed throughout the room. "Your answer is very simple. Guilty or not guilty. Now, I will ask you again. What is your plea?"

"Well, not—"

"Don't answer that!" a voice cut in. An eight-foot-tall slender dragon, walking upright like a man, entered the room. His eyes were blue as ice, and he wore a small satchel around his waist. Of all the dragons, Slivver was the most human. He walked upright like a man, spoke in common more than he did dragon, and even sat at tables and ate with utensils.

"Slivver!" Nath said with a sigh. His brother had shown up at the perfect time. He tried to hug the approaching dragon, but Slivver held him off.

"Just be silent, Nath," he said eloquently, "and let me do the talking for a change."

Nath nodded. Balzurth had many children, but none like Nath. Slivver was one of Nath's many brothers and sisters who were full dragons hatched from eggs. Though Slivver was gone most of the time, he was one of the very few who spoke with Nath like an actual sibling, friend, or person, for that matter.

"High council dragons," Slivver said, pacing with his arms behind his back. "I would like to remind you that the evidence does not point to Nath. You are aware of this. Our findings have concluded that the Trahaydeen are solely responsible for this act and Nath, the son of Balzurth, the Dragon King, was framed. Poorly framed at that."

Karnax stretched his neck. "Regardless, he must enter a plea. That is our law."

Slivver lifted a clawed finger. "As Nath's representative, I will advise you that he will not be entering any plea. A guilty plea would certainly satisfy our tragically hurt and wounded brethren, with a swift and certain justice. But a not guilty plea will lead to a trial, building up more tension, unrest, and the appearance of guilt, and that would be wrong. Your charges against Nath are without foundation, and I move that they be dismissed."

"No!" Karnax said. The other dragons nodded in agreement.

Slivver spread out his arms and wings. "High council dragons, we have proven without a shadow of a doubt that Nath is not involved in this foul conspiracy. And you cannot try to hold Nath accountable for tragedies of the past."

Nath whispered at Slivver, "What tragedies?"

Slivver shooed him away. "Though I hate to put it this way, in more human terms, this is a witch hunt. Nath is not the witch. He is our brother and guiltless at that. All of you knew this before you even came in here, yet you are trying to pin the murder on him still." Slivver punched his fist in his hand. "It... Is... Wrong!"

The council of dragons conferred with one another in their own dialect. As they convened, Nath went to work on Slivver. "You know I'm grateful, but can you please tell me what in the mountain is going on? Why would the Trahaydeen kill the fledglings and pin it on me?"

Putting his clawed hands on Nath's shoulders, Slivver said, "They had bad seeds, brother. All races do, and you can never fully trust them. Even the dragons have bad seeds. But the important thing is that you are innocent. I know this, as does the council, and many others, but it's not so easy to convince all of the dragons. They don't trust you or the elves. As it turns out, the culprits not only slew the fledglings, but many of their own kind as well. They wanted it to look like you went into some sort of rage. They framed you as a distraction and fled the mountain."

"But why, Slivver? I just don't understand it. Elves killing elves. That is madness within madness." His jaws clenched. "It was led by Chazzan, wasn't it?"

"I can't say for certain, but he was one of the many who fled. The others are incarcerated but most likely will be banished."

"What about Maefon? Where is she? I need to see her."

"She is one of the ones who fled with the others. She is a suspect." Slivver patted Nath's head. "I can see the blood running from your face, Nath. Are you all right?"

Ashen-faced, Nath replied, "I don't know."

CHAPTER 21

A s the High Council of Dragons deliberated, Nath's thoughts raced through the rapids of the tragedy. Never in his life had he seen anyone die. The Trahaydeen were always in good health, even though many came and went. As for the dragons, the most ancient of them were rarely seen, and when it was time, they would move on to the land beyond the murals. Now, the most innocent of creatures, fledgling dragons, had been slaughtered by the most trusted of the races, the Trahaydeen.

Maefon couldn't have done this. She just couldn't have.

Nath rubbed his temples. His head hurt, and his heart ached. But deep within him, an anger burned. He wanted vengeance for the dragons. Justice would have to wait.

Slivver nudged Nath, breaking his train of thought. "The council," Slivver said quietly.

The High Council of Dragons broke from their conversation and turned their attention to Nath. Karnax spoke. "We have deliberated. The votes are split as to whether or not to dismiss the charges against you or not."

"Split?" Nath said with shock.

Slivver cut him off with his hand. "Let me do the talking." He stepped toward the high council. "Split? That is the most absurd judgment I have ever heard or witnessed. We have proved without a doubt that Nath is innocent. We know who the murderers are."

Karnax banged the round stone of the rock. "Order! Order, I say! There will not be any more outbursts from you, Slivver, or the defendant. A decision has been rendered. And you will be silent so I can complete it."

Slivver looked back at Nath and shook his head.

Nath stopped breathing for a moment. Were they really going to put him on trial for murder? *Why are they always against me?*

Clearing his throat, Karnax continued, "Given the split decision, I will make the final call." His yellow eyes locked on Nath and narrowed. "Nath, you stand accused of murder. We have weighed all of the evidence, and I have given every detail heavy consideration. The charges against you will be… dismissed."

Frozen in place and not believing his ears, Nath said, "Slivver, did he say dismissed?"

Slivver's quick jovial nodding confirmed the news. "Yes. You are free, Nath. No case will be made against you!" They hugged.

Nath slapped the folded wings behind Slivver's back. "Thank you for being here for me. I didn't know what to do." A loud banging of rock on rock echoed inside the chamber. Nath, along with Slivver, faced the High Council of Dragons again.

"We have a very egregious situation on our hands, Nath and Slivver," Karnax added. "Given the vile nature of this incident, coupled with the absence of King Balzurth, the dragon council has decided to enact Pwaunlow. It is effective immediately."

"Pwaunlow? What is Pwaunlow?" Nath asked Slivver.

"Dragon Home will be locked down until King Balzurth returns," Slivver replied. He clicked his teeth. "Interesting."

"Interesting? What do you mean? I really don't know what a lockdown is."

Karnax bent his long neck toward Nath. "Pwaunlow means that no dragons may enter and no dragons may leave until King Balzurth returns. If they depart, they will be exiled. The remaining Trahaydeen will be banished immediately."

Scratching the back of his head, Nath said, "I don't understand. What about the pursuit of the Trahaydeen? Certainly, the dragons are hunting them down and bringing them to justice. How can they do this if the dragons are not allowed to return?"

"Pwaunlow is Pwaunlow." Karnax banged stone on stone. "This meeting is adjourned." He departed the room first, followed by the other dragons.

The gray scalers released Nath and left as well. Nath faced Slivver, gaping. He shook his head. "That's it? They are just letting the elves go free. No pursuit? That can't be, Slivver. It just can't be." He punched his fist in his hand. "They must be brought to justice."

"Nath, let's walk, and I'll do the best I can to make sense of this." Slivver nudged Nath along with his hands. Jaws clenched, Nath moved along with him. They exited the chamber into the tunnels. "First off, the Trahaydeen who fled the mountain are gone. And when I say gone, I say they vanished. Their trail went dead at the base of the mountain. There was no evidence. No scent. It was as if they vanished into thin air."

"Magic?" Nath said.

"Certainly. And for all we know, they could be anywhere in all of Nalzambor. As far as the east is from the west in regards to Dragon Home. It might take decades to find them." Slivver moved down the corridor at an easy pace. "But the dragons are patient, and they will have vengeance, and they will have justice. It will be very slow going. When our father returns, I have no doubt that he will act on this event immediately. The important thing is that you are not among the accused anymore. You need to be patient and wait until Father returns."

Nath shook his head. "Patient? I'm not going to sit here and wait while a pack of murderers is out there. They don't deserve to get away. And Maefon is out there. I bet she's scared. She will need me to clear her name. There is no way she could be responsible for this act. I would know it in my heart. No doubt Chazzan has something to do with this. He's deceived her. I know he has. He's a shady elf."

Slivver stroked a loose slab of skin under his chin that looked like a beard. "Yes, I suppose he is. There are many strange goings on among the races, always. I tell you, Nath, they fascinate me. In all truth, I envy you, born a man. I wish it had been me."

"Really? Well, that's the dumbest thing I've ever heard. You would give up flying, not to mention all sorts of other things."

"True, but as you have a strong fondness of Maefon, I too have a heart's desire for one much like her." Slivver's ice-blue eyes sparkled. His taloned hands covered his heart. "She is radiant."

"No offense, Slivver, but that is kind of weird." Nath took a split in the path that led him back toward his home. "I suppose I should understand it, but I don't. I adore Maefon, but I still want to earn my scales and become a dragon. Like my father. Like you." Nath eyed his brother. He was truly one of a kind. "I envy you."

Slivver sighed. "I don't suppose anyone will understand my predicament."

"Nope, probably not." Nath climbed the steps into his cave. Slivver waited at the bottom with a perplexed look on his face. "Are you coming up? You don't have to, because I'm coming right back down. I've decided I'm leaving." He went into his little home and opened a wooden chest on the floor. There were many special items Balzurth had given to him. He quickly examined them one at a time. A small lantern, some candles, a leather gauntlet, and some rope. *I can't wait to use these again. There has been little use for them here.* He tossed them into a smallish backpack with dark zigzag shapes and designs woven into the leather and headed back outside with the pack slung over his shoulders.

"Nath, what is on your mind?" Slivver said.

"I'm going after the Trahaydeen." Nath hustled down the steps. "And don't try to talk me out of it. My mind is made up. I'm not letting them get away with this, and Maefon needs me. I know it."

Slivver seized his arm. "Nath, you cannot do this. You will be exiled."

Nath shrugged him off. "It will only be until Father returns. Just a few years or so. That should be plenty of time to rescue Maefon and bring those murderers to justice."

"No, Nath, you don't understand. You cannot leave. If you do, you won't be exiled for a few years. You'll be exiled for a century."

Chapter 22

"WHAT?" NATH SAID, LOWERING HIS pack to the ground. "Did you say a century?"

"Yes." Slivver nodded. "Nath, you are thinking with your heart and not your head. You are not ready to leave Dragon Home. Trust me. And the High Council of Dragons has ruled for our safety. Even if Father returns, he will not overturn their ruling. He trusts them. You must wait until Balzurth comes back. I'm sure he will release you on this hunt then."

Balzurth's last words echoed in Nath's mind. *Do not depart from the mountain, no matter what.* "I have to go, Slivver. I must know what happened. This is the right thing to do. Father will have to understand."

"No, Nath, this is the foolish thing to do. You are a dragon, and dragons can be patient. More patient than a man. When the time comes, we will have vengeance, and we will have justice." Slivver grabbed him and gave him a serious look. "There is more to this conspiracy, Nath. I can feel it. And I don't think it has anything to do with those dragons so much as it has to do with you."

Nath pulled away. He headed toward the throne room. "What do you mean?"

"First off," Slivver explained, "I believe the High Council of Dragons enacted Pwaunlow hoping you would leave. It's not what they all want, but it's what most dragons want. You saw how the council was split. Even though we know you are innocent, most of the dragons feel that you are guilty, and with Father gone, they are trying to get you to leave. Stay here and prove yourself. Show them you are a true, obedient, and just prince. You have a big enough burden, given what you are, on your shoulders."

Stopping in his tracks, Nath faced his brother. "Do you know why they despise me so? Is it just because I look like a man? Or is it something else? I can't help but feel like there is something that is not being told to me that I should know."

Slivver's dragon features had a long look about them. When he spoke, his voice was soft. "I always figured Father would have told you more by now. After all, you are a hundred, and it's time that things are revealed to you. Nath, you have a brother."

Making a puzzled look, Nath said, "Yes, I have you, as well as other dragon brothers and sisters that don't ever speak to me." Nath marched down the hall. "How is this news?"

"No, you have a brother that is just like you. He's... human."

"Don't jest with me, Slivver," Nath said with a feeble smile.

"I wish I was, but I am not."

"And you know him? You've seen him?"

"Neither. I just know *of* him. He was on the scene before my time."

Grabbing Slivver's arm, Nath asked, "Well, who is he? What is his name? What does he look like?"

"I know of him, but I know little about him. He is not spoken about in Dragon Home. In truth, I wouldn't have even known that he existed if not for our brothers and sisters who explained to me why the dragons shun you so. It seems that your brother, our brother, committed an atrocity in Dragon Home."

"What kind of atrocity?"

"He was accused of killing dragons, but it could never be proved that he did it. Sound familiar?"

Nath was at a loss for words at the stunning news. He had a brother, like him. He'd always wished he had a brother or even a sister the same as him. It would have made life much easier in Dragon Home if he did. But at the same time, maybe he wasn't so special after all.

Slivver continued in a grim tone, "You see, Nath, that is why the dragons shun you. They fear that you will turn out like him. And now, fledglings are killed, and if not for the elves, every talon and tail would be pointed at you. So yes, the dragons have always watched you with wary eyes and suspicion. They fear the worst in you."

Suddenly, all of the dragons' ire toward Nath made sense, but he just didn't understand why Balzurth couldn't have told him. If he had known, things could have been different. "Well, I am not my brother, whoever he is. My actions should have spoken for themselves. So what happened to him?"

"He left. I'm not sure if he was banished or if it was of his own accord, but as I understand it, no one has seen him since."

"And this was a long time ago?"

"Perhaps three hundred years, maybe longer. Again, the dragons' lips are as sealed as bark to a tree." Slivver patted Nath's back. "I wish I could have told you sooner."

"No, that's fine. At least now I know something, and in truth, it does give me some relief." Nath stood in front of the throne room doors. He pushed the one on the right open.

"What are you going in there for?"

"To get Fang."

"And why would you be getting this Fang?"

"Fang is the sword that Father made me. I'm taking him on my journey."

Slivver reached for Nath's collar. Nath evaded it. "You are still going? Why? Be patient. I'm telling you there is more to this than we know. You need to stay put. At least give it a few months, if not years. Nath, don't go."

Nath walked into the throne room. Fang was lying in front of Balzurth's seat, sheathed in his scabbard. He picked it up and slid the blade halfway out. "Hello, Fang. We have work to do."

"Please do not do this, Nath. You are too young to go on this journey. And you will be gone a hundred years, if you even last that long. I'm telling you, stay put until Father returns. You have been cleared of this matter, and it is not your responsibility. You need more time to develop."

"Develop what? I've been training all my life. And another hundred years of it? No, I can't just sit and wait while Maefon is out there. And I'm not going to let those murderers get away with what they did. They killed fledglings, Slivver. Fledglings! In cold blood. Doesn't that outrage you?"

"It wounds us all. But vengeance and justice will only come with patience and a best-laid plan. You have no plan at all." Slivver stood in a pile of treasure. He pulled a steel breastplate out of the pile and dumped the coins and gems out. "Or protection, for that matter. Put this on."

"I don't need that. It will just slow me down."

"You are in an awful big hurry for someone who has no idea where they are going." Slivver spun Nath around. With quick hands, he dropped the breastplate over Nath's head and buckled the leather straps tight. "Perfect. It fits like a glove."

Nath inspected it. "Well, it is light." He knocked on his chest. The steel plate had a dull shine to it. "What is it made of?"

"Moorite."

"Huh, that's dwarven. I've read about it. I find it strange that it was crafted for a man my size. I thought they didn't like to share."

Nath slung Fang over his back and looked up at Slivver. "You aren't going to try and stop me?"

The silver dragon didn't hide the disappointment in his face. His frown was as big as ever. "Didn't Father command you to stay in the mountain?"

"I'm not sure that he specifically said that." Nath knew exactly what Balzurth had said. He was not to leave.

"Disobedience has consequences, Nath. You will face them."

"You can come too."

"As much as I'd like to, I'll await Father's return. Besides, you need to know that you won't have a ring of safety around you. You are protected here, and you won't be out there. This is your last warning."

Nath gave his brother a fierce hug. "See you in a hundred years."

Slivver pulled something from a leather pouch he kept around his waist and stuffed it into Nath's backpack. "When you find the time, read it. It might prove helpful. It's a theory of mine."

"Of course." He made his way out of the throne room. As he crossed the threshold, the doors quaked and groaned. The door closed behind him. Fang suddenly felt like an anvil on his back. Balzurth told him that he wasn't supposed to take Fang out of the throne room. It seemed that Fang didn't want to go either. He pulled Fang free with a grunt. Looking at the sword, he said, "Fang, I have to do this, and I'll need you. But if I have to leave you, I will. What will it be?"

Fang's blade hummed.

The heavy blade lightened in Nath's grip.

"Thank you, Fang. Thank you." He set his eyes on the path out of the mountain. "We have a mission to fulfill."

CHAPTER 23

NATH EXITED DRAGON HOME NEAR the base of the mountain. He turned back, looking down the long corridor he'd just taken. Slowly, rocks filled in the gap until nothing but stone remained. An archway made up of glowing ancient runes etched in the rock faded. Nath touched the rock. The stone was cold beneath his palm. It was the door he always took to come and go when he'd sneak out onto the mountain to watch the sun rise and fall, though there were others vastly bigger.

"Am I banished or am I not banished? That is the question." Nath took a breath. He recited the ancient words that let him enter. Long and flowing, the words came freely from his mouth. When it ended, the mystic runes in the archway did not appear. The stone remained. There would be no coming. There was only going. Emptiness filled him, a longing to be inside the warmth of the mountain. A chill breeze rustled his hair. He faced the horizon, set his shoulders forward, and walked. "One hundred years, here I come."

Nath traveled north. His journey took him over narrow paths, crossing over a moat of lava that circled Dragon Home. From there he traversed the rugged terrain of the lakes of lava. It was a slippery trek that only seasoned mountaineers, bold adventurers, or wingless dragons with strong claws would take. Climbing out of one steamy ravine after another, he noted the red rock dragons half buried in the hot muddy banks of the lakes. Their green eyes were fixed on Nath like he was their next meal. Nath came to an halt. "Huh, I've never been this far out before."

Standing on the bank, Nath watched the boiling red waters surge by. There was a wide gap, over one hundred feet. The treacherous terrain wasn't meant to be crossed to the mountain. It was a barrier between mortal and dragon that kept the races away. Nath searched the lava rocks that jutted up out of the fiery stream. There was a fair distance between them, but he was confident he could hop from one to another.

"I should have known that leaving the mountain would be difficult. One slip, and I'll be charcoal." He considered going back and taking another way, but one way in would be as troublesome as another. The Mountain of Doom was laid out that way, to keep the races' curiosity at bay. He gathered his legs beneath him. "Here goes!" In a flat-footed hop, he jumped ten feet to the nearest stone. He hopped from one to another, going forward and backward in a zigzag pattern. Halfway across, he landed on a rock and slipped. His boot toes dipped toward the boiling waters. "Whoa!" He flailed his arms, regaining his balance. "Whew! That was close."

He sucked the blistering heat in as he swiped sweat from his brow. Rivulets trickled down his back. He peered through the steam, searching for his next spot. He jumped from rock to rock, still advancing, but his own youthful energy began to fade. The lava was draining him. "Come on, Nath, only a few more to go." He jumped to the next rock. There was one more ahead, and then he'd have plenty of room to make the final leap to the other side of the bank. He huffed out a breath of relief and wiped the stinging sweat from his eyes. "This would have been easier than walking if I didn't have all of this gear on me."

Nath jumped. His landing spot moved. It wasn't a rock. It was a red rock dragon. "Gah!" The wingless dragon was as big as a Haversham hippo he'd come across in his studies. Its massive jaws opened wide. Pulling his feet up, Nath landed on the tip of the dragon's snout. It snapped. Nath jumped. Timing it perfectly, he jumped as the dragon bit, landed on its closing jaws, and jumped again. It became a dance between the two in the swirling river of flame.

"Quit trying to eat me! I am not your enemy, brother!"

Out of the corners of his eyes, he saw red rock dragons close in.

"You mindless brutes! You aren't supposed to eat your own kind!" Nath jumped. The lava waters rippled as the dragon heaved upward and snapped at his toes. Nath landed once again. Thinking on his feet, he decided to use the brute strength of the dragon in his favor. The dragon surged upward again. Nath leapt, using the dragon's momentum to propel him. He landed on the back of another red rock. It bit at him. He jumped again, twisting in the air toward the awaiting back. He landed face first in the hot dirt and soft clay, exhausted. He pushed his face out and saw the red rocks closing in on his position. He scrambled up the steep bank and climbed over the rim, just as the nearest red rock dragon nipped at his toes. Its jaws clacked together. Nath kept running, not stopping until the brown ground turned green.

Finally, standing in a field of grass and wildflowers up to his knees, he turned back toward the mountains and sat down. Dragon Home loomed miles away. Lava seams flowed out of the stark mountain between the ridges. Its peak waited beneath the rolling clouds, daring them to draw closer and be swallowed up. It was Nath's home, or at least it used to be. And from where he sat, it didn't look very pretty. If he didn't already know better, he would have thought Dragon Home looked scary.

He picked at the grasses and plucked the wildflowers. Bees moved from flower to flower, making a gentle buzz. The wind rustled the high grasses. A flock of bright-blue birds streaked through the skies above. A huge vulture-like bird, with the appearance of two heads, fell out of the trees, gliding over the grasses before disappearing in the lazy fabric of the meadows.

A chill crept through Nath. His eyes swept over his surroundings. He felt as if he was being watched. Finally, it passed.

Nalzambor was full of vibrant life. Nath had never witnessed it before at close range. At least, not at length. Most of the time, he was in the sky with his father. Wiping the mud off the best he could, he said, "This doesn't seem like it's going to be a dangerous place. It's kind of nice, actually."

A large drop of water splattered on his head. He looked up. Storm clouds formed overhead. Thunder rolled in. The winds picked up. The sky flashed, and a downpour of rain began.

CHAPTER 24

SOUTHEAST OF DRAGON HOME, FAR away and forgotten, a fortress of stone was dug out of the rocks. The fortress overlooked a rushing river of rapids. A suspension bridge, barely wide enough for two, swayed over the river as the chronic stiff winds tore at its planks. With the rain beating against their faces, Maefon, Chazzan, and four other Trahaydeen elves made the risky trek across the bridge.

"The last time I was here, it was storming," Maefon shouted against the wind. She stepped forward, right behind Chazzan, clinging to the bridge as she moved forward, hand over hand on the ropes. "It's been storming since we left. I hate being wet."

"It rains often here, but I don't imagine Lord Dark Day will let us take up residence. He'll have plenty of work for us. As he says, 'A Caligin's work is never done until all of his enemies lie dead.'"

"Yes, I know," she said, reaching the end of the bridge. She hopped on the ledge and looked up at the fortress. Water cascaded from its crevices like a waterfall. The face of the stone complex was a hundred feet wide and a hundred feet high. Stone balconies jutted out from its sheer face. An iron portcullis behind the archway entrance in the middle was closed. The elves gathered underneath one of its arches, out of the hard rain, but huge drops of water still dripped on them. Shivering, she said, "It better be dry in there. And a fire would be nice. For some reason, I am freezing."

From behind, Chazzan wrapped his arms around her waist. "Either way, I will warm you up."

She touched his cheek. "I know you will."

Still holding her, Chazzan kicked at the portcullis. "Hello? I know you are there. I can see you hunched over your lard-filled belly."

Sitting against the wall with his face between his knees sat an ogre. His head, as round as a boulder, lifted up. More shoulders than neck, the chinless brute got up. Wearing nothing but trousers made from animal skins, the greasy-haired brute strolled over. His arms swung at his sides, knuckles almost scraping the puddles on the stony ground. Standing a full nine feet tall, he glowered down at the group with a milkly yellow eyes. "I am Monfur, warden of the portcullis of Stonewater Keep. State your business," the ogre said in a voice that sounded more monster than man.

"Whew!" Chazzan covered his nose. "What do you eat? Manure pudding? Add some fruit to it or something. Foul, so foul."

Maefon pinched her nose and backed away. "I don't think fruit will do it. He's an ogre. He was born rank. He'll die rank. Not even the salt of the seas could wash his stench away."

"Anyway, I don't care who you are. We are Caligin, faithful servants of the Lord of the Dark in the Day, and without further delay, you need to let us in." Chazzan produced a neck chain on which hung a platinum ring with a black stone set in it. "Cast your eyes on our insignia, and open this gate with haste."

The ogre stared at the black rock. "Hmmm... you may enter." The ogre bent over and removed a pin from the floor with his fingers. With one arm, he lifted the heavy iron portcullis that would have taken a dozen elves to lift.

All of the Trahaydeen gaped as they hustled inside.

"You know, if the ogres were half as smart as they were strong, they could possibly rule the world," Chazzan said to Maefon. All of the elves tossed their heads back in laughter. The gate dropped down with a loud bang, cutting off their laughter.

"Take the stairs," Monfur said, securing the pin in the portcullis. "He stays up." He walked back to the wall where he came from and hunkered down in his seat. "I stay down, but I always remember, elves are delicious."

Stonewater Keep's stone walls were slick with green-gray moss and dripping from most of the crevices. Maefon's feet splashed in puddles of water as they traversed the damp interior and made their way up the stairs. The wood beneath the elves' light feet creaked and groaned beneath them. Many of the wood planks were soft and rotting as the staircase crossed over and up, floor by floor. Rain dripped from above into the gap in the middle. They passed different doors on their way up, each sealed shut. Finally, they made it to the top level. An oak door strapped together with iron banding blocked their entrance into the room.

Chazzan wrung out the sleeves of his dripping-wet robes, tossed his hair back, and said with a clever smile, "Our destiny awaits." He knocked on the door.

The metal door on the square portal slid open. The person on the other side had no face. Instead, their head was covered in a sack of dark-crimson cloth. The eyes were cut out like slits. The prying eyes inspected the six Trahaydeen elves.

Chazzan held up his signet ring. "Hail to the Lord of the Dark in the Day."

The person in the mask let out a snobby snort and slammed the portal door closed. A few seconds later, the door's locking bolt popped. The heavy door swung inward. The six elves were bathed in warm firelight as they entered.

The entrance led into a grand hall where two fireplaces were burning. A long table made of ancient mahogany and fit for fifty people ran the length of the floor. Standing at attention behind most of the empty chairs were the guardians in crimson hoods. The cut-out eyelets were different for all of them, designed in a self-gratifying, sinister way. They had no mouths or nose holes. They all wore a set of black leather armor. A long sword and dagger dressed all of their hips. They were elves, the same as Maefon and the others in her group, but they were disciples of the Caligin, going through training. A feast of food spread over the table. There were roasted beasts, dates, fruits, nuts, and crystal decanters of apple wine.

Maefon's stomach rumbled. She needed food to settle it. The journey hadn't been long, but the teleportation spell that whisked them away from Dragon Home's mountainside turned her belly upside down.

At the far end of the table, the Lord of the Dark in the Day was seated. A scenic mural of the entire world of Nalzambor covered the wall behind him. By far the largest person in the room, the big-boned man wore crimson robes that partially covered his muscular arms. A chrome mask fashioned with the sharp features of a frowning elf covered his face. In his left hand, he held an orb made of solid iron. His head was tilted to one side. He banged the orb casually on the table.

Chazzan glanced back at Maefon. Together, all of them took a knee. Heads down with arms up and fingers outspread, all together, they said, "Our service is yours, Lord Darkken. Now and forever."

Lord Darkken spoke in a commanding voice. "Welcome home, Caligin. Enter. Feast."

CHAPTER 25

AEFON AND CHAZZAN SAT AT the very end of the table. The other four Trahaydeen were beside them. Quietly, they ate. Even the disciples lifted their hoods over their noses and indulged in the meal.

Lord Darkken broke the uncomfortable silence lingering in the foreboding room. "They can eat, but they can't talk. You remember those days, don't you, Chazzan? Maefon?"

"Those days were unforgettable." Chazzan toasted his crystal goblet in the air and drank. "Has much changed since I trained, Lord Darkken?"

"Please, you can dispense with the formalities, brother. Lord will do." He let out a rusty laugh. "Ah-haha."

Maefon dabbed the corners of her mouth with a napkin. She never could tell when Darkken was joking or not. "I prefer Lord Dark Day."

"Oh, how I have missed your wit, Maefon." Darkken reached over and squeezed her forearm with an iron grip. "Dark Day, hah. Honestly, it was a consideration, but Darkken is suitable. And you both have earned the privilege. But whatever you are comfortable with will do. The Caligin are not explicit on formalities unless needed.

It's best to keep it casual among the races. Adopt their culture and win them over." He locked his fingers. "Hence, I like to keep our conversing more casual in nature. The Caligin want their enemy's guard to be down before we strike. As it turns out, the word *Darkken*, Maefon, is old dwarven for dark day. Besides, I like to condense words where I can, given my upbringing."

"Understood," she replied with a nod but not fully understanding Darkken's meaning. "The dragon recitals, though fascinating, almost made my ears bleed at times. It wouldn't have been so bad if they didn't fully recite their names at the end to give credit. I could hardly keep my eyes open."

Chazzan rolled his eyes. "Oh, those were dreadful. They could be such boring creatures on occasion, and they moved so slowly."

"Yes, truly a waste of time. Often that is what the dragons do, waste time." Darkken's coppery eyes flickered like light behind his mask. "So you have brought new recruits, I see? Only four, after what, eighty years of work, Chazzan?"

"The Trahaydeen were hard to crack. Given the mission, Lord Darkken, I focused on exactly what I needed for fear that I would arouse suspicion." Chazzan smiled from ear to ear. "The mission was pulled off to perfection. Though I started to wonder if Balzurth—"

Darkken slammed the iron orb on the table. *Bang!* "Do not say his name."

"Yes, yes, absolutely," Chazzan said, shifting in his chair as the smile vanished from his face. "Apologies, Darkken."

Maefon shifted in her seat. She and Chazzan only knew the mission, but they did not know its purpose. For whatever reason, Lord Darkken wanted to take the dragons down or do them harm somehow, and Nath was the link in the chain that needed to be broken. Why, she didn't know for certain as of yet, but Darkken clearly had a grudge against Balzurth.

"It's Lord Darkken," the dark lord warned.

Maefon's heartbeat skipped. The edge in Darkken's voice sent chills down her spine. She'd trained in the keep for a full five years before becoming a full Caligin. Darkken had a voice that would cut right through her. He pushed, prodded, and demanded excellence. Stonewater Keep was a training ground where the elves learned to spin lies and deceit. They learned how to use weapons of wood and steel, as well as the weapons of the mind. There were potions and poisons brewed. The physical training pushed her to the limit. The tests of the mind were anguish. The devotion was pure because, as the Lord of the Dark in the Day liked to put it, you were purified in darkness. Their mission was to spread chaos throughout Nalzambor and take over the world. There was no better way to spread the deception than through the blood of the most trusted race of all... the elves. Maefon, from the moment she met him, thought he was brilliant.

Lord Darkken pushed back from the table. The chair legs ground over the floor. He stood up, a tower of a man, seeming even bigger than he already was. "As you can see, many of the chairs at the table remain empty. Both of you know how customary that is. Many wash out. I begin with fifty, train them for five years, and finish with sometimes less than twenty. But this class, as you can see, with forty left, has been remarkable. The Caligin's numbers are growing. Over a thousand strong now poison the fields and sow the seeds of deception through the land."

"Does that include this class?" Chazzan asked.

"No." Darkken faced the huge painted map on the wall of Nalzambor. "But it only takes a few to topple a kingdom. And I have many." He pointed to a spot on the map where the home of the elves, Elome, was. The city blended in with the trees and natural rock. "In Elome, our brethren keep the elves divided, for they have penetrated the highest of councils. Their policies agitate the dwarves who could be potential allies, and the skirmishes with the orcs will never cease. Of course, that is a given." He paced back and forth, poking the different locations as he spoke. "In the human city of Quintuklen, elven envoys and minsters give bad counsel. In Narmum, the melting pot of most of the races is stirred. Bad trade deals, failing crops, goblin raids in foreign lands. It never ceases, and words cannot describe my delight in these matters. Eventually, all of the kingdoms will crumble from within. Self-destruction is in their nature, even the elves and dwarves—one just has to know how to ignite it." He leaned on the map with his hands. His chrome skull turned all the way toward them. "Oh, how I delight in causing trouble."

"We delight with you, Lord Darkken," Maefon said. Standing up, she lifted her goblet. "May I propose a toast?"

Lord Darkken turned. "Yes, Maefon, and please, didn't I tell you to call me Darkken?" He eyed her. "But I agree! A toast is in order, though it will be difficult for me to drink due to this finely crafted mask." He approached the table, leaned down, and removed the mask. Long locks of flowing hair that matched his rust-colored eyes spilled out over his shoulders. His handsome face, without blemish or scar, was perfection. He set the mask down, picked up a goblet, and showed a radiant smile of pearl-white teeth. "Go on, Maefon."

With bated breath, she lifted her goblet higher. Everyone at the table stood. Her eyes were fastened on Lord Darkken. The only man she'd ever seen who rivaled his enchanting looks was Nath. They were different, Nath something brighter, and Darkken something darker. Her heart fluttered before the captivating man. "To deception and conquest!"

"To deception and conquest!" all present replied.

"Long live Lord Darkken," she added. "May his new kingdom reign supreme forever!" She touched glasses with Darkken beside her and Chazzan across from her. The crystal made a loud *tinnng!*

"I enjoyed that toast," Lord Darkken said, after taking a long drink. "And speaking of deception, I look forward to hearing more about your seduction of Balzurth's son, Nath."

Chazzan's eyes grew big. As Darkken was about to continue his conversation, he interrupted, "Lord Darkken, no disrespect, but I was just given a stern impression that you don't like the dragon king's name mentioned. Did I miss something?"

"Of course not, Chazzan. I just wanted to build more tension. It was merely a lesson for the disciples. You remember those mind games, don't you? How to control the room?" Lord Darkken set his glass down, moved behind Chazzan, and placed his hands on his shoulders. His fingers massaged the elf's muscles. "So now that we have gone around the horn, tell me how you executed the demise of the fledglings."

"Certainly, Lord." Chazzan smiled at Maefon. "I'd be happy to share. After all, deceiving the races is one thing, but misleading dragons is quite another. I cannot express what an honor it has been to be chosen for this mission. And having Maefon at my side was a boon." He winked at her. "In more ways than one." Chazzan recounted at length everything that he planned and executed to the last detail. He started the story with all of the flair and intensity one would expect from a master storyteller and stage performer. It included luring away the dragons from the nursery and pinning the murder on Nath. With everyone in the room captivated by his words, he finished by saying, "We fled the Mountain of Doom, used the talisman at the bottom, and arrived within a league of the keep." He drained his goblet of wine. "And here we live, and here we breathe."

Darkken's eyes narrowed for a moment.

"An interesting choice of words, Chazzan." Darkken slapped the elf's shoulders on the sides. "And I owe you a *well done*. Now, not wanting to interrupt such a delightful story, I wanted you to go back. You said that you framed Balzurth's son, Nath. I clearly stated that the fledglings were to be killed. I know I didn't mention Nath's involvement."

"Yes, but I saw an opportunity to deflect attention from us by implicating him." Chazzan refilled his goblet. "I pride myself on that kind of forward thinking. And I did have decades to come up with it. I just wished I could have remained to see the dragon's son squirm."

"I see." Darkken resumed massaging Chazzan's neck. "But I was very explicit. Explicit in meaning that you shouldn't take any liberties with this carefully planned project. I sent you in decades ago, Chazzan. My plan was not to be altered."

"Apologies, Lord Darkken. Is something wrong? I'm confident that all will turn out in your favor as always." Chazzan winced. The shoulder rubs were getting deeper. "Has Nath not departed the mountain as you surmised? I just wanted to borrow more time. Keep the dragons off our trail."

"Yes, he has departed. My eyes have told me that. That is not the problem. The problem is you not following my explicit orders." Lord Darkken's brows knitted together. He massaged harder. "You risked destroying everything I planned for."

"Lord Darkken, I swear, I would never cross an order—*hurk!*"

Lord Darkken's hands closed on Chazzan's neck and squeezed. Chazzan's eyes bulged. He dropped his glass. His knees banged against the table. Darkken ripped the man out of his chair. He held Chazzan high in the air.

In a heated voice, Lord Darkken said, "My orders were explicit." His arms flexed. Chazzan kicked his legs. He clawed and pounded on Darkken's arms. His pleading eyes flitted to Maefon. There was a loud crack that sounded like a dry tree limb being broken. Chazzan's neck sagged. His toes kicked a few times and stopped.

"Open the door," Lord Darkken said. A hooded disciple opened the door. Lord Darkken marched through it. "Monfur! Incoming!" He dropped Chazzan into the gap between the stairs. A delayed *thud* followed a moment later.

"To the washout?" Monfur hollered back up.

"Yes, along with all the other washouts. And don't let it dam up the river this time." Lord Darkken reentered the room. The door closed behind him. He had Chazzan's signet ring and necklace in his hand. He set it in front of Maefon. "For you," he said.

Fighting her trembles, she said, "Thank you, Lord Darkken."

"You're welcome. And I hope that you won't miss him, Maefon. You won't, will you?"

"No, Lord Darkken." Using her fork and knife, she sawed into her slice of meat. Her hands trembled. She fought against it. Her heart pounded like galloping horses. She loved Chazzan, and now she'd lost him, forever. She forced a devilish smile. "Of course not. I have you, don't I?"

"Of course. Heh-heh-heh."

CHAPTER 26

SITTING ON A STREAM BANK, Nath took off his boots. The storms had passed, but the pathways through the forests were muddy. He'd learned that he didn't care for mud or the rain. It made him wet and his boots muddy. If he could avoid it altogether, he would have. He moved out to a flat rock, sat down, rinsed his boots off in the water, and dipped his toes in the cool depths. With the setting sun shining in his face, he said, "Ah!"

Nath was used to seeing the world from above, not below. His only time in the world came when he flew with his father, and they never landed. Things were different when they weren't from a dragon's point of view. The trees were bigger, the land vaster, and the signs of life were overwhelming. In the mountain, things were quiet, very quiet most of the time. But now there were bugs chirping, varmints slipping through the grasses and climbing the branches, and the constant sounds of birds calling, except at night when the owls would hoot, but not as frequently.

"Nature sure is busy." Nath set his boots on the rocks and watched the stream rush by. "I suppose I'll get used to it, though. After all, I don't have much of a choice." Looking down at his clothing, he noticed mud splatter all over it. "I don't think looking like a vagrant will make a very good impression on whoever I meet, either." He waded into the water and sat down. The waters massaged his neck. "This isn't so bad." He rinsed off his face and hair. "I like it. I wonder why swimming in the water is different than getting rained on. This is much more pleasant."

Closing his eyes, Nath went over his plans to find the Trahaydeen. He knew what they looked like and who they were. He would go from village, to town, to city and ask the people if they had seen them. He had no doubt that someone would have seen something. Elves would stand out anywhere that wasn't elven. And the murderers wouldn't be safe in Elome. The elves were a tight people, and if the banished Trahaydeen immediately went to Elome, there would be questions.

Nath's eyes popped open. "Wait a moment. Won't the elves be looking for them too? Ah, I'm so stupid." He hit the palm of his hand on his head. "Of course they will. At least, I would. But maybe, like the dragons, they take forever making a decision. Yes, I need to be doing what I am doing, because the longer I wait, the farther away they get. And I have to find Maefon. She's in danger. I can feel it."

Nalzambor had five major cities. Quintuklen, the human city in the North; Thraag, the home of the orcs in the northeast; Elome, the home of the elves; and Morgdon, the westward city in the rocks. Then there was Narnum, the free city, where all of the races were welcome, so long as they were tolerable. If there were elves abroad in places like Narnum, then that was where Nath would start. He'd try his fortune there, and if he didn't have any luck, there were hundreds of smaller cities and towns he could look into. Someone somewhere would know something. He just had to ask.

"Well, lounging in the water isn't going to find me anything but fish," he said. At that same moment, a salmon leapt up out of the water over the rocks. Nath snagged it out of the air. The large fish wiggled in his hands. Nath held on. "Oh, no you don't. I'm hungry, and I'm going to eat you." The fish squirted out of his hands. "Ah! Blast!"

Nath climbed out of the water, pulled on his boots, readied his gear, and started back upstream.

"Help! Help!" a voice cried out from the other side of the stream. A vision of a woman raced through a clearing in a weathered cotton dress that clung to her body. Behind her, a two-legged man with four hairy arms and the head of a beast chased after her. It closed in on the screaming woman, who vanished into the willowwacks, still screaming, "Heeelp!"

Chapter 27

ITHOUT GIVING IT A THOUGHT, Nath crossed the
stream and burst out of the water. He chased after
the monster into the woodland. Cutting through the
brush and forest, he heard the woman still screaming, "Help meeee!"

Nath followed the sound of her voice. Branches slapped his face,
and briars dug at his legs as he pushed toward the woman's cry for
help.

Where did she go?

The forest darkened the deeper he went. The leaves were a deep-
green roof over his head. Losing the sound of her voice, Nath slowed
down. He reached behind him and drew Fang. The blade hummed
in his grip and gave off a very faint shade of blue. Hearing some
scuffling in the bushes and branches, Nath advanced.

A loud grunt was followed by a woman's scream.

Nath took off in a straight line. He didn't stop until he entered
a cove where the beastly four-armed man had the woman cornered
against the rocks.

"Get away from her, monster!" Nath shouted.

The monster whipped around. Its four oversized hands with
talons like metal spikes clenched in and out. Its wide, hairy face

was like a dog. Its big ears pointed up into tips. Its earlobes almost touched the layers of brawny shoulder muscles, and it stood a full foot taller than Nath. Wide jaws slavered with drool. "Go away, or die, little man! She is my prize, my prey, my dinner if I wish."

Flanking the beast, Nath said, "You speak well for such an ugly thing. Now use those big ears of yours. I will turn your four arms into two quicker than you can blink. So back away from the woman. Otherwise, I won't hesitate to slay you, whatever you are."

"I am Rond, the bugbear. I do not fear your metal. You might cut off one hand, but I will crush you with the others." He bared his teeth. "Come on then, give it a try."

Nath circled around, coming between the woman and Rond. The woman's tattered dress did nothing to conceal her beauty. She was young, fair skinned, with salt-and-pepper-colored hair and a full and fetching figure. Over his shoulder, he said back to her, "Stay close, lady. I am here, and I will protect you from this beast."

Sobbing, she said, "You are so brave, warrior. I owe you my life. Thank you for protecting me. My hero!"

Flashing his sword from side to side, Nath said, "Rond, I will only warn you one more time. Flee, or suffer the consequences of a single lethal strike. You see, I could take your arms, which seems helpful, seeing how you have two too many, or I could bury my blade in your heart. That will resolve all of your problems, and hers, and one of mine." The woman wrapped her arms around Nath's waist. "I don't think you want that, so begone."

Hugging Nath from behind and nuzzling her cheek in his back, the comely woman said, "You are my hero. A great, great hero."

"Did you hear that, Rond? I am a great, great hero, and I aim to live up to that. So last chance. Back off, or die. What will it be?"

Rond's narrowed eyes ran the full length of Fang's blade. He looked Nath in the eyes, made a hawking sound in his throat, and spit snot on the ground. "I'm going to pull that flame hair from your head, one handful at a time." He beckoned Nath forward. "Come on, give me your best."

"Stay here, lady." Nath broke away from her. "And you might not want to watch this."

"You are so brave." The woman touched his arm. "And foolish. I never met a brave man that wasn't."

"Huh?" Nath said. A shock ripped through his body like a jolt of lightning. His teeth clacked together. Fang fell from his fingers, and his legs wobbled beneath him.

CHAPTER 28

REGAINING HIS BALANCE AND TRYING to shake the stars from his eyes, Nath said, "What did you do to me?" Charges of energy flowed from the young woman's hand and into his arm again. "Ow!" Nath fought to stand on his feet, swaying from side to side.

"Why aren't you falling?" She slapped his arm again. *Zzzzt!* Nath still stood. Her arms grew bigger. "Fall, mind you, fall!"

As she reached for Nath again, he grabbed her by the wrists. With a thick tongue, he said, "What is woong with yooou? I'm trying tooo heeelp yoooo!"

"Rond! Rond!" she called out, trying to twist out of Nath's grip. "Get this stubborn fool off me."

"Nooo, nooo," Nath said. "I am trying to help you. Why are you trying to hurt—" Rond's shadow fell over Nath and the woman. The bugbear's big fist collided with the side of Nath's face. Pain exploded through his cheek. He hit the ground face-first. The taste of dirt and grass filled his mouth. He fought to stay awake. He couldn't push his sunken face out of the dirt. Between the shocking and the heavy-handed blow, his limbs had nothing left.

"Bind him to the tree." The woman rubbed her hands with a scowl on her face.

"Why not kill him, Calypsa?" Rond said in his gruff voice. He dragged Nath by the hair and pushed him into a tree then looked at Calypsa. "I don't have any rope. What shall I tie him to the tree with?"

"Just hold him still." She faced Nath. She was very pretty, with a tiara made from twigs in her hair. The cotton dress she wore had living leaves woven into the fabric. Holding her hands out with her palms to the ground, she chanted, "Evergreen, evergreen, lend me your root. Evergreen, evergreen, life flows from your shoots."

The ground came to life. Like a snake, roots crept out of the ground, slithered around Nath, and wrapped him tight to the tree. He grimaced. The small veinlike roots felt like steel coil. They bit into his arms. His face ached, his tongue was swollen, and his energy was sapped. It took everything he had to keep from blacking out.

Calypsa and Rond huddled over Nath's gear. His leather pack lay on the ground, and Calypsa emptied out the contents. With big eyes, she said, "What have we here?" There were some potion vials, a leather purse, a small hooded lantern that fit in the palm of his hand, candles, a coil of rope, and a gauntlet with a gem embedded into the leather. She held it before her. "That's a big stone."

Rond handed her a knife. "Let me dig it out. The leather is useless."

She pulled away. "You just keep your twenty sticky fingers back, Rond. Even though the glove is too big for my hand, it is quite fashionable." She petted her face with it. Her nose crinkled. "It stinks a bit." She held out her hand. "Let me see that knife. I'm starting to think that digging it out is the right call."

"Don't ruin it," Nath mumbled.

The bugbear stormed over to Nath and pulled two hands back for a backhanded slap. "Silence!"

"Oh, Rond, leave him be. He's incapacitated now." Calypsa bit her tongue as she tried to dig the stone out of the leather glove. "My, this thing is really mounted in there well. Rond, go ahead and take a crack at it."

As Rond headed toward Calypsa, Nath managed to lift his boot and trip the bugbear. The bugbear fell hard to the ground. He jumped back up, chest and shoulders heaving. "You'll pay for that!"

Calypsa giggled. "Now that was funny. Just leave him be, Rond." She opened up the strings on Nath's purse and dumped the contents into her hand. Gold, silver, and precious gemstones poured out. "Oh my!"

Rond turned toward her. His long ears wiggled. He came to her side and fell to his knees. "It's a fortune. I've never seen such treasure." He held up an emerald that looked like a pea in his fingers. "What a score! We are rich!"

"Yes," she said. "This is the robbery of a lifetime!" She punched Rond in the arm. "I told you our day would come."

"You are thieves?" Nath said as his head began to clear. "You tricked me with a false cry for help only to steal from me?" He was aghast. "What is wrong with you?"

"We are not thieves," she argued. "He is a bugbear, and I am a dryad." She inspected the treasure in her hands. "Actually, I'm part dryad—my mother was a dryad, and my father was a man." She winked at Nath. "Not so very different than you, handsome."

"What you are doing is wrong," Nath said. "You can't just lie to people and steal from them."

"Why not? It's what we do. After all, we have to use our gifts for something," she said.

"Yes, why not," Rond said flatly. He started shaking one of the ceramic potion vials that was colored orange with black specks. "What is this?"

Calypsa snatched it away. Every move she made was graceful. Her way was captivating. "Besides, how does a lone man like you come by such treasure? Hmmm? I'll tell you how. You stole it. You stole all of it. For you are too young to have all of this wealth. It's a princess's ransom."

Brows knitted together, Nath said, "It's mine. Gifts from my father."

She burst out laughing. "Ah-hahahaha. Who is your father, the king of Quintuklen? You are going to have to come up with a better explanation than that, but I don't have time to listen." She started putting all of the items back in the pack. "Rond and I will be going. But it was nice robbing you, uh... What is your name?"

"Nath," he said with a frown.

She walked up to Nath and slung his bag over her shoulders. "Well, Nath, next time you see a gorgeous woman screaming for help, perhaps you should avoid it." She gave him a sweet kiss on the lips. "Most heroes wind up dead. Don't be one of them."

Suddenly, Nath felt very sleepy. He started to yawn. "What did you do to me?"

"I gave you the dryad's kiss. Just go to sleep, have sweet dreams of me, and enjoy it."

"But I don't want to go to..." As his words trailed off, his lids became heavy, and Calypsa and Rond walked away with his belongings.

CHAPTER 29

"STOP," NATH MOANED. HE SHOOK the cobwebs out of his head. "Don't leave. You are thieves." As his vision became clear, Calypsa turned toward him. There was confusion on her face. She marched toward him.

"Why are you not sleeping? You should be asleep!"

"I'm not tired anymore."

She got down on her knees, grabbed his face, and kissed him again. "You will sleep. Every man I kiss sleeps."

Nath closed his eyes for a moment then popped them open again. "Not me. Perhaps your kiss isn't as powerful as you think it is. Or as good, for that matter."

"What? There is no better kisser than me." She kissed him fully with her soft lips.

Nath returned the kiss. In truth, she was a great kisser. When she broke it off, he said, "You are improving."

She jumped to her feet and stomped them on the ground. "What kind of man are you? Are you a sprite? A trickster?" She shook the bag. "Is this treasure even real? Rond! Choke the truth out of him!"

Rond fastened his big hand on Nath's neck and started squeezing. "Tell Calypsa what she wants."

Gagging, Nath tried to spit out the words. "I can't talk if I can't breathe."

"Loosen it up, Rond. Now, tell me who or what you are." She shook her head. "And is this treasure real, or is it bewitched?"

Rond's fingers loosened on Nath's neck. Nath started to get the feeling that neither Calypsa nor Rond was very bright. Either that, or she was paranoid. He considered telling her a lie. Perhaps he could be a sprite or a trickster, but lying wasn't the way he wanted to go. He decided the truth would be better. In a hoarse voice, he said, "I'm a dragon."

"A dragon? Really?" She looked at Rond. The bugbear squeezed Nath's neck again. "And if you are a dragon, then where are your scales? Your tail? I don't see any sharp teeth in your mouth. What about the horns and wings? You are a liar."

Red-faced, Nath shook his head. "I'm not."

"Just let go of him, Rond," she said. "I want to hear more of what he has to say. I have to admit, I'm a bit curious about this golden-eyed man that I cannot shock or put to sleep. That is abnormal."

"We should kill him. Cut off his head and go."

"Just let go of him." She crossed her legs, put her elbows on her knees, and propped her chin up on her hands. "I could use a good story. It's been a while."

"I disagree, Calypsa. I say we go. He smells of trickery." Rond stepped away but kept a wary eye on Nath.

"Out with it, Dragon Man," she said.

Clearing his throat, Nath said, "I am from Dragon Home."

"You mean the Mountain of Doom?"

"I suppose."

"Hah, this fairy tale is getting richer. Go on."

"I am the son of Balzurth, the king of the dragons. Recently, I was exiled for a hundred years because I am hunting down a pack of elves, called Trahaydeen, that murdered over a dozen dragon fledglings."

Nath shifted against his natural bonds. "You see, I was not supposed to leave, and when I did, I became banished. So I cannot return, but I will find the murderers and avenge my brethren."

A little smile played on Calypsa's lips. Her big chestnut eyes probed his.

"What?" he said.

"You really are convinced that this is truth. I have to admit, your words are convincing. Either you are the greatest liar I have ever met, or what you say is true, which is preposterous." She glanced at Rond. "What do you think?"

"He lies." Rond punched two of his fists into both of his other hands. "Let me kill him."

"But I'm not lying," Nath pleaded. "Think about it. Your magic has little effect on me. How can you explain that, Calypsa? I know it perplexes you. The only explanation is that I am what I say I am. And that treasure you have, it could only come from the mountain. After all, I know you have not seen the likes of that before. How can you explain that?"

Calypsa's eyes looked up to the left. Rond scratched his chin. Finally, she said, "I suppose some of the story is plausible. And don't you think for a moment that I haven't witnessed many wonders. I am a dryad who has seen many things. But your story about the elves is ludicrous. Elves would never do such a thing. All of Nalzambor knows this. They might be aloof, but cold- blooded killers? I don't think so." She patted Nath on the ankle. "Sorry, but whatever you are and whoever you are, I think it's best that I keep my distance from you. So long, Nath Dragon, and thanks for all the treasure."

CHAPTER 30

MAEFON STOOD BEHIND THE BATTLEMENTS on the top of Stonewater Keep. The wind tore at her robes, but the rain had stopped. The chronic dampness in the air lingered. Still damp, she shivered. It was always damp at the keep. Always. Below, the river rushed over the rocks, creating dangerous rapids. Her eyes followed the water. It carried large sections of branches down the channel, where it bent away from the sheer face of the mountain before turning, where it ended in a waterfall that spilled into a chasm below.

That was the washout. It was where the Caligin disciples who failed wound up. They were never told about it until they had become Caligin or it was too late. Now Chazzan was the latest elf to take the plunge into a watery grave. She rubbed the signet ring. The black stone had the distinct features of an elf etched into it. It reminded her of Chazzan. She truly had loved him.

If that can happen to him, then it can happen to me.

She couldn't shake the memory of Chazzan's limp body dangling in the might of Lord Darkken's hands. Chazzan was the best. She'd trained with many Caligin and known others, but there were none like him. He was gifted and unique. Now those blessings were in the pit of the river where countless others had failed.

She slipped the ring on her slender finger. It was too wide to fit. She looped it back through the chain and hung it over her neck. "Good-bye, Chazzan," she whispered. "You were the love of my life." She wiped her eyes and turned away from the battlement. She gasped then said, "Lord Darkken!" She gave a quick bow. "I'm sorry, I didn't know you were here."

"That's because you weren't supposed to know that I was here, Maefon," he said without feeling. He was dressed in the same robes, but his hair was braided over his shoulders in a ponytail. "Mourning, are we?"

"I-Well..." she sputtered then got a grip on herself. "Yes, I was. I'm sorry, but my heart and thoughts deceive me. I know that I cannot fool you."

"No, you can't, but you should at least try to fool me. After all, that is what Caligin do." He draped the blanket in his hands over her shoulders. "Take a breath, Maefon. I'm only jesting with you. In truth, I want the Caligin to be cold, ruthless, and compassionless. Emotionless would be delightful, but it is those emotions that drive me, and you. I hunger for power, vengeance, and supremacy. You would probably kill for Chazzan because you have passion for him. Perhaps I killed him because I was jealous of the spark that he shared with you. Now, wouldn't that be something."

"I'm flattered that you are so fond of me," she said, pulling the blanket over her shoulders and offering him a smile.

"Please, don't be flattered. I was only using that as an example." He petted her cheek. "You see, Maefon, the world is run on emotion. The Caligin were created to use them and abuse them, turning one against another by pulling on heart strings and levers." He moved to the battlements, raised his arms to the skies, and lifted his voice to the air. "It's intoxicating!"

"I agree," she said, "and invigorating. I enjoyed leading Nath along. He was very naive."

"Yes," he said with a dashing smile. He leaned against the battlements. "Tell me more. I want to hear this story. All of the details. Don't leave out a bit."

"That will take hours."

"You've been working on this for decades. I have the time, and you have the time. Time is a Caligin's ally."

Maefon started with the day she was taken in as a Trahaydeen, and the moment she met Nath. "Aside from you, I never imagined a man could be so handsome." She went on, talking about the friendship they built over the years, and the longer it went, the easier it was to deceive him. "But it wasn't easy. If Chazzan wasn't there, I think I might have been swept away by Nath. Chazzan kept me grounded. I struggle with why you would kill a brother that was so instrumental to your cause."

"Ah." He lifted a finger. "You just answered the question yourself. You called Chazzan an instrument. Or more clearly in his case… a tool. A big one. You see, he was there to keep you grounded and focused on your mission. He accomplished that, and I didn't really have any more use for him. So I killed him."

"Are you telling me that his feelings for me were not sincere?"

"If he was as good a Caligin as we thought he was, then no, he didn't have any feeling for you whatsoever. Henceforth, you shouldn't miss him." He looked between the battlements. "I'm certain that he's not giving you any more thought these days."

"But—"

"Now, don't let your heart get all twisted up. This is a learning experience. You will have other elves, men, or who knows, maybe a precious halfling in your life. It's all part of the game. Just enjoy playing it."

The weight of his words was staggering. Her shoulders drooped, and she stared at the ground with glassy eyes. How could what Chazzan showed her not be real? It felt real. She was enthralled with him, and he with her. Quietly, she said, "I have a lot of learning to do."

Lord Darkken clapped his hands and spread them wide. "There you go! You see, you are learning."

Maefon stepped back. "But if I completed my mission, then—"

"Then why don't I scoop you up in my arms and pitch you over this wall? Well, I have thought about that, but purely for entertainment's sake, and that wouldn't be practical. Besides, the disciples foul things up often enough to keep me treated." He gave her a big hug. "No, I still need to keep you around. You are the reason Nath left the mountain, are you not?"

"I'm certain that he would be worried about me. He tires of life in the mountain. He just needed a reason to leave. I'm a good one. I planted the seed of friendship deeply."

Lord Darkken lifted his eyes, cupped his mouth, and let out a squawk. A huge vulture circled down from the sky and landed on top of the battlements. Big as a man, it had two bald heads with rough and ugly reddish skin. Its feathers were black as a crow's. The nasty-looking bird's eyes were burning emeralds. "This is Galtur. My eyes, my ears, my familiar. Handsome, isn't he?"

"For a vulture, I suppose."

"Ha, good jest."

"So now are you going to tell me what you want from Nath?"

Rubbing the bird's belly of ruffled feathers, Lord Darkken smiled. "Perhaps later."

CHAPTER 31

NATH BUTTED HIS HEAD AGAINST the tree. "I'm so stupid!" He'd been fighting against his bindings for almost an hour. The more he wriggled, the tighter the roots became. "Come on, her spell can't last forever." He closed his eyes, breathed deeply through his nostrils, and let his body relax. The roots slackened. Nath flexed his muscles. The entanglement of foliage tightened again. "Gads."

On and off, he tried to relax, exhale, and narrow his body. Slowly, he shifted his shoulders, trying to inch his way out. Like living things, the roots tightened with every move. "Oh, it's no use. By the time the spell wears off, if it wears off, they'll be long gone." He leaned back and sighed.

So far, his life abroad in Nalzambor hadn't gone too well. He was certain when he left that he'd fare better, but already he'd been duped by the first people he'd encountered. And he was trying to help them.

What kind of world is this, anyway?

He thought about Calypsa and her captivating smile. He'd read a little about dryads in Dragon Home. Dryads were wood nymphs, born of the trees through magic, but she claimed to be different. She said she was part-dryad, with a human father. It seemed strange, if not impossible. Regardless, she wielded enchantments, two of which failed against Nath, but the third, the roots, got him. As far as he understood magic, it didn't have a lasting effect. So the spell was bound to wear off sooner or later. But that might be hours, or even days. He couldn't wait that long. Not only did Calypsa and Rond have his belongings, but they had Fang too.

"I'm not going to just sit here!" Nath heaved against his bonds. "Hurk!" His biceps and shoulder muscles bulged. The veins in his temples pulsed. His jaws clenched as new sweat beaded on his forehead. He gave it everything he had. The roots tightened. "I can do this! Mind over matter, Nath. Mind over matter!"

The vines cut the circulation off in his arms. His fingers started to turn blue.

Nath gasped. His taut muscles slackened. "Fine, you win, snakes of the ground, you win!" Panting, he noticed a woodchuck saunter into the clearing. It was a big one, with its little black nose to the ground. It sniffed the grass and the shrubs, gave Nath a glance, found a tree, and chewed at the bark.

"Say…" Nath said out loud. When he was younger, he was told that dragons came from magic and magic was in them all. They all had varying abilities. One of those abilities, he recalled, was speaking with other creatures. Not sure how to go about it, he spoke in dragonese. "Excuse me, woodchuck, can you hear me?"

Coated in a healthy brown fur, the woodchuck stopped chewing on the bark in his hands and looked at Nath.

"You hear me, yes, you can hear me. Woodchuck, will you come over here and free me of these vines?"

The woodchuck dropped from its hind legs onto all fours and came at Nath.

"You understand me. Yes, keep coming," Nath said, feeling a thrill go through him.

The woodchuck stopped at his feet. It sniffed the toe of his boot then opened its jaws and bit into it.

"Ow! Don't chew me—chew the vines!"

The woodchuck scurried away.

"No, no, no, no," Nath said more politely, "please come back. I need you to chew these vines and roots." He nodded toward it. "Please, chew them."

Head down, the woodchuck waddled forward and passed Nath to the other side of the tree.

Nath couldn't see it. With his head twisted to the side, he said, "Are you doing it? Yes? Chew them. Chew them away." He didn't hear anything. Turning his head from one side to the other, he said, "Are you there? Woodchuck, are you there?" He turned his head left, right, left. "Gah!"

"Gaaaaah!" the woodchuck said back to him, except it wasn't a woodchuck. It was a small, very hairy little man, with big brown eyes and sharp ears that pointed downward.

"What happened to the woodchuck?" Nath said, recoiling from the weird-looking little man, who was so thick in hair he didn't need clothes but wore mud-red fur trousers that covered his knees. "Who are you?"

Jutting his head in and out like a clucking chicken, the little man said, "Who are you?"

Nath arched a brow. The weird little shaggy man didn't seem dangerous. He carried nothing in his little hands. The skin on his face was smooth, but his features were large. He had a triangular snout and wide mouth. "I am—"

"Yes, I heard, you are Nath Dragon."

"Just Nath," he said. "Uh, you heard all of that? You saw Calypsa and Rond rob me?"

The little man gestured with his hands when he talked. His voice was pleasant, somewhat husky, but shady. "Oh, yes, the nymph and the bugbear. I see them rob all the time. I listen. They are greedy but not as smart as they think they be. I watch. I know." He flicked his pointed earlobes and popped out his eyes. "I know all in the forest." He made clicking sounds with his mouth as he poked and prodded Nath with his fingers and bare toes. "I heard your story. Yes, very interesting. Son of the dragon king. I believe you." He made a giggle. "Very interesting."

"Then you'll free me? Please free me."

"I will free you, but first, you must tell me what my name is."

CHAPTER 32

NATH SHOOK HIS HEAD. "WHAT? Is that a jest? There are
a plethora of names out there. I couldn't begin to guess
that. What sort of creature are you, anyway? I don't recall
learning about something like you. Are you some mix of woodchuck
and pixie?"

"Hahaha." The hairy man sat on Nath's thighs like they were a
bench. "I'm no part woodchuck, though my pelt resembles them."
He picked bark out of his chest. "I'm a hermix. A part gnome, part
hermit, part varmint, some say. Hee-hee. So guess my name, and I
will free you."

Rolling his eyes, Nath said, "I don't have time for this. What you
ask me is impossible."

"Nothing is impossible, and in truth, I want to help you out. So
I will make it easy. My name is Rumple."

"You are telling me your name, and it is Rumple?"

The hermix's caterpillar eyebrows lifted as a smile full of teeth
took over his face. "Is that your guess?"

Nath shrugged. "I'll bite. I guess Rumple."

Rocking back and forth and stomping his little hairy feet, the
hermix said, "No, that is not it. It is Ruffle. Not Rumple. You are
wrong. Tee-hee."

"Is anyone honest outside of the mountain? So far, everyone I've met has lied or deceived me in one way or the other. No wonder the dragons find this world amiss. This is ridiculous." Nath kicked his legs.

Ruffle bounced up and down. "Oh, that is fun. Like riding the rapids. Life is filled with troubled waters. *You* will always paddle against the stream."

"Just get off me if you won't help."

Ruffle stabbed a finger in his face. "Ah, ah, ah, I will help you, but you, dragon prince, must help me."

"Help you how?"

"I need your promise that you will help me when the time comes. Your word, Nath Dragon."

"It's just Nath, and I'm not going to agree to do something if I don't know what it is."

Ruffle cupped his ear. "Hear that?"

"No."

"Yes, it is the sound of Calypsa and Rond getting farther and farther away. Soon, they will be gone, and you will not find them. Heh-hee."

Nath's fingers fidgeted. Ruffle was right. The longer he waited, the more likely his belongings would be gone forever. And he didn't want to spend his time tracking them down. He wanted to focus on finding the betrayers. Besides, what demand could the silly little creature picking his ear while he sat on Nath's lap really want? "I won't kill anyone for you. Is that clear?"

"Oh yes, perfectly." Ruffle eagerly nodded. "So you agree?"

Unable to stand the thought of Calypsa getting away, he said, "I agree."

Ruffle clapped his hands. "Hah-hah! Perfect. I will see you in the future, Nath Dragon. Be ready." The hermix faded along with his voice. In a moment, he was gone, as if he'd never been there at all.

"Hey!" Nath said, narrowing his eyes on the spot where Ruffle vanished. "You need to free... me?" The roots and vines that had constricted him were gone. "Yes!"

In no time, Nath was on his feet and running. He moved through the forest, hopping fallen trees and creeks like a deer. As he recalled some of Master Elween's teachings that—at the time—he never thought would have any application, his keen eye followed the disturbed branches and bushes where Rond must have passed. There were big footprints in the soft ground too. There was no sign of Calypsa's footprints, but he had no doubt that she was with Rond. Rond's body odor still lingered. Nath ran for a full thirty minutes before he caught up with them. They were sloshing through an ankle-deep stream. Calypsa had Nath's pack slung over her shoulder. Rond clapped. She stopped and turned.

Nath sank behind the bushes.

CHAPTER 33

ALYPSA'S EYES PASSED OVER NATH. As Rond crossed to the other side of the stream, she looked away, started singing again, and finished crossing.

Nath let out a breath of relief. He wasn't going to rush into this. He would follow along and see where they went, and once he saw an opening, he would take it. All he needed to do was snatch his pack and sword. Once he did that, he'd run. He knew they couldn't catch him, and he wouldn't be dumb enough to let them trick him again either.

Patience, Nath, patience. They might fool me once, but they won't fool me twice.

Calypsa and Rond moved at a brisk pace. Neither of them seemed to have a worry in the world as they both walked with their arms swinging. No, the two bandits of the willowwacks seemed to have delusions of grandeur in mind as they talked back and forth, laughing at one another.

It rankled Nath as he darted between the elms and blueberry bushes. He would get them. He just had to wait for the right time and then pounce. At the same time, the longer they walked, the more he worried. He envisioned them having a hideout of some sort, perhaps a cave along the grounds or a fort in the trees where it would be difficult to sneak up on them.

When will they stop walking? They have to stop sometime, don't they?

Tirelessly, the odd pair kept going onward, upward, downward, through channels of moss-covered rocks and huge ferns that filled the forest. Nath's biggest issue would be retrieving Fang. The brute had the blade and scabbard strapped over his back. His pack wouldn't be an issue. Calypsa carried it over one shoulder, with her flowing hair tossed to the side of the other.

Finally, shortly after night had fallen, they settled down in a clearing and made camp. Rond stacked up sticks. He broke big sections of branches with his arms. Calypsa touched the wood with her fingertips. There was a loud pop, and the campfire came to life. With the warm glow of firelight on her face, she talked with Rond and left the pack beside her. Nath listened in from only a couple dozen feet away.

"Rond, do you suppose that Nath really was what he said he was?" She had a brush carved out of wood that she ran through her hair. "I can't get over him still standing after I sent a charge through him. Several times. And those eyes. No man has eyes like that."

"I don't care what he is." Rond's four hands were filled with different things. On the top left, he held a hatchet, and in the bottom left, he held big branches. He chopped them into pieces while with his hands and arms on the right, he ate dried meat and drank from a canteen. "I hope a wild thing comes by and kills him. I didn't like him. He had a smart mouth. Everyone thinks they are smarter than Rond, but they are not."

"No, of course not, Rond. You are, after all, the smartest bugbear I know." She smiled at him when he stopped doing what he was doing and cast a wary eye at her. "You're smarter than most people too. But you want to kill everyone you meet. You would make a fine murderer if you wanted to be."

"I am a warrior." Rond beat his chest with the cheek of his axe. He shrugged. "But being a bugbear, we do like to kill things. We are good at it. Strong. Mighty. Hah." He flexed all four of his arms. "I am mightiest of them all."

"I've never met one mightier. You are a true warrior, Rond. The best. Just think, now you can buy whatever you need thanks to this treasure." She patted the backpack. "It is a fortune, but didn't he say there is more where this came from? I'm curious."

Rond tossed his sticks into the fire. With his heavy, gravelly voice, he said, "Stop thinking about that man. He is trouble. A liar. He stole it the same as we stole from him. We will be the better for it."

"He seemed innocent, though. If not for that far-fetched story about the elves—"

"I hate elves." Rond sat down in front of the fire across from Calypsa. He sneered. "They think they are so perfect. Scrawny little men that run and dance like they have wings on their feet. Hate them very much. I agreed with the flame hair. They are evil. I'm not surprised one bit."

She laughed. "A bugbear calling an elf evil. Well, if that's not the pot calling the kettle black."

"I'm not evil, entirely." Rond's ears bent as he spoke. "Misguided, perhaps, but not evil. I like things my brethren don't, such as you. That's why I'm outcast."

"You are an outcast because you are not some mindless slayer that kills whatever he is told to kill. You thought for yourself, Rond. You should be proud of that. You are a gem."

His head sagged. "No, I am outcast. My kind hate me. I'll have no home in the rocks and caves again. Not with them."

"Some of them might come around to your way of thinking. You never know." She made her way over to him and wrapped her arms around his shoulders. "Don't give up on your people. People change. You did."

"No, I still want to kill people." His face clenched. "It's just not the same mindless urge. I think about it first. If it's me or them, I let them have it." He punched his hands several times. "I still like it."

Nath picked up a stone. He chucked it far over Calypsa and Rond. The stone crashed through the forest.

Rond came to his feet. Pushing Calypsa behind him, he said, "Wait here. Probably a critter, but you never know." He vanished into the woodland, leaving Calypsa alone and peering after him.

On cat's feet, Nath crept into the camp. With Calypsa turned away from him, he grabbed his bag. He pulled open the neck strings, reached inside, and fished out the leather gauntlet. The leather was thick and supple. The tips of the fingers were cut off. The blue gemstone mounted on the glove above the wrist shone like the moon. He slipped it on. The gem glowed more brightly.

Calypsa turned. "You!"

CHAPTER 34

"N O, NATH. BUT I HAVE to say, I'm a bit offended that you've forgotten my name so soon." Nath stretched the gauntlet over his left hand and flexed his fingers. He shouldered his pack. "I believe this belongs to me."

Calypsa's fists balled up at her sides. "You put that back. We stole it honestly."

"What? *Stole it honestly?* How can you steal something honestly? That is preposterous. What is wrong with the people in this world?"

Calypsa gave a sad look. Clasping her fingers together, she came toward him, pleading. "Oh, Nath, we are hungry. That is why we steal. The world is harsh and cruel. Please, let us share it." She went down on one knee. "I am at your mercy, but don't leave us starving. We'll die out here. Let me have the sack."

Nath couldn't break her hypnotic stare. His mind wanted to give her what she wanted. The words that came from her mouth were so convincing. The forest became a blur around her. "I... I..." He shook his head. He wanted to break her stare but could not. "I can't."

"*You must give me the pack, Nath.*" Her words were a tapestry carried through the air, dropping an unseen blanket over Nath. "*It is the right thing to do. Just set it down.*"

Nath started to take the pack off his shoulders. He couldn't feel his body. Some unseen force moved his body on its own. Her suggestions turned what he came to do completely around. *Stop. Don't let her do this. This is my gear. My possessions.* He stared back in her eyes. "No."

"*Look at me, Nath. Listen to me. Nath, leave the pack and go,*" she said with big beautiful eyes that could make men's hearts waxen. "*It is for the best. Trust me.*"

He stood rigid, with sweat dripping down his face. He fought against her words, an inner war waging in his mind. She was so beautiful, pleasant, soft, and convincing. All he wanted to do was help her.

"*You don't really need it, Nath. This would be the right thing to do,*" she continued in words soft and warm like a fireside blanket. "*Help me.*"

The backpack slipped down his arm. Completely unaware of his surroundings, Nath let the pack fall to the ground. All he saw was her with a smile growing on her face.

"Thank you, Nath," she said, crawling toward the pack. She looked up and over his shoulders. "Be still, Nath."

The blue gemstone on his gauntlet shone bright as a star. Nath's thoughts became lucid, his awareness keen. Someone crept in behind him. Like a striking snake, he turned and punched Rond square in the chest. The four-armed bugbear's entire body left the ground. He flew back twenty feet and slammed hard into the trunk of a tree.

Calypsa snatched the pack.

Before she could dart away, Nath grabbed her arm. "You aren't going anywhere with this." He ripped the pack free of her grip and slung it over his shoulder. "And I think I've had enough of you."

"Look at me, Nath," she pleaded as she tried to pull away. "Look at me."

Nath looked her dead in the eye. "I'm looking." Her hypnotic stare was there, but it had no power over him. "And I don't like what

I see." He dragged her by the wrist toward Rond. The bugbear was sitting on his behind, rubbing the back of his head and chest. "Give me my sword, Rond, or I swear I'll punch you so hard next time that you won't land until tomorrow."

Grimacing as he moved with shaky limbs, Rond laid the sword and scabbard down at Nath's feet.

"You tricked us, Nath Dragon. You used magic." Calypsa's cheeks were rosy, and her hair hung in her eyes. She strained to break Nath's grip. "Let go of me!"

"I will when I'm ready." Nath held her with his right hand and looked at the gauntlet on his left. The fires in the blue gem died. "Thank you."

"What is that?" she said, shooting a glance at his glove. "Tell me. You are a warlock, aren't you?"

"No, I'm a dragon. And this," he said, holding up his left hand and spreading his fingers, "is the Gauntlet of Goam, a gift from my father. Though I never had any use for it before today. Frankly, I wasn't even sure of the full extent of its strengthening power." His brows lifted. "I think I know now. Hah! I'm glad I brought it." He swung a look behind him. "Aren't you, Rond?"

Rond clutched his ribs with all four arms. He feebly shook his head.

Nath released Calypsa. As she stood beside him, flatfooted and gaping, he slung Fang over his back, adjusted the strap, and put the pack on top of it. He looked down at Calypsa. "We are finished here. I wish we could have met under better circumstances, Calypsa. What you do is wrong. You should use your gifts for a greater purpose."

"That's just silly." She crossed her arms over her chest and turned her nose up. "You are no better than we are. You tricked us all the same."

"I didn't trick anybody." He shook his head. "I'm leaving now. Don't follow me. Don't chase me. I don't want to see either of you again. I won't be so merciful next time. I hope I'm clear." Giving them both a lasting look, he said, "This is normally where I'd say goodbye, but it doesn't seem appropriate for thieves and robbers."

CHAPTER 35

NOT WANTING TO BE FOLLOWED, Nath ran on and off through the night and through the day, never stopping to rest. He crossed the highland plains and ran by herds of cattle. He wanted as much distance between him and the thieves as he could get. He'd been tricked and cheated, but he'd learned his lesson.

Making his way down a hillside, he finally stopped at an overlook. The rising sun settled on his face. Down in the valley was a large city with streets paved in stone and tall buildings over three stories tall. The main city was built by large cut stones, and outside of its border were homes made of logs, surrounded by miles of farmland where crops were growing and livestock grazed.

Nath tingled. It was clear to him that this city was rather big, with tens of thousands of people living together. From where he sat, a mile away, he could count the farmers in the fields. Men and women worked together, along with halflings, and even though he wasn't completely sure, possible part-elves too. The men wore wide-brimmed straw hats and had their sleeves rolled up. The women were in modest dresses and white cloth hats decorated with flowers. Wagons pulled by horses came and went on the main roads to the city.

"I suppose the time has come to dip my feet in the city." He headed to the bottom of the hill and angled toward the dirt road. Passing by the farmhouses and fields, he came to a huge wooden sign mounted on a boulder that read Riegelwood. There was a crest with an oak tree growing out of a rock. Shields were in the leaves.

Nath politely waved to everyone he passed. Most of the people waved or smiled. Others didn't look his way. The actual city started where the dirt road became paved with stones. Buildings stretched into the distance as far as he could see. Most of them were made from stone with wooden porches and walkways. There were decks on the top of the roof. People leaned over the rails. Flowers decorated the windows, and clothing was hung on lines on the very top roofs.

Nath nodded and said hello to a group of women who were walking toward him. They all blushed, giggled, and walked on by. One of them tripped over her dress as she passed. She spilled a basket of apples on the road, but she still couldn't take her eyes off Nath.

"Will you quit gawking, Candice?" A woman who seemed like the young lady's mother helped her daughter up. "You are making a fool of yourself."

Nath came over to help. "Let me lend a hand." He picked up the apples and loaded them into the basket. The other women giggled as he handed the basket to the girl. "Here you go. Sorry for the trouble. Could you tell me—"

The mother cut in front of him. "She's spoken for, lad. Now move it along." She gave Nath a long look up and down. "Quickly, before I forget I'm spoken for as well."

"Mother!" the young lady said, embarrassed.

"Well, I might be older, but I'm not blind. Let's go, girls. We have fantasies... I mean chores to do."

Nath waved as they hurried away. He turned and found himself face to face with two soldiers. They wore metal skull caps and a red tunic with the city crest sewn on the front over chainmail armor.

Their hands were on the pommels of their swords. One was tall, black-haired, and had a short thick beard, and the other younger, shorter and clean shaven.

"Hello," Nath said.

"What brings you to Riegelwood, traveler?" the older soldier said.

"Just passing through." Nath could tell by the soldier's tone that he took his business seriously.

"I see." The bearded soldier's eyes landed on Fang's handle. "That's quite a length of steel you have strapped on your back. Are you a soldier or another one of those adventuring types who likes to create a ruckus in our city?"

"Yes, well, neither, I suppose," Nath replied as the younger guard moved behind him. "My father made this sword, and I'm a bit of a blacksmith myself. It's the last gift I have from him, and I go everywhere with it. That said, I'm just looking for a place to settle for a bit. I have money, and I won't be any trouble. If you could show me where I could find a place to eat and sleep, I'd be grateful."

The soldier clawed at his beard. "What do you think, Kevan?"

"He sounds honest, Hartson." The young man reached toward Fang's handle. "This craftsmanship is astounding. Look at the crossguard's detail. I swear, the little dragons are staring at me. May I touch it?"

"Uh, I wouldn't," Nath said, but it was too late. The young soldier's fingers were on the crossguard.

"That isn't real gold, is it?" Kevan said.

"Of course not. No fool of a blacksmith would make crossguards out of gold. It's too soft."

"It's gold plated," Nath said.

"It will chip," Hartson replied, "but that's probably more of a decorative sword, right? It's too fancy and big for fighting."

"Well, I haven't had to use it yet."

"Good. See to it that you keep it that way." Hartson knocked on Nath's breastplate. "What kind of metal is that?" He rubbed his knuckles. "Oh, never mind. Listen, you seem decent enough. Take this road five blocks down, turn left, and you'll find the Oxen Inn. Tell them Hartson and Kevan sent you. But don't make me look bad. Understand?"

"Yes, sir. Thank you, sir."

Hartson pointed at him. "I mean it. The city lord won't tolerate troublemakers, and I won't either. Come on, Kevan. We have work to do."

CHAPTER 36

THE OXEN INN WAS A quaint establishment. Men sat out on the porch underneath the deck, rocking in rockers and smoking tobacco made from polished wrynnwood pipes. They made small talk about the weather and the trades they represented. Nath gave them a nod on his way up the steps. Some of the men glanced his way but continued on with their lively conversations. Entering the tavern, Nath nearly bumped into a waitress. She slipped by him with a tray of food on her shoulder and kept on going.

Almost every chair at the tables was filled. Men and women were talking, laughing, and eating. There was a small stage in the corner near a fireplace. Three red-headed halflings sat on tall stools. One sang to the melody the others played on the violin and flute. The song was peppy, and several patrons clapped to the beat.

The day they robbed the dragon is the day the dread men died...

Fire came and swallowed them up, no water could quench the flame.

The disgraceful men of Run Tilllamill, were brave and bold, not wise.

For the day they robbed the dragon, is the day the foul men died.

The dragon took the treasure back,

The men's coffins were filled with ash...
Cause the day they robbed the dragon is the day the unwise died.

Nath gave a winsome smile as he made his way over to a lone stool at the bar. Men hunched over their food, gobbling up piles of steamy eggs covered in cheese, thick strips of bacon, and slabs of ham. Biscuits the size of Nath's fist were smothered in gravy. Nath scooted the stool back. His belly roared.

A very heavy man in nice clothing, tastefully wearing a lot of gold jewelry, cast a tired eye at Nath. "If you're hungry, this is the place to be." The man let out a belch. "Pardon me. Best food in the little kingdoms. Always stay here in my travels and try to stay as long as I can." He spied Nath's sword. "Uh, that's a big sword. Are you a henchman? Henchmen eat in the back."

"No, I'm checking in." Nath watched the women and men coming and going from the kitchen. The place was a hive of activity. Behind the bar, three women were working. Their hair was in buns, and they wore powder-blue aprons. They refilled coffee and switched out empty plates with plates loaded down with food. Nath waved at them. They paid him no mind. "Sir," Nath said, but the man turned his back and crammed half a biscuit into his mouth. Nath felt a tap on the shoulder. He turned. "Oh my."

A woman as tall as him and built like a blacksmith stood in front of him. Her brown hair was back in a ponytail, and her muscular arms were crossed over her chest. She wore an apron like the others but seemed more menacing than the rest. She cast a wary eye on Nath. "Excuse me, but we don't allow the adventuring types here. No offense, but this is a different kind of place of business. As you can see, our customers aren't loaded down in weaponry, just money, and we keep it that way." She took Nath by the elbow. "Try the Fox's Pit. Out you go."

Nath tried to ease his arm out of her grip. She held him fast. "I was told to tell you that Hartson and Kevan sent me."

Her grip eased. "They did, huh? Tell me, what did Hartson and Kevan look like?" He gave a quick, accurate description of the two men. "I see," she said. "Well, I'm Nina. I run the Oxen, and I won't have any trouble. You look like trouble with that hardware on your back." She let go of his elbow and gave him a friendly pinch on the chin. "But *you* don't look like trouble—anything but, actually." She smiled and stared right in his eyes. It went on for an awkward amount of time.

"Excuse me, Nina?" he said, sitting back down.

"Oh, oh yes," she said, blushing as she flattened out her apron with her hands. "Were you wanting to stay or eat?"

"Both, actually."

"Well, listen, you can't be down on the floor with that sword and wearing the stove door on your chest. I'll get you a room, but you need to change."

Scratching the back of his head, Nath said, "I don't have another shirt."

"You have money, correct?"

He nodded.

"I'll send a shirt up." Nina searched the room. She caught a tiny girlish woman as thin as a stick crossing the floor. "Little Shirl, get him a room and a shirt, and bring him down here while I fix him up."

The little woman nodded and hurried away.

Nina helped Nath out of his seat and sat down. "I'll save your stool and have a plate of hot food ready for you. Make it quick."

CHAPTER 37

Upstairs, Nath's room had a single bed with two quilts stacked up at the foot of the bed and a pillow. There was a small chest of drawers, and an oil lantern on a nightstand. He dropped all of his gear on the bed, closed the window, locked it, and drew the curtains.

"Here is your key and shirt," Little Shirl said, holding up the key while her eyes stayed focused on the floor. "You should change quickly. Nina doesn't like to wait. She is very demanding."

"Yes, well, this looks like a very busy place." He removed his breastplate and shirt and set them on the bed. Little Shirl stole a glance at him. "I believe I can find my way back, Little Shirl."

"Of course," she said flatly. "But do hurry." She opened the door, stepped out, and closed it behind her.

Nath slipped on a royal-blue tunic, adjusted the leather strings at the neck, and stared at the length of the sleeves. "This is a fine fit."

He took out his coin purse, exited the room, locked the door, and put the key in the purse. Heading down the hallway, he noticed Little Shirl waiting at the top of the stairs, adjusting the bun in her hair. "I told you I could find it, Little Shirl."

She held out her hand. "Yes, but you forgot my gratuity."

"Your what?"

"Have you ever stayed in an inn before? I could tell by the look about you, you hadn't. You seem as innocent as a sheep." She spoke in a spooky, quiet, and dull manner. "A gratuity is when you pay someone like me for the little help I do for you."

"You handed me a shirt and key."

"Yes, but I'll always clean and care for your room. Look after other needs. Just ask. It's how I make my living."

"Oh, I see. Please, excuse my ignorance. I haven't been to a city so big before."

"I could tell."

Nath fished out a gold piece from his purse. "Will this be adequate?"

Little Shirl's unblinking eyes hung on the coin like it was a diamond of comparable size. She swiped it out of his hand. "Yes. Thank you." She hurried down the steps and vanished through the doors leading into the kitchen.

Nath joined Nina at the bar. The man in the stool beside her had cleared out, and she switched to it.

Patting Nath's stool, she said, "I kept it warm for you." She snapped her fingers. A girl brought over a plate of steaming food, a wooden tankard filled to the brim with milk, and a glass cup and saucer of coffee. "Little Shirl hustled into the kitchen with a smile, I think," Nina said. "I'm curious as to why."

Nath stuffed bacon and ham inside his biscuit. "She introduced me to gratuity. I think she was pleased with what she had earned."

"Which was?"

Taking a bite out of his biscuit, he said, "Just a gold piece."

Nina's eyes grew big. "Nath, that is excessive. Only a silver at most. A few copper pieces would have been more than adequate."

"I don't have any of those." He drank his milk. "Ah, all of this is wonderful. Sometimes I forget to eat, but when I do eat, I eat a lot in a single sitting. You might have to keep the plates coming."

"Yes, well, that won't be a problem." She dusted the crumbs off his chest. "Nath, if you don't mind me asking, where do you come from? I've seen people from all over Nalzambor, but you are not like any of them."

"Why is that?"

Nina eased back against the bar. The gruff exterior she had carried earlier had been replaced by a lovely woman who carried herself in a very polite manner. "For starters, I've never seen a man with eyes the color of gold. Your hair, well, I'll just say, would make a princess jealous."

Smiling, with a mouthful of food, he said, "It would, wouldn't it?"

"Oh yes. Listen, it's not my business where you are from. After all, we are strangers. But I am glad that Hartson sent you here." Her legs were crossed, and hands clasped on her knees as she kicked her foot. "Are you going to be staying long?"

"Possibly." He dipped his biscuit into his gravy and ate the whole bite. "I'm from the south, and from a place that isn't a large city such as this. I want to get a feel for how life operates in a place like this, and I'm looking for some people. The truth is, I don't even have any idea where to find them. I'm just looking." Nath didn't want to say too much. He didn't know much about Nina, but she did seem friendly. He didn't want to make her suspicious either. He decided to fill her in a little more. "You see, I have some friends that ran away. I need to find them."

"Did you stop to think that they might not want to be found? Do you even know why they ran away?"

Nath told a half truth. "They were scared."

"Now that is interesting. Of what? I hope not you."

Nath wiped his hands on his cloth napkin. "No, not me. I feel that one of them was forced to flee because of the actions of the others. I want to make sure they are safe."

"A kidnapping?"

"Maybe."

"Nath, I've been dealing with people for over twenty years. The Oxen Inn is my family, and it is my home. And when you mingle as much as I do, you get a deep understanding of people." She took his hand in hers.

"This person you are looking for, it's a woman, isn't it?"

He gave a terse nod.

"And you love her, don't you?"

Feeling a little foolish, he said, "Yes."

CHAPTER 38

ONCE THINGS SLOWED DOWN IN the Oxen Inn, Nina offered to take Nath through the city. They strolled down the streets together. People stepped aside as she passed, even the men. Nina carried an air about her, and her towering presence was formidable as she stood a couple inches taller than Nath. She filled him in on Riegelwood and its people.

"The five major cities have kings and queens that rule them," she said, "but even though Riegelwood is vast, we don't have kings and queens. Instead, we have city lords and ladies. Our city lord is Jander, a fair-minded man whose family has been in charge for centuries. He keeps Riegelwood in order, but there is only so much he can do. We aren't without our problems, the same as any other town, municipality, or province."

Nath noticed beggars in the corners and men huddled in the shadows of the alleys. His nose crinkled when they passed certain places in the city. "Yes, there are some odors that I'm not accustomed to."

"Yes, the safest place to be is the places that don't stink, unless it's a barn, or something. It's understandable there." Nina walked with her arms behind her back. She was heading toward the castle that stood out at the end of the road. The stonework was white, and it had three ivory towers behind its walls with red roofs made from baked-clay tiles. The flag of Riegelwood billowed on the tops of all of them. From the main road, scaffolding held up workers that labored on the castle's wall. "That is Lord Jander's home. They are always building on it. It's a big family, but they really don't need that much room. My inn holds one hundred comfortably, but that castle could hold a thousand."

"I thought you said he was fair-minded."

"There have been worse than him. Jander hasn't become completely power hungry yet, but he is paranoid. That's why you can't be wandering around this city, asking questions. Adventurers pass through all of the time and are tolerated, but if they step out of line, they can easily wind up in the dungeons. If you don't like the stink up here, then you'll be in for a real shock when the stink greets you down there."

A flock of pigeons flapped away when they walked by. "I'm just looking for a friend. Certainly, there have been lost people in this city before."

"Yes, lost people and kidnapped ones as well." She led them to a small garden park across the street from the castle. Small trees and bountiful flowers flourished, and an assortment of colorful winged chirping birds fluttered about. They sat on a black marble bench. "There is a lot of wealth that flows through this trade city, and it's not all honorable. Things happen behind the scenes. People can be robbed, killed, or even disappear altogether. Gone without a trace. The city lord has to take care of his people, but there are always threats to his castle. Recently, one of his own daughters went missing. She was returning home from Quintuklen when tragedy occurred. She didn't make it. Her armed escorts were found dead less than a league from here. They had no wounds. They stood where they were, as solid as stone. There was no sign of Lord Jander's most beloved daughter, either. He called her Princess. Janna is what we like to call her."

"That's very sad," Nath said, watching the soldiers who were posted on the castle walls. "So are they still looking for her?"

"Certainly, but the more time passes, the colder the trail gets. I haven't seen Lord Jander in quite some time. I fear he is brokenhearted. Janna was very special to him." She sneezed. "Sorry, sometimes the flowers get me. Where was I? Yes, Lord Jander, I hear, secretly blames a rival family. He thinks they are trying to take him down and took Janna to wound him. Anything is possible. If she's not found, it's possible that a feud between the families will break out. That can get very ugly as well as bloody."

"There was no sign of her at all?" Nath asked. "Someone must know something."

"The trail went cold. I don't know how much you know about Nalzambor, but—"

"I know plenty if you are going to mention magic, Nina. When you mentioned the princess vanishing, it reminded me of what happened to my friend. She vanished very much the same. My brethren had no sense of what happened to her."

Nina shooed a bird off the side of the bench. "Go away, little nibbler. I don't have seeds today. Sorry, Nath. I come here often and feed them. They know me." She gasped. "Nath!" Small birds who had perched themselves on Nath's shoulders and legs scattered. "How did you do that?"

He shrugged. "I don't know. I just thought the birds liked me. Is that not ordinary?"

"No." She let out a laugh. "But I don't think you are ordinary either. You have a very charming quality about you. I think you will be well accepted by people."

Nath pulled his shoulders back. "Thank you. Nina, do you think you could take me to the place where the woman vanished from? The princess?"

"I don't see why. Listen, what you are talking about is adventuring, and that's a very risky affair." Nina stretched out her fists and yawned. "Excuse me. As I was saying before, adventurers, heroes for hire, henchmen, fortune hunters, and mercenaries are a dangerous and often sordid lot. They claim good intentions, but what they do, they do for treasure and glory. And it can be very competitive. You see, Nath, there is a reward for the princess, and there are men and women, around and about, that are trying to solve this mystery. You don't want to cross them."

"But I want to help," he said. Sincerely, he did, but he remembered his father's stern warning about getting mixed up in the affairs of men. *They will tempt you, and they will try you, and there is little honor among most of them.* "I at least want to look. Perhaps it will give me some new perspective on things. After all, it sounds like the city lord is dealing with the same kind of circumstance. Will you take me?"

She stared at the highest tower in the center of the castle. "I'll tell you what. We can ride out in the morning, but I want to hear more about this woman you are determined to find. I want to know your story. You don't have to tell me all of it, just something to delight me. Besides, your words are so pleasant when you speak. I'd enjoy more of your company."

Nath didn't see any reason to tell the domineering woman no, and he did like her company. He nodded. "I'll see you in the morning then."

"Meet me in the stables behind the inn." She kissed his cheek. "See you then."

CHAPTER 39

NATH SAT ON HIS BED in the Oxen Inn with his pack on his lap and his eyes closed as he leaned against his headboard. He'd been trying to sleep, or at least get a little catnap, but his excitement about the coming day was overwhelming. He couldn't wait to see where Nina took him. He opened his eyes. The oil lantern burned low, leaving the room very dim.

"I can't wait hours until the morning. I'm ready to go now." He moved to the window, drew the curtains, and opened the window. His window overlooked the back side of the inn. The barn roof was below him. In the star-filled sky, the bright white moon was at its zenith. "Great Guzan, the morning birds won't be out for hours still."

Nath paced the room. Typically, a few hours meant very little to a dragon. He'd seen dragons spend hours just yawning, and they were very slow about doing things. Since they lived so long, they tended to operate as if they had all the time in the world. Growing up in Dragon Home, Nath was used to it, though it did annoy him from time to time. There were very long stories, lectures, conversations, and training lessons. But outside of the mountain, inside the cities of men, life moved faster. The people moved about as if the sands in the great hourglass of time were about to empty out.

He plopped on his bed. The backpack rattled with the distinct clinking of the potion vials inside. He emptied out the contents by removing each item one by one. There were three potion vials in tubes made from a clear, thick glass, a thin coil of golden-brown rope, and some wax candlesticks. He held the hooded lantern in his palm. It looked like something that was more decorative, being so small that it could be hung from a tree like a seasonal ornament. The last thing was the Gauntlet of Goam. The soft, durable leather was broken in. The blue sapphire set in the leather showed a wink of fire burning deep within. All of the items were gifts from his father, but they wouldn't be anything that an actual dragon would ever use. Instead, Nath had come to the conclusion that the items were gifts that were brought to the dragons by the races long ago when dragons and men were friends.

Nath had some other common supplies in the bag too that he fished out. Among them were strips of cloth he used to wrap around the potions so they wouldn't rattle. He bound the vials up together all as one. Stuffing them back inside the pack, he felt something scratch against his knuckle. He pulled out a sheet of parchment rolled up like a scroll.

"Oh, Slivver, I'd forgotten about this." He unrolled the parchment. There were words written that only a dragon could read and a drawing in the corner. It showed a picture of a face with very sharp and distinct elven features carved into a black gemstone. The elven face had a deep scowl etched in it. Slivver's handwritten words read, "In my ventures abroad, I have discovered that there are elves that have aligned themselves with evil. They call themselves Caligin. Operating from the dark of the night and the shadows of the day, they strike from anywhere and at any time. Be wary, Nath. The friends you make might not be what they seem. Beware of the dark in the day. Slivver."

A chill breeze rustled the curtains. Goose bumps rose on Nath's arms. He studied the image and read the note again.

"What is he saying? Is he saying the Trahaydeen were Caligin? Maefon is Caligin?" The note slipped from his fingers. "She couldn't be, could she? No, that couldn't be what he is saying." He combed his fingers through his hair. Maefon was so beautiful and always loving toward him. She was his best friend. Then he thought of Chazzam. "He must be the Caligin."

CHAPTER 40

MAEFON ENTERED LORD DARKKEN'S STUDY. Like the rest of the keep, it was a dreary octagonal room made from the dark stone. The walls were bare aside from a single wooden bookshelf ten feet tall and over half full with leatherbound tomes. Lord Darkken stood in the center of the room, looking down into a large copper bowl that sat on a stone pedestal.

"Please, Maefon, come and gaze into the Pool of Eversight with me." Lord Darkken faced her from the other side of the bowl. The rims of his eyes glowed like shiny copper. "I've been looking forward to your company all day."

"And I yours, Lord Darkken," she said, stepping up to the Pool of Eversight. The copper bowl was bigger than she could get her arms around. The water in the bowl was clear as glass, showing the copper basin at the bottom. "What do you require of me?"

"A drop of your blood, and repeat my incantation, and you will then see all that I can see." He handed a dagger handle first over the bowl, which looked like it was carved from either a dragon's tooth or dragon bone. Taking the dagger, she quickly pricked the tip of her index finger. Fresh drops of blood plopped into the waters, making ripples and staining the clear liquid. "Close your eyes. Repeat after me."

The ancient incantation she repeated were words from a time long forgotten. The eloquent words took life of their own, lending new strength to her body. A spring of energy coursed through her the moment the incantation ended.

"Open your eyes. Gaze into the pool, and tell me what you see," Lord Darkken said.

The waters swirled, shimmered, then formed a clear image. "I see fertile lands as if a bird flies over them." She held her stomach. "My tummy twists."

Darkken let out a chuckle. "That will subside. If it does not, perhaps this duty is not something that you are suited for. There are others who might prove more capable if I give them a try."

"No, I'm fine, lord."

"Of course you are. I knew you would be. What you are seeing is indeed a bird's-eye view. This is what Galtur, my vulture, sees. Though sometimes he doesn't like it. It gets his feathers *ruffled*, so to speak, and I end up having to use other methods. Linking to him is one of the uses of the Pool of Eversight. Using Galtur, I have learned, gives me more flexibility. You see, I can command his actions from where I stand. Soon you will learn to command him as well. Have you been practicing your magic, Maefon?"

"Yes," she said, leaning farther over the pool. The image barrel-rolled, dove down toward the tall grasses, and swooped up again. Her knees buckled as her stomach turned. "Uh, it's all coming back to me, and I'd forgotten how much I'd missed it. It's good to have the magic back on my lips and fingertips."

"Indeed." Lord Darkken waved his entire arm over the bowl. The image faded. The spell broke off.

Blinking, she said to him, "Have I done something wrong, lord?"

"Of course not. The pool is power and takes some getting used to." He put his arm around her waist. "You did well. You didn't faint. I knew that you had the strength in you to withstand the power. Of course, if you had collapsed, I probably wouldn't have any use for you whatsoever."

Maefon felt like a child in his arms as he led her in front of the bookcase. Some of the books were as thick as the breadth of her hand. The spines were lettered in many different languages. "It's an impressive collection. Are they all spell books and histories?"

"History books are elsewhere," he said. "No, these are books of magic in every language and from every race that I can get ahold of. Of course, most of it is miniscule, and filled with a variety of concoctions and silly spells. Primitive, one might say, but every culture has something to offer. Most particularly the elves and humans." Up on tiptoe, Darkken grabbed a book from one of the higher shelves. He handed it to Maefon. "Heavy, isn't it?"

She nodded at the tome that now filled her arms. The muscles in her back pulled a little. Unlike the other books, this one wasn't bound in leather. It was bound with black dragon scales and skin. With awe, she said, "Where did you get this?"

"I made it. I want you to study it. There is much about dragons and men that you need to learn. I put it all together in there. Spells and lore. But the book remains in here."

"I'm honored."

Putting his hands on her shoulders, Darkken said, "I know you are." He took the book and put it back on the shelf. "You may come to this study as you please, when time away from your duties permits. But for now, there is another place I want to take you. I've gotten a bit bored, and I want to play around a little. Close your eyes."

The moment she closed her eyes, a warm breeze stirred her hair and clothing. Her stomach felt like it spun a full circle. Dizziness assailed her. The only things that kept her from falling were Darkken's strong hands.

With assurance, he said, "Open your eyes, Maefon."

With the sun on her face, she squinted. They stood on rolling grass hills as far as the eye could see. Darkken gave a handsome smile. He was dressed like a commoner, wearing a cotton white shirt under a brown vest. The shirtsleeves were rolled up over his forearms. His forest-green trousers were held up by a belt with a copper buckle. He wore leather traveling boots too. "Is this the field we saw?"

"Yes," he said, taking her hand and leading her through the meadow. "You look very pretty in your new clothing."

Maefon wore a pale-yellow blouse and forest-green skirt that covered her ankles. "I'm dressed like a milk maiden."

"I know. We need to blend in where we are going. Have you ever milked a cow before?"

"No," she said, frowning. Maefon touched the white cotton cap on her head, which was tied underneath her chin. She might be Caligin, but she preferred to maintain a certain style about her attire. Dressing like a human wasn't something she cared for. In addition to that, her mind raced. Darkken had just transported her across the countryside and changed her and his clothing in the wink of an eye. She knew he was powerful, but she never imagined his abilities were so vast. It scared her and thrilled her at the same time. A hunger for knowledge built inside her. She squeezed his hand. "But I'll milk a thousand for you if I have to."

"Good, because it will probably come to that."

CHAPTER 41

JUST BEFORE DAWN, ARMED AND ready to go, Nath headed to the barn. As he entered the barn, a horse nickered and another whinnied. Nina led two horses by the reins. Harnessed and saddled, the beasts were ready to go. So was Nina. The long strands of braided hair were curled up on the top of her head. She wore a leather tunic over a coat of chainmail. A broadsword and dagger were belted onto her full hips. She smiled at Nath. "Good morning. I hope it's not too early of a start for you. Is something wrong?"

"Er... no, it's just that you look like a warrior. I thought you were an innkeeper, but I'd swear by the looks of you, you are an adventurer."

"Who? Me?" she said, touching her hands, covered in leather riding gloves, to her chest. "Why, I'd never!"

Nath batted his lashes at her. Approaching the horses, he said, "What are you up to?"

She climbed into her horse's saddle. "We'll talk about it on the way. Have you ever ridden before?"

"Ridden what?"

She gave him a funny look. "A horse, of course. What else would you have ridden?"

Nath was thinking about riding dragons, but he said, "No, I haven't ridden a horse, but I'm fairly good with animals and get the hang of things quickly." He stuffed his foot in the stirrup, mounted, and turned the horse toward the barn exit. "Is this this how you do it?"

"Yes, that is how. Just be sure to keep up." She led the way out of the city at a trot. They headed northwest, following the roads to Quintuklen. As Nath got a better feel for his horse, Nina did the talking. "So you figured me out. I'm not just an innkeeper. I do my fair share of adventuring too."

"So you deceived me."

"No, you didn't ask. I just keep a very low profile, and given the notoriety of adventurers, I have to. After all, the Oxen Inn is my family business, but I'm not married to it." Her forehead wrinkled. "I'm not married to anyone. Are you mad at me?"

As the horses crossed over a small creek, he said, "No, I understand your reasons. And why would you be forthcoming with a stranger? You know little about me. I'd probably do the same."

"Speaking of forthcoming, tell me more about this woman you seek. I imagine she is very beautiful. A possible wife, perhaps?"

"No, I don't believe so. You see, she is an elf."

"An elf?" Nina said, unable to hide her shock. "Why would you chase an elf? They are the snobbiest race in the realm."

"Sorry, but I haven't been around many other people," he said.

"Raised by elves, huh?" she said, shaking her head. "Now I've heard it all. So what happened to your own parents? Clearly, you are not an elf. What did you become, a charity case they took on? The ones I've known are picky and often try to make things better."

"What's wrong with making things better?"

Red-faced, she said, "And you defend those pompous pointed-eared fiends." She took a breath. "Sorry, Nath, I had a bad experience with them. It still sticks. If I were raised by elves, perhaps I'd side with them too. So you have elven parents?"

"No, I don't have elven parents. I don't know my mother, but I've been with my father all of my life—until now, that is, since I left home to find Maefon."

"Hmph. Tell me more about her."

"She's elven, blond, and very friendly. She likes to joke a lot, and her laughter is delightful. She makes these little dimples when she smiles."

"That's enough. I get the picture. Come on, we're close." Nina dug her heels into her horse and snapped the reins. "Yah!"

Nath gave chase. Finally, Nina came to a stop at a bend in the road where the tree branches hanging over the road on both sides formed a tunnel. Nina dismounted. She led her horse off the road. "Did I say something to offend you?" he asked.

"No, I just don't care for men blustering over women unless it's me. Now, are you going to sit up there all day, or are you coming along?"

Nath hopped off his horse. "I'm coming."

Together, they entered the forest. Just inside the rim of the brush was a clearing. There were statues of soldiers in a circular ring, facing inward. In some cases, weapons were drawn. Shock and horror crossed their faces. Fear filled their wide eyes.

Nath's neck hairs rose. "I thought what you said about them being turned to stone was just a figure of speech. I never imagined..." He touched a man's face. "I've never seen faces so scared before. They are absolutely terror-stricken. Look, this man has goose bumps still standing on his arms."

"I know. I want to believe they aren't real, but I know better. They were found on the road just like this." She kneeled down. The forest had overtaken the stone men's feet. "They were dragged over here and made into this creepy memorial. I don't get it, but Lord

Jander wouldn't allow them in the city. He's still investigating. He keeps leaning toward the rival families who want to take his scepter. Personally, I think the Riverlynn monks had something to do with it. I just can't prove it."

There was a wreath made from twisted sticks embedded with flowers hanging from one man's neck. The flowers had withered. Nath plucked wildflowers from the ground and began replacing them. Nina did the same. "So who are the Riverlynn monks?"

"Well, that's what they call themselves, but in truth, they are nothing more than a motley band of brigands and rogues pretending to be holy men. The lowest of the low are among them. And they are notorious snatchers," she said then shrugged. "But Lord Jander won't touch them without cause. If we could find some evidence, I'm sure he'd challenge them. Until then, he blames the other rival families. No one is as blind as he who will not see."

Snap.

Nath and Nina looked up as a dozen brigands dropped out of the branches.

CHAPTER 42

NATH DREW FANG.

Nina snaked her sword and dagger from their scabbards. "Stay in the circle, Nath! Stay with me."

One statue lay on the ground at Nath's feet. He stepped over it, coming back to back with Nina as the brigands closed in. Nath's eyes swept over them. This wasn't some motley band of wayfarers, but a well-organized group, dressed in clothing and armor that blended in with the woodland. Twigs and leaves were pinned to their garments. They carried swords, spears, and crossbows. There were twelve hard-eyed men, part-elves, and halflings. They lurked behind the cover of the statues, weapons poised for destruction.

A somewhat pleasant, even-keeled speaking voice with an edge to it cut through the tension. "Let's make this easy, shall we?" From behind the rank and file of bandits, a tall, broad-shouldered man came forward. He had more beard than face, piercing eyes, and a crossbow in his hands. "All we want is your steel, your purse, and your horses. Put the metal on the ground and drop your pack, and we won't put fresh holes in you. Do you understand?"

"I won't be surrendering anything to you." Nath turned the tip of his sword toward the ranging man, who stood even taller than Nina. "I've lost once, and I swear I won't lose again."

"Son, you've lost already. Look around you. Heh?" the leader said. "Not even the finest soldiers can escape from this. Not when we have a bead on you. No, do what makes sense and drop your weapons. Both of you."

"You lawless curs!" Nina said. A brigand poked through the statues and took a stab at her legs. She knocked the jab aside and chopped at the man. Quick on his feet, he sprang backward behind the statues, giggling hysterically. "Come back, you cowering, mangy dog! I'll split you like a log."

With one hand, the leader pointed his crossbow at her head. "You won't be splitting anything if you have any sense about you. Let me be clear. This is a robbery. I have no intent to kill you, but I will kill you if that is what it takes to achieve my goal. I'll do anything for my brothers, and they for me. Blood stains all of our hands. The less I feel, the better. What will it be?"

"He's bluffing," Nath said, searching their eyes. "I can see fear lurking in their eyes. They are uncertain. Doubt swells in their loins. Thieves are liars, and I bet this bearded fellow hasn't even butchered a cow."

Thwack!

A crossbow bolt tore into the back of Nath's thigh. "Argh!" He glared at the halfling behind him. His little fingers were reloading a crossbow. Another halfling, with a crossbow and bolt ready, stepped in front of the other.

"Nath!" Nina cried, looking down at his leg. "You're wounded. It looks bad."

Grimacing, he reached behind him and yanked the bolt out. "It's not as bad as theirs is going to be."

The brigands cast a few nervous glances between themselves.

The leader gave a lazy shake of his head. "I warned you, and now you bleed. You are a foolish young man. Lady, you seem reasonable. I asked, in exchange for your life, for your goods, all of which are replaceable. I'll tell you what. I'll even let you both keep your armor. I don't think it will fit any of us. That way you can return home with your britches on."

Nath's knuckles were white on his sword. "I'm not giving up my belongings. You'll have to kill me first."

"No, Nath, I can't let you do this." Nina tossed her sword and dagger down. "I'm not having your blood on my hands. Let them take it. Whatever you have, I'll replace it."

"You can't replace this," Nath said of Fang.

"It's only a sword," the brigand leader said. "Who knows, maybe you'll be able to acquire it one day after we sell it. It's very distinctive. It shouldn't be too difficult to track down unless some knight acquires it."

"Nath, please," she said, "just let this go. I'll make it right somehow. I'll help you find your friend."

The lot of brigands snickered.

Nath swallowed down his pride. Red faced, in pain, and sweating, he lowered the blade. "I'm sorry, Fang."

"You see, you are wiser for the robbery," the brigand said, giving an approving nod.

Fang's tip hit the stone statue of the man on the ground.

TIIIIIIIINNNNNGG!

A shockwave of sound carried out of the blade like a tuning fork being struck. Pushing down the grasses, the sound slammed into the statues and the surrounding brigands. The grubby bandits dropped their weapons. They fell to their knees, clutching their heads. They screamed against the growing sound.

Nath lifted the sword. He stood over top of Nina, who lay on the ground, curled up in a ball. He could hear the distinctive sound, but it didn't have any effect on him. It was just a low ringing. Before his eyes, Fang's blade quavered. Blue light coursed through it. "I don't know what you've done, but I'm glad you've done it."

The leader of the brigands begged, "Make it stop! Make it stop!"

TIIIIIINNNNGGG!

Even if Nath could make it stop, he wasn't so sure that he would. As for Fang, what he was doing, he seemed to be doing on his own. "You'll think again before you ever cross me, won't you?"

The brigand leader shook his head, turned his back, and on jittering limbs, ran away. The other brigands staggered away, falling over and scrambling to regain their feet. The farther they got, the faster they moved. Without looking back, one and all disappeared into the forest.

The ringing sound ended. Fang's glowing metal cooled. One handed, Nath flipped him around a few times then sheathed him. "Well done." Nina lay sprawled out at his feet. Her eyes were closed. Her body spasmed. "Nina!"

CHAPTER 43

K NEELING, NATH SHOOK THE WOMAN, calling her name. "Nina! Nina! Can you hear me?"

Suddenly, her eyes snapped open. She gasped for breath. Broken out in a cold sweat, she panted. "What was that? I felt like I was trapped in a ringing bell tower. Oh, thank the lord it has ended." She clutched Nath's arm. "Tell me that won't happen again."

"That's not up to me. That's up to Fang." He put a waterskin to her lips and let her drink. "I didn't even know that he could do that. Sorry."

"You speak of your sword like it's a person," she said, wiping her mouth with her hand.

"Is that out of the ordinary?"

"I suppose not. I've known many warriors who talk to their weapons like friends." She searched the woodland. "Are they gone?"

"As far as their clumsy feet will take them." Nath glanced at the abandoned weapons on the ground. "I don't think they'll be coming back for them anytime soon."

"They won't be here when they do," she said, holding out her hand. "Help me up."

Nath hauled her to her feet, grimaced, and helped her steady herself. Nina swayed a bit. "Maybe you should sit longer."

"No, I'll be fine. Just embarrassed. And you need a bandage! They shot you," she said, red-faced.

"I'll manage," he said, taking a potion vial longer than his finger out of his pack. He drank down the clear bubbly contents in the little glass flask. "Ah," he said, able to feel the skin, muscle, and sinew in his leg beginning to mend. He put the half-empty vial back in the pack. "Much better. I might limp a little bit."

"Another surprise," she said. "Nath, I truly feel ashamed. Nothing has ever taken me down like that before. I just wasn't ready." Her eyes swept over their surroundings. She picked her sword and dagger up and slid them back into their sheaths. "You are full of surprises. I thought they had us for certain. I apologize for letting you down."

"Don't be silly. I think you were right to tell me to stand down. My actions could have gotten either one of us killed."

"I suppose we should go," she said, holding her stomach. "I'll gather up their weapons."

"That sounds like a good idea, but I'm not ready to go back yet. We still need to search around a bit." Nath reopened his pack. "Perhaps something was left behind that the others missed." He took the small hooded lantern with a brushed-nickel finish and green lens out of his pack. "This might be of some help."

"I don't see how a lantern is going to be of any help in broad daylight. And it's so small." Nina picked up swords, daggers, and crossbows and put them in a stack. Her eyes kept scanning the woodland. She glanced at Nath. "Even for a halfling."

"I haven't used it before, but it's a gift from my father. It was my thirtieth celebration day present. He called it Winzee's Lantern of Revealing. Supposedly, it's an all-seeing eye. If something was missed, we should find it."

"Who is your father that bestows upon you such magic?" Nina asked. "Was he a wizard?"

"Er… well, I suppose you could say that. But this has been in our family quite some time." Nath twisted the key on the lantern's side. A watery green light spilled out, casting new light around Nath in a ten-foot radius. "Whoa, now that is interesting." He picked up a silver piece hidden in the ground near his feet. "I didn't notice that before. And I have a very keen eye."

Nina's eyes were the size of saucers. "Nath, that is incredible. Can I use it?"

"I believe anyone can." He passed it to her. She took it by the handle. "I'll follow you."

"I'm going to start at the road where the scrum occurred." She pushed through the brush, back toward the road, and picked up several coins and a rusted horseshoe along the way. "This is impressive. I bet this little lantern would come in handy locating secret doors and passages. I wish I had it years ago. Huh, I might have avoided falling into a pit."

"You fell in a pit? Where did this happen?" Nath said, limping to catch up with her.

"It happened in an abandoned dungeon. We were treasure hunting. I'm just glad we made it out alive."

"You were a prisoner?" Nath asked.

"No, just searching ruins from cities abandoned long ago." Nina started on the dirt road and walked in a slow outward circle. With her eyes scanning the green hue covering the ground, she said, "This is like seeing the world with a new pair of eyes. Magic eyes. I've dealt with mystic items before, but never one such as this. Or your sword. This is fascinating."

"I'm glad you are enjoying it. It makes me happy."

"You have no idea how this thrills me. The uses are countless. The possibilities endless." She took a knee on the edge of the road, across from where they'd first entered the forest. Her fingers brushed over the dirt.

"What is it?" Nath asked, leaning over her shoulder.

"A button," Nina said, holding it up to his face. It was a steel button the size of a knuckle. Three wavy lines, like water, were engraved in the metal. "But not just any button." The lantern's light dimmed. "No!" she exclaimed. She slapped the lantern's side. She twisted the key. "Nath, what happened?"

"I suppose its use is limited." He took the lantern from her and twisted the key. Nothing happened. "I don't know."

Standing up, she gave him a serious look. "This is horrible." She kicked the dirt. "We need more proof than this button."

"What is so special about that button?"

"It's from the robes of the monks of Riverlynn."

Chapter 44

B ACK AT THE OXEN INN, Nath waited to hear from Nina. He sat on a tall stool on the wraparound deck that overlooked the barn outside his window. The back of his wounded thigh still burned beneath him. He'd been sitting for hours, waiting for a knock at the door, but one never came. After Nina found the button and the lantern went out, they spent another couple of hours searching for more evidence. Nath found lizardman skin that had peeled. Nina found a strip of leather cord. She said she thought it might have been used to tie someone up and that she'd run it by Lord Jander, but it was unlikely, given the lack of evidence, that he'd support a mission.

The drifting clouds blotted out the sun on and off throughout the day. The sun set, the moon came. Nath was still sitting. He'd gotten a feel for the city and made a friend. He liked it. Nina was an interesting person. She wanted to help people. Nath wanted to help people too. He'd convinced himself that if he could find Janna, then he'd be better prepared to find Maefon. He could make new friends and allies. Nalzambor was a big place, and after getting jumped by the brigands, he realized having some allies and friends could make a difference.

Little Shirl appeared on the deck. The tiny lady walked up to Nath, head down. "Nina says you need to come with me. You can bring your arms."

Smiling, Nath said, "Well, I never go anywhere without my arms."

"You know what I mean," she said flatly.

"Yes, of course." Nath reached inside his room and grabbed his sword, belt, and pack. He closed the window. "After you, young lady."

"I'm not as young as I look," she said, walking down the deck and heading down the stairs at the end. "I'm as old as Nina but look much younger. I don't do those things that she does. You should not either. It will fill your comely face with wrinkles well before their time."

"I'm more worried about scales than wrinkles," Nath said.

Little Shirl shot him a confused glance. "Scales?"

"It's an odd condition that runs in the family."

"Sounds horrible."

"I guess it depends on one's perspective. Anyway," he said, catching up with her brisk pace, "where are you taking me?"

"I'm taking you where you need to go," the spooky girlish woman replied. "Keep up now."

The Oxen Inn was located on the eastern side of the city. Little Shirl took him west. The burning oil in the streetlamps gave the city a warm, shadowy illumination. The people who strolled over the cobblestone roads were lively. After a hard day of working, they walked arm in arm, some singing, and others staggering. On the balconies, women with long lashes and colorful cheeks, wearing silks and flimsy linens, waved and whistled at Nath.

"Traveler," they called. "Come visit. We want to greet you!"

Five of them were hanging over the balcony rail, waving their silk sashes and scarves and giggling.

"Yes, Red Hair, we welcome all who come here!" The women blew kisses and winked at him.

Nath waved back with a smile. "Perhaps later, when I return."

Little Shirl pulled his hand down. "Have you no sense at all? You don't consort with those women. They are trouble."

"Trouble how? They seem very friendly."

"Stay away from the ladies with the painted faces. I told you once. I won't tell you again." With both hands, she held his hand. "It's best I keep you close. We don't have far to go." She stayed on the main road, took a corner left and the next corner right. With storefronts on both sides, she stopped halfway down the street where an alley split the stores on the left. She pointed. "At the end is a door. They will meet with you inside."

"They?" Nath said, peering into the darkness of the alley. His nostrils flared. "And there is a stench."

"Yes, you are very observant. There is a stink, but that is very common in most alleys. More so in this area of the city. Good-bye, Nath. I bid you farewell." Little Shirl bowed, turned, and quickly walked away.

As Little Shirl faded into the crowd, Nath said, "That was a little cryptic." He stepped out of the streetlamp's light and into the alley. He let his eyes adjust to the darkness and crept forward. A rat darted across his toes. A cat chased after it. He weaved his way through the abandoned wooden crates piled up on the sides of the building. He made out the outline of the door at the end. Stopping at arm's length of the door, he gave it closer study. The door was made of metal and painted brick red. Extinguished torches covered in webbing hung on the sides.

Why would Nina want to meet me here? This is deplorable.

Nath took a backward glance. He peered up both sides of the walls. He'd learned a hard lesson from the brigands who ambushed them. He should have been more alert. He survived, but he had a limp to show for it. He wouldn't make that mistake again. Seeing no immediate threats, he faced the door and lifted his fist.

The door swung open, hard and fast. An unseen force yanked him inside, and the door slammed hard behind him.

CHAPTER 45

NATH'S ENTIRE BODY SLAMMED INTO the wall of a pitch-black room. Shaking his head, he fought his way back to his feet and reached for Fang's handle. A hard punch to the jaw sent him sprawling again. Lying flat on his belly, someone jumped on his back. Heavy as an anchor, the man locked his hands under Nath's neck and pulled.

"He's strong as a young bull," the person on his back said in a gruff voice. "But I can hold him."

"Just hold him still, Cullon, while we kick him all over." The person speaking made a high-pitched giggle. He kicked Nath in the legs with a hard-toed boot. "Did you feel that? Huh? Did you feel that?"

Muscles bulging in his neck, Nath fought to pull his chin down. He pushed up on his hands. "Auugh!"

"Be still," the person on his back said. "Stop wriggling, or we'll hurt you more!"

Nath heard the shuffle of more feet and others breathing. He guessed there were at least four people inside the room, plus him. One was kicking the daylights out of him. Another, whom he thought was called Cullon, had strong, calloused hands locked underneath his chin, trying to pull his head off. He made out four warm bodies in the darkness. Pitch black or not, Nath could make out the warmth of the living in the dark as if it were day. "Get off of me, thieves. I'm warning you!"

Cullon let go of his chin.

Nath's face hit the floor. His lips busted. He tasted blood in his mouth. He twisted to his back, threw a punch, and connected with a jaw as strong as iron. With pain shooting through his fingers, he unleashed a flurry of punches. His hard blows smacked into Cullon's face.

"That's enough of that!" In the dark, Cullon grabbed him by the collar of his breastplate and jerked him up. He head-butted Nath right between the eyes. "How does that feel?"

Bright spots exploded in Nath's eyes. Pain streaked down his neck. His temper boiled. Hearing a soft scuff of a boot near his head, he lashed out. He grabbed someone by the boot and yanked them down. They landed hard on the planks. "Ow!" the person said. "Let go of me!"

"You let go of me!" Nath hollered back. He pulled them closer and punched them in the ribs.

"Ulf." The person groaned.

Nath hit Cullon in the chest with everything he had.

Cullon made a low chuckle. "You'll have to hit harder than that."

In a swift move, Nath brought up his feet, hooked Cullon by the shoulders, and thrust him down. He pinned Cullon on his back. Cullon tore free and flipped to his belly. Nath put him in a headlock. He couldn't clamp down on the neck the way he wanted. Cullon was covered in hair. He hip-tossed Nath.

Nath hit the ground. Before he could get up, he felt the sharp edge of a weapon on his neck. "Stay down," a calm voice said. "Virgo, may we have some light, please?"

"As you wish," a woman with a velvety voice said.

A greenish glow filled the room as candles in an iron candelabrum hanging in the center of the ceiling caught fire, the flames a dark-emerald color. He was in a large storage room with many shelves loaded with boxes, jars, and wooden vegetable crates. There was a second door, and he could hear the faint rumblings and movements of other people. He was certain there was music too. Nath locked eyes with the man who held a dagger to his throat. "What are you waiting for?"

"Introductions, actually," the man said. He offered a nice smile with perfect white teeth. His brown hair, moustache, and sideburns were neatly trimmed. His chest and shoulders were covered in deep-brown leather armor. "I'm Tobias. Believe it or not, we are friends of Nina, who sent you. She'll be along shortly." He tucked his dagger into its scabbard. "This was a bit of a test. We wanted to see how you would handle yourself in a dangerous situation."

"I could have killed you," Nath said, propping himself up on his elbows.

"Not likely. We held back, way back."

"Aye!" Cullon's voice was loud and harsh. He was all dwarf, standing just shy of five feet tall and built like a rock. The very top of his head was bald. His black hair came to his shoulders, and a thick beard covered most of his chest. Belts of knives crisscrossed under his beard, hand axes hung on his hips, and a white scar crossed the side of his prominent nose. "I could have killed you. He's too young, Tobias. Soft. We don't need him."

"What's he talking about?" Nath said, coming to his feet. "I'm not soft." He pointed at the wiry man wearing a loose-fitting gray outfit who lay on the floor, holding his ribs. "He's soft. Look at him, squirming like a worm with ribs."

Slapping Nath on the back, Tobias let out a delightful laugh. "Ah-haha. I couldn't have put it better myself. Worm with ribs. It's perfect! Nath, meet Worm."

The scrawny man on the floor waved. He didn't look much older than Nath, but it was hard to tell because his messy light hair covered his eyes. "You have quick hands. You surprised me."

"He is really named Worm?" Nath said, slipping out from Tobias's hand.

"Yes," Tobias replied. "And last of all, meet Virgo. She is the one that so skillfully whisked you in here. Dashing, isn't she?"

Virgo, older than the rest but without a wrinkle, had straight, silvery hair down to her back. She leaned against the doorframe with her arms crossed. Her hypnotic eyes soaked Nath in. She wore a long black gown made from nicely woven cotton, giving her pale and slender figure a fuller look. She had a little smile as she seemed to glide across the room toward Nath. She took his hand. "I hope I didn't hurt you when my powers flung you into the wall." She made a pouty face. "But I do what I am told to do." She kissed his hand.

"You have very cold hands," Nath said, unable to break her stare or grip. "Not that it is a bad thing. I heard that cold hands make—"

"Warm hearts?" she said. "That's something cold and old women say. But I can assure you, my heart is very warm now." She brushed Nath's bangs aside. "Your hair and eyes are like nothing I've ever seen. You are dazzling."

"Yes, I think it's fair to say that he has above-average qualities, Virgo." Tobias, who was a good-looking man himself, peeled her fingers from Nath's and nudged her aside. "But we didn't bring him here to be fawned over. Nina thinks he'd be a welcome addition to our party." Studying Nath, he combed his moustache with his fingers. "But I agree with Cullon. He seems too soft. Too young."

CHAPTER 46

"I AM NOT TOO YOUNG," NATH exclaimed. "I'm older than you." He caught himself as the others started laughing. Aside from the dwarf, he was certain that he was older than the rest. He pointed at Worm. "Well, him, anyway."

"Don't be so sure of yourself," Worm said in a silky voice. "I am much older than I appear." He cackled. "But I coat myself in rare silks and oils when I slumber." He glided over to Nath. Staring at his face, he said, "May I?"

"I suppose," he replied.

Worm ran his fingers down Nath's face. "I've never seen one without blemish. His skin is smooth, yet there is thickness to it." He rubbed a lock of Nath's hair between his fingers and thumb. "My, the wig weavers would give a fortune for this. It has more sheen than even Virgo's."

"When did you stick your dirty little paws in my hair?" Virgo said to Worm.

Worm cackled. "Ah-hah, most likely it happens when you snore so soundly."

Arms crossed over her chest, Virgo rolled her eyes.

Nath brushed Worm's hand aside and stepped back. "When I say

I'm old enough, you must believe me. And I'm a fine warrior, as good as any."

"Hah!" Cullon laughed. "Tobias, I say that we be done with this redheaded rogue. I say we vote now. My gut tells me that we need to move on. And we don't need him to do what we do." He clawed at his beard. "Saying he's older than us. There is something foul about that."

"Appearances aren't everything." Tobias combed his hair over a distinctive ear with a point on it.

"You're part elf?" Nath said.

"Quarter elf would be more accurate," Tobias said. "My grandfather on my father's side was full-blood elf." He motioned to a long table at the edge of the room. "Let's all have a seat, shall we?"

Sitting at the table, Nath asked, "Where are we? And where is Nina?"

"She'll be along." Virgo took a seat beside Nath and scooted close to him. "Don't worry, you have me to keep an eye out for you. And don't let Cullon bother you. He's a dwarf, born with a poor disposition chockful of rotten as his manners."

"Aye." The dwarf took a small wooden keg off the shelf, plucked out the wooden plug, tipped it up, and started drinking. Ale splashed all over his face and beard as he guzzled it down. "Ahh!" He replaced the plug and sat down at the table. His sausage fingers beat the barrel like a drum. "Go on, keep talking about how rotten I am. I like it."

Tobias sat across from Nath, leaning forward with one elbow on the table. "Have no fear, Nath. Nina will be along. She most likely will enter from the front entrance of this tavern. There are many types that haunt this not-so-refined establishment. That's why we had you come through the back—to avoid prying eyes. You tend to stand out a bit, like a candle flame on a dim night. It can stimulate provocation in a place such as this."

"So this is an adventurers' cove?" Nath's fingers tapped on the table.

"There are many sordid people in this den. Trust me when I say you are in good company, for there is a rotten brood out there."

"And in here." Cullon pulled the keg plug and drank more.

Tobias kept his eyes fixed on Nath. "Tell me a little more about yourself, Nath. You are from the south, as I understand it. Do you have a family name? We are all seasoned travelers. Perhaps we would recognize your family name?"

"Uh, I doubt that. There are thousands of names, and you couldn't possibly know them all," Nath said. *Or say them, for that matter.* Dragon names tended to be as long as a river, not to mention in an entirely different language. "Nath should be fine. I don't see a need for so many formalities."

"Nath, to be a part of this, we need to know much about one another. It's called trust." Tobias leaned back in his chair. "But if you really aren't that interested in saving Janna or receiving our help, I can't fault you for going it alone." He got up from his chair. "So sorry for all the trouble we put you through. I'll inform Nina that she was wrong. It was nice meeting you, Nath whoever-you-are."

CHAPTER 47

"NO, WAIT, PLEASE SIT BACK down, Tobias," Nath said. "It's not that I don't want to share my last name. It's just I'm a bit embarrassed about it."

All eyes were fixed on Tobias, who sat back down. "All right, I'm listening. Though I can hardly think of a last name that would be so embarrassing."

"Orc would be an embarrassing last name," Cullon said. "Are you Nath Orc?"

"No." Nath shook his head. If these people could really help him find Janna, he wanted to be a part of their group, and he didn't want to disappoint them. Thinking of the first thing to come to mind, he made up a lie. He recalled a long word that he'd learned in one of the books he read in Dragon Home. "Olifflinursagewahn. It's hard to say, and we would typically go by Olifflin, but it's meaning is even worse."

"Yes, it is a mouthful. It must be from a very old tongue," Tobias said, scratching the corner of his mouth. "So what does it mean?"

Nath could have given it any meaning, but he said the truth. "Dragon."

Cullon erupted in laughter. Holding his stomach, he said, "That is worse than orc!"

Worm cackled insanely. He banged his fist on the table. "Nath Dragon. Oh, that is rich!"

"Well, they don't call me that," Nath argued. His cheeks turned rosy. "Stop laughing. It's just a name."

Virgo rubbed his arm. "Well, I like it. It fits."

"I concur." Tobias rapped his knuckles on the table. "Nath Dragon—it has a nice ring to it."

"I don't want to be called that. Can we just stay with Nath?" he said.

Virgo laid her head on his shoulder. Batting her eyes at him, she said, "I'll call you whatever you like."

"Please, Virgo," Tobias said with a frown, "give this young warrior some space." He pushed back from the table and glanced at the door that led into the tavern. "Nina should be here by now. Anyway, Nath, I don't question your heart, but I don't want to endanger you right away. And frankly, my gut says you aren't ready. I say we have a preliminary vote, as Cullon requested. Do I have a second?"

"Aye," Worm said with a grin.

"Good." Tobias nodded. "All in favor of allowing Nath into this group, on a probationary basis, raise your hand." Virgo and Worm lifted their left hands briefly, the greenish light glinting off their fingers eerily, and dropped them down on the table. Their palms were both tattooed black. "And those not in favor?" he continued, lifting his left hand. His palm too was black. Cullon raised the same hand. It was black on the palm as well. "It seems the decision is split at this point, and I'm fairly sure where Nina the tiebreaker will lean."

"You can't cast a vote on account of her absence," Cullon growled. He glared at Virgo and Worm. "The both of you are ignorant. All you will do is get this boy killed."

"I'm no boy!" Nath said, looking at Tobias's hands. "I do have a question. Why are all of the palms of your hands stained black?"

Tobias showed a clever smile. "That is who we are, Nath. We call ourselves the Black Hand."

"So my hand will be tattooed?"

"Again, it's a probationary basis."

The door from the tavern opened. Nina hustled inside. The tall woman closed the door behind her and caught her breath. "Sorry I'm late. The city lord was being very chatty. He was quite interested in what I had to say, for a change. Then he slipped me out. He's so paranoid about who comes and goes. Hello, Nath. Are my friends treating you well?"

"I suppose," Nath replied.

"We took a vote, Nina," Tobias said. "The decision is split. Are you ready to cast your vote?"

"I think he's ready. At least, I've never seen a man so young and able, or well-equipped," Nina said, taking a seat at the table.

"I concur," Virgo said, keeping her eyes on Nath.

Cullon shoved the table. "I don't care what kind of equipment he has! He ain't ready, and I don't like him. You have too much of a thing for newcomers, Nina. It's a weakness. The Black Hand requires veterans."

"Worm is hardly a veteran. And none of us were perfect when we came along," Nina argued. "Every initiate is new."

"He's green." The dwarf slammed the keg back onto the shelf. "Green, I say."

"The only one that is green is you. Green with envy," Virgo quipped. "Not that I blame you."

"Speaking of equipment, Nath, now that you are part of the Black Hand, do you care to show us what equipment you have to offer?" Tobias said as he got up and walked to the nearest corner behind the table. A sword belt hung on a peg. He drew a falchion blade with a curved end and razor-sharp tip from the scabbard. The brass pommel was fashioned like a wolf. "This is Splitter, an enchanted blade passed down to me from my grandfather." He twisted it from side to side and made some quick cuts. "Splitter never slips from my grip. It's a marvelous piece of work, the same as my armor." He tapped his chest. "Leather from the weavers of Rodingtom. It can't be cut."

"Fascinating." Nath looked at Virgo, who was right in his face. "And do you carry a weapon?"

"You'll have to search me yourself, Nath Dragon," she said.

"I can just take your word for it."

"Oh, that is a shame," Virgo replied. "But I have a staff. I don't carry it always. It makes me look old."

"It's the wrinkles, not the staff," Nina said. "The staff is more polished than you."

Virgo shot a look at Nina. "I don't have wrinkles! Watch your tongue, you overgrown innkeeper!"

"Ladies! Let's not get into this again, please," Tobias said as he sheathed his sword. "We are the Black Hand, planners, not squabblers."

"I have many interesting items, Nath," Worm said. He had a parchment under one hand and three potion vials in the other. They were Nath's items from his pack. "And I thank you for them."

Nath flung his body at Worm. "Those are mine!"

CHAPTER 48

ORM VANISHED. NATH CRASHED INTO the young man's chair. Rolling to his feet, he found Worm sitting in Nath's chair beside Virgo. "You trickster!"

Cackling, Worm said, "I wouldn't call me that." He looked up. "I prefer prankster." He looked at the parchment Slivver had given Nath. "This is intriguing. Are you an artist? Virgo is an artist. Aren't you, gorgeous?" He planted a kiss on her cheek.

Virgo slapped at Worm. He vanished a split second before she made contact. "You dirty little rogue. I'll have you."

Worm reappeared behind Nath. He started stuffing Nath's items back into his pack. Quickly, he said, "I was only toying with you, Nath. Just fun."

"No one steals from me!" Furious, Nath spun around, launching a punch as he did so. Worm ducked underneath the swing. "Hold still." Nath threw several haymakers. Worm slid away from them all.

"Enough!" Tobias said, standing eye to eye with Nath and coming between them. "Apologize, Worm, and make this right. Offer the left hand of honor." He turned his attention to Nath. "You have to understand, Worm has very sticky fingers and an alley cat's curiosity. He's plucked us all more than a time or two."

Peeking from behind Tobias's shoulder, Worm said, "Yes, you just saw me steal a kiss from Virgo. And I'll steal one again." He held out the parchment from Slivver. "Here is your paper."

Tobias took the parchment. His eyes grew big when he glanced at it. He cleared his throat, rolled up the parchment and handed it to Nath. "Uh, sorry, but that's an interesting image on the paper. You can share all with your comrades here. Our lips will be as sealed as a boat that's watertight."

Nath snatched the parchment. Turning his back, he took out his items and placed them on the table. "There is all you need to see of me." He lifted the coil of rope and the lantern and showed them the Gauntlet of Goam that he'd put on his hand. He had the three potion vials again and his candles. "Wait a moment, where is my—"

Clink!

His purse of coins landed on the table. Nath looked inside the small sack. All of the coins and gems appeared to be intact. He turned and stabbed a finger at the rogue. "Worm, you better never steal from me again."

The slender young man slid out from behind Tobias with his head down. "I wasn't stealing. It was a prank. A jest." He looked up into Nath's eyes. "I can't help myself. It's what I do."

"Steal? I don't want to be in the company of thieves," Nath said with his eyes sweeping over all of their faces. "There is no honor in that."

"No, Nath, you don't understand," Tobias explained. "We all have different skills that we rely on to get us through the horrors that await us in tombs, caves, and ruins. Worm can find traps and disarm them. He has a very special gift for that. We need him. We need each other."

Worm offered his hand. "It won't happen again."

In the blink of an eye, Nath locked his fingers around Worm's throat. Squeezing, he lifted the young man up on tiptoe. Looking the rogue right in the eyes, Nath said, "No, it won't." He shoved Worm into Tobias's chest. Tobias couldn't hide the shock on his face. No one could.

Coughing and wiping his watery eyes, Worm said, "That was fast. Very fast."

"Yes, I'm very, very fast. What would you expect from a man named Nath Dragon?"

"Breathing fire would be a good trick," Cullon remarked.

Nath shook his head. "These are my belongings. Well, this and my sword and breastplate. Is there anything else you would know of me?"

All eyes were glued on the items on the table. The three other men in the room came closer with a glint in their eyes.

"Those appear to be very serviceable magic resources," Tobias said, looking at Virgo. "Am I correct?"

She spread all ten fingers out, closed her eyes, and began to hum an incantation. The skin on her hands illuminated with radiant light. She passed her hands over the items one at a time. Opening her eyes, she said, "It's all magic. Very strong magic."

"I told you what the hooded lantern could do," Nina said, standing up. She put her arm over Nath's shoulders. "I think our items and skills, combined with Nath's, are just what we need to rescue the princess. It will give us the edge we need. If Nath truly wants to help, we will succeed. What do you say, Nath? Do you want to be a part of the Black Hand?"

Nath gave an affirmative nod. "I believe I do. But how is it that your hand is black now when it was not before?"

"I can explain that," Virgo said with a playful smile on her lips. Getting up from her chair, she moved under the candelabrum and passed her hand beneath it. Arcane words spun from her lips. The candles' fires flickered. The colors shifted from an ambient green to natural orange. Holding up her hand, she turned and winked at

Nath. Her black palm was the color of natural flesh again. "It's a little spell that I created to identify those who are marked. Your time will come, I hope."

"Everything seems to be in order, then," Tobias said to them all. "Black Hand, it's time to rescue a princess."

"Oh, there is one more thing I need to mention," Nina said. Her brows creased. "Lord Jander wants this done quietly, and he wants it done now. I suggested we leave at first light."

"Agreed," Tobias said. "We'll just have to make plans on the way to Riverlynn then." He smiled. "Dismissed."

The three men departed, leaving Nath alone with Nina and Virgo.

"Let's go, Nath," Nina said, yawning. "I need some rest. We'll get up early and have the horses ready."

"I'm not tired," he said. "The truth is, I'm tingling. I won't be able to sleep tonight. I don't sleep much anyway."

"Me either," Virgo said, hooking her arm in his. "Nina, please, go ahead. I'll walk him back to the inn later."

Casting a wary eye at Virgo, Nina said, "Remember the code, Virgo."

"Yes, I know the code. No romance among members."

Yawning, Nina gave a nod and departed.

Once the tall woman was gone, Virgo giggled. "But you're not a full member yet, are you?"

CHAPTER 49

NATH SAT ON A STOOL inside Virgo's apartment. Her place was nicely furnished, smelled of fresh flowers, and was very warm. Framed paintings hung on the wall in an assortment of sizes. Others were leaned against each other along the walls. Some of the paintings were of the trees in the woodland, snowy and sunny, and others were groups of people, in a tavern, or a parade or celebration, gathered together. But most of them were portraits of people, posing the same as Nath was.

"Sit up straight, Nath, and lift your chin a little higher. And a smile would be nice, you know. Flash a few teeth. You have a dashing smile. I want to capture it." Virgo had put her silver hair up in a bun and stood behind a canvas on an easel. She looked younger with her hair up, revealing more of the rich features of her beauty. She painted with easy strokes. The board with a palette of paints was in her left hand. "You might be my masterpiece, Nath. I can feel it. You are the one I've been waiting for."

Nath stuck his chest out and smiled. "I didn't imagine that when you brought me up here, it would be to paint me."

"Really, and what did you imagine, Nath?"

"Er... well," he said, wiping his sweating palms on the thighs of his trousers. "I thought you wanted to kiss me."

She laughed softly. "Well, the thought did cross my mind, believe me. But there is a code. Are you disappointed that I haven't acted on my passions?"

"Well, no, I'm more relieved, actually," he said.

"Relieved? That's not at all what I expected you to say."

"No, no, it's not you. You are divine. It's just that I haven't kissed many before, and well, I'm spoken for, sort of."

"Chin up," she said sharply. She chewed on the end of her brush as she eyed her painting. She took a few glances between the canvas and Nath. "This isn't turning out so well after all. Something is missing."

"I'm sorry, Virgo, have I offended you? I didn't mean to. I just, well, I don't really have much experience in the company of women. And—"

"Oh, stop it, Nath. It's refreshing having you in such a naive and innocent state of mind. So often, the men I paint can't stop begging for my attention. They grovel for my hand and my time. They vow to leave their families and offer me their fortunes. Shameless, they are. I just want to paint them."

Keeping his head still, Nath scanned the portraits on the wall. The details were incredible. There were many handsome men with strong lines in their features, and women, each a different kind of beauty, varying in their gorgeous hair, lovely eyes, or perfect smiles. "You have an amazing talent. They are so realistic."

"Indeed, but I feel I am falling flat on this effort." She approached Nath, palette and paint brush in hand. Eyeing his chest, she said, "Your armor. It is so... bland. Would you be offended if I were to paint a design on it?"

"Er... I don't see why not. It wouldn't be too showy, would it?"

"No, I just think it needs a bit of flair. Everything about you stands out, but the armor is dull. It doesn't fit. It needs some splash to it."

Nath shrugged. "If it makes you happy, then it makes me happy to let you do it."

"Breathe easy, but be still," she said as she began painting.

Nath could hear the soft brush strokes on his chest. Virgo's perfume filled his nose. Her soft breath kissed his neck. His mouth became dry. His eyes searched for hers. They found her soft pink lips, which had a glossy look on them. *I really do want to kiss her. She is so exquisite.*

"Just a little longer," she said. Her paintbrush moved with a quick and gentle ease in her hand. She carried on a few more minutes. "There, that will do it."

Nath let out a breath he hadn't realized he'd been holding. "So you are finished. May I see?" He looked down at his chest. He flexed one eyebrow. "What is that?"

"Come over here and look in this mirror," she said, walking over to a full-length mirror standing up in the near corner of the studio. She stepped alongside it. "Take a look."

Nath stood in front of the mirror. Two black lines, like partial wreaths, partially enclosed a brick-red design of a sword and a dragon. The sword resembled Fang, with the dragon crossguards, and the dragon profile was a large face with a smaller tail. They overlapped one another. He tilted his head to one side, then the other.

"Do you like it?" she asked.

"I think so."

"I can remove it," she said, frowning. "I understand if you don't care for it. But I really do like it."

"It looks like the symbols form a *D*."

She giggled. "Yes, it's subtle, but it is a *D*. A *D* for dragon. Nath Dragon."

His mouth hung open.

"You hate it. I'll take it off."

Eyes frozen on the symbol, he said, "No. No, don't." The corners of his mouth started to rise. "I actually think I do like it. It's flattering in an odd sort of way."

"Then I shall seal it!" Virgo said, setting down her brush and palette. She put her hands over his chest. "This might get a little hot, but only for a moment. It will keep the paint from peeling or chipping off." She closed her eyes and muttered an incantation. Her hands turned the color of fire.

Nath's chest warmed. Perspiration broke out above his brows. There was a sizzling sound, and a puff of stinky smoke rose from his chest.

"It is finished," she said. "Did that hurt?"

"A little, but I'm fine."

Virgo draped her slender arms over his neck and gave him a quick kiss. "Go back to the tavern and rest, Nath. I'll see you in the morning. We have an important journey ahead."

"But your painting of me. Don't you need to finish it? I'm not sleepy."

She broke off the embrace. "I have to prepare for tomorrow myself. And a little rest does keep away the wrinkles. You can find your way back, can't you?"

"Yes. See you in the morning, Virgo. I look forward to it." He backed toward the painting. "However, I would like to take a quick look."

"No, no, no!" Virgo rushed into his path. Pushing him back, she said, "You cannot look until it is complete, Nath. Now go."

"You're sweating all of a sudden," he said, wiping the perspiration running down the side of her temple. "It can't be that bad. You are a great painter."

"Nath, just go. I need to prepare for tomorrow." She pushed him toward the door. "In the morning, then?"

"In the morning." As he passed through the doorway, he turned back to say good night. The door slammed shut in his face. "Uh... good night."

CHAPTER 50

Late at night, Maefon watched a bridge that tied one side of the creek to the other burn. Men and women rushed from their village cottages in a mad scramble. They filled buckets of water from the nearby shallow river and passed them along a row toward the fire. The people hollered back and forth at one another. Lord Darkken stood among the villagers, talking with encouragement, passing the filled buckets from hand to hand. The bridge was consumed in flames. The timbers cracked and popped. A black plume of smoke darkened the sky, making a thick haze between the desperate people and the passing clouds.

"Maefon! Maefon!" a woman cried out, swing her arms wildly. "Lend a hand. Fetch more buckets from the storage houses!"

Maefon nodded. She sprinted toward the streets of Ferly. Dashing into a barn, she swung open the storage door and fetched three more milking buckets. For the past few days, she'd been helping out in the barn, milking cows and cleaning stables. Lord Darkken lent a hand to the men who built the bridge. The bridge tied two feuding villages, Ferly and Starnly, together. They'd finally come to terms and agreed to work with one another, opening up a road for trade and expanding commerce. The bridge, a sturdy wooden structure, not even a hundred feet long and wide enough for two wagons, was a symbol of the communities coming together. Now, it burned.

She ran back to the river and handed the buckets down to the crowd. The woman who had called out to her shook her head. Tears streamed down her cheeks. "It's too late. Too late," she said.

From one end to the other, the bridge became an inferno. The black cloud of smoke blossomed in the night.

The coughing and crying men and women's efforts to extinguish the flames came to a stop.

Flaming hunks of wood collapsed into the water.

A man clutched his head. "No, no, noooo."

On the other side of the stream, the people from Starnly shared the same distraught reaction. They had been working together for weeks, building a bridge that now had been burned down. Lord Darkken came over to Maefon. "You did a fine job setting that bridge on fire. And no magic. Impressive."

"I mixed hay and tar with oil," she said as they walked back toward the abandoned village. "I packed it underneath the joists last night. It was a simple thing, really. These people really took a shine to me."

"Yes, well, you are elven and often fascinate many people. You did well in your seduction of them. But not everyone slept," he said. "I, for one, didn't, and I witnessed the entire event." Lord Darkken stopped and turned toward the stream. "You see, a man spied you from the other side of the river. He was out wandering, drunken and smoking a pipe. I killed him. I used one of this village's marked chisels to complete the authenticity." He pointed to the bank south of the bridge on their side and made a little motion with his hand. "They should find their brother's body any moment now."

From her elevated position, she saw a bulk detach from the bank and float down the stream. The bloated body arrived among the squabbling people. A woman let out a bone-chilling scream.

The dead body was dragged out of the river and onto the bank. A woman from the other side of the bridge dropped to the ground, and from her hands and knees, she wailed, "My husband! My husband! They murdered my husband!"

Angry village folk waded through the stream toward one another. Shouts echoed over the burbling stream but quickly turned into an exchange of heated words, pushing and shoving, and punches thrown. Within seconds, the men and women from both villages were going at it.

Lord Darkken smiled down at Maefon. "I think that should create a grudge that will last a few generations. Don't you?"

"Agreed. You've created a fine stream of discourse."

He put his arm over her shoulders. "In this case, we both did. Now, let's go find another peaceful community with hopes and dreams we can destroy."

CHAPTER 51

O N HORSEBACK, NATH RODE WITH the Black Hand southeast from Riegelwood. In the distance, two mountain ranges merged together, forming a V-shape in the rocks. Stormy skies were beyond the vast gap. Flocks of birds flew over them in waves, every hour or so. Riding tall in their saddles, Nina and Tobias led, with Nath and Virgo in the middle, and Cullon and Worm brought up the rear.

Aside from Worm cackling from time to time, the journey had been very quiet. Nina and Tobias's eyes were fixed ahead or scanning from side to side. Their horses were loaded with plenty of gear, including bedrolls and saddle bags. Swords hung in scabbards off their saddles. Tobias also had a bow and quiver of arrows.

Riding beside Nath, Virgo carried next to nothing. She rode with her gown up over her bare knees, and a bedroll behind her. She looked at Nath and smiled from time to time. Aside from greeting her in the morning, she hadn't said a word to him. The Black Hand seemed to be all business.

Worm cackled.

Nath looked back at him. Worm wore loose-fitting clothing and showed nothing else of use. The young rogue made big eyes at him and laughed again. Even Cullon chuckled.

"Is there something that I should be aware of?" Nath asked.

"Oh no, of course not, Nath Dragon," Worm said, trying to hold back his laughter. His eyes drifted to Nath's chest, and he started laughing out loud again. "Bwah-ha-ha-ha-hah!"

Tugging the reins, Nath turned his horse around to face the man and dwarf. "I don't know what your problem is, Worm, but if you are laughing at me, I demand to know why."

"Just let it go, Nath," Virgo said, coming along his side. "Worm has a very twisted sense of humor. He laughs at and teases everyone. Don't take it personally. We all put up with it by ignoring it."

"I don't like it," Nath said, staring the man down. Worm had already stolen from him and tried to make a fool of him. Now, his cackling was getting under Nath's skin. "I want him to stop."

"I can't," Worm said, trying to look away, but his eyes remained on Nath's chest. Pointing at Nath's breastplate, he made a circle motion with his fingers. "It's that."

"My paint? What about it?"

"It's a bull's-eye," Cullon growled. The bushy-bearded dwarf with a bald top rode a horse loaded down with hand axes, short swords, a crossbow, saddle bags, two quivers, a coil of heavy rope, and a morning star. He spit black juice on the ground. "What kind of adventurer puts a mark like that on his chest? It's red. It has 'aim here' all over it. Hah!"

Glancing at the mark, Nath frowned. "No, it doesn't."

Cullon and Worm looked at each other and began laughing again.

Virgo touched Nath's bare arm with ice-cold hands. "Don't let them bother you. They are envious of the attention I've shown you. Especially Worm. He begs for me to paint him, but I don't." Worm stuck his tongue out at her. "He is childish, and Cullon should know better than to encourage him."

"And you should know better than to paint a bull's-eye on Nath Orc's chest," Cullon fired back. He unhitched his crossbow and pointed it at Nath. Closing an eye, he said, "Too easy. Of course, those bright-red locks aren't doing him any favors, either. Heh. That's two bull's-eyes in one." He squeezed the trigger. *Click.*

"Let's keep it moving!" Nina hollered back at them. "Or do you want Tobias and me to handle this all alone?"

"That would be fine by me," Worm said.

"What was that?" Nina yelled back.

"Nothing, Nina. We're coming." Worm led his horse by Nath, snickering along the way. Cullon did the same, leaving Nath and Virgo behind.

"I'm sorry, Nath. I didn't think my little design would create such a stir. I honestly don't think it stands out so much. I can make it duller," Virgo said, holding up her hand. Her fingers turned into a rainbow of alternating colors.

"No," Nath said, offering a smile. "I like it the way it is. Very original, and I wouldn't change a thing. I should have handled it better."

"Yes, be the bigger man, Nath." She squeezed his forearm. "And don't worry about Worm and Cullon. They are reliable, even if they are difficult to get used to. Believe me when I say that we have all had our bouts. What we do is a dangerous business, and it makes us all edgy. We all release it in one way or another."

Nath nodded. Following the leaders, they moved on. Nath wasn't very used to dealing with actual people. All of his life, it had been dragons and the Trahaydeen. All of them tended to go about their business in a very orderly fashion. Dragon Home was peaceful. Every day, Nath knew what to expect, but that all changed the day he left to find the murderers of the fledgling dragons. The people in Nalzambor, so far, had proven to be unpredictable. He was determined to get used to it. He wanted to be a part of people that he could count on. He might need someone's help to find Maefon and avenge his brethren.

Nina and Tobias led the group to a stop about a hundred yards from where the dirt road entered the narrow channel through the mountains. All of the riders made a row beside Nina. The dark passage between the rocks rose hundreds of feet high. Black birds with bright-yellow beaks flew in and out, sometimes landing in their nests high on the ridges. Addressing them all, Nina said, "This is the Channel. On the other side lies Riverlynn, where we shall find the monks and, hopefully, Janna. But the Channel is not without its dangers. Over the mountain is much longer," she added, pointing where the road split off and eased up the mountains in a long and winding path. "Does anyone object to taking the shortcut?"

"Quit trying to frighten the boy," Tobias said with a smile. "We've navigated the Channel dozens of times without incident. There's no need to be dramatic, Nina."

"Aye, let's just go," Cullon said, moving forward. "It's not the Channel—it's what lies on the other side that is a problem."

"I just want Nath to be wary. Anything can happen, and you seem to forget there was that one time," Nina added. "That I'll never forget."

"That was an accident," Tobias said, leading his horse forward, "and we swore to not speak about it ever again. Now, let's get moving before that storm hits."

Shaking her head, Nina looked at Nath. "Just stay alert."

"Always," Nath said. They rode into the Channel, and the day seemed to turn to night.

CHAPTER 52

THE CHANNEL BENT LEFT AND right in ridged angles. A light rain started to fall. The rock enclosing them was sheer in many places. Any climb up to the mountain would be steep and require the skilled hands of a mountaineer, or climbing equipment. It didn't take Nath long to understand the concern of traveling the Channel. Fifty feet above their heads were overlooks and ledges. Heavy in thick brush from the mountain terrain and showing the natural cover of boulders, it was clear it was the perfect place for an ambush.

Birds darted through the gulch, zipping over the tops of their heads. The horses climbed up steep banks and through narrow passes barely big enough for a wagon to pass through. Thunder rolled in the distance, louder than normal as it echoed throughout the canyon. Nath's horse whinnied.

"Easy," Nath said, petting the beast's neck.

The Channel widened again, big enough for ten wagons side by side. The walls were as sheer as they'd passed in any part of the canyon. A few spots sloped steeply upward. On the other end of the expansive stretch was another narrow neck leading out. Nath surmised they were a mile deep with at least another mile to go. Nath adjusted his gear and subtly patted down the items in his pack. He slid a glance Worm's way. Concerned the thief would try something sly, earlier, Nath had also slipped the candles from his pack into his trousers, as they were small, no bigger than a finger and easy to conceal.

All items accounted for.

Nina raised her arm as she led her horse to a stop. She cast her eyes all over the upper ledges. A mountain lion prowled the upper ledges. It vanished over the rim.

"What's the holdup?" Nath said to Nina. "The big cat doesn't worry you, does it?"

"No," she said. Her eyes narrowed as she cast a glance toward the neck in the canyon ahead. "Do you hear that? Someone comes."

"Don't get so antsy, Nina," Tobias said in a whisper. "We aren't the only travelers in the Channel. We should always expect someone. I'm sure it's just some merchants not wanting to get caught up on the mountain during the storm. It gets a bit slippery, and sudden mudslides have sent many off the mountain only to perish in the Channel." He pointed toward the walls where the debris of wagons had crashed long ago. "Whoever it is, I'll do the talking."

"Well, don't take too long. We know how you like to gab," Virgo said, placing a cloak over her shoulders. Droplets of water splatted down around them. "I'd like to find shelter before I get soaked. You know I hate getting wet. It tampers with my spellcasting. Not to mention my hair and clothing."

A jackrabbit darted out of the narrowing passage. In a blur of brown fur, it hopped right at them. Nath and Nina's horses reared up as it weaved through the beasts' legs. The long-eared rabbit bolted for the passage where they just came from and disappeared through the rocks.

Nath fought at his reins, steadying his horse.

Worm cackled.

"Thanks for the warning, Nina," Cullon commented in a dusky tone. "That little rabbit just about made me brown my britches."

Everyone started to laugh.

With deep creases in her forehead and a new rosy hue on her cheeks, she said, "That certainly wasn't what I expected." She fought to control her horse, tugging the reins from side to side. All of the horses snorted and nickered. "What has possessed these beasts?"

On horseback, a barrel-chested orc with a lumpy face and coarse, stringy hair rode out of the passage. The horse was the biggest Nath had ever seen, at least half a head taller than the one he rode. Coming to a stop, the horse snorted and clawed at the ground. Its hooves were covered by hair that grew from its ankles. Behind the orcen rider, another group filed out of the passage on horseback, splitting to either side of the orc. They were a multitude of races with faces that Nath recognized. It was the same hard-eyed brigands from the encounter at the memorial of statues. Nath's blood ran cold as he reached for his sword.

CHAPTER 53

"**B**E STILL, NATH!" NINA COMMANDED. Her hand was on the pommel of her sword, as was Tobias's, but none of them moved. Her eyes were fixed on the brigands on horseback easing out of the passage and spreading out before them. "Let Tobias do the talking."

Nath had his arm over his back on his pommel, with Fang slid out a few inches. "These are the men who tried to rob us. I won't go through that again." He scanned their faces. There was the orc, brawny and ugly, who carried an air of command that came with his great size and girth. The big steed beneath him made him even more formidable. Beside the orc was the tall, slender brigand who did all of the talking when they were robbed. He had his loaded crossbow leaned back against his shoulder and a cocky look on his face. There were part-elves and orcs, the wiry rogue who cackled much like Worm, and three red-haired halflings who seemed familiar. Nath eased his sword out of his scabbard a little farther. "We can take them."

Moving his horse between the orc and Nath, Tobias looked back to Nina, who was beside Nath. "Settle down our new addition, please, Nina, while I talk us through this."

Nina grabbed the reins of Nath's horse. "I'll handle it," she said in a dangerous voice.

Cullon and Worm backed behind Nath and Nina. They turned their horses to face the enemy. Virgo stayed to the left of Nath, Nina on the right, and Tobias in front, facing the orc less than thirty yards away.

Nath counted twenty brigands in all, excluding their leader. All of them were dressed in soiled woodsman garb, many with traveling cloaks covering their shoulders. Three of them skirted the edge and trotted to the other narrowing in the passage, blocking off any avenue for escape. The Black Hand was closed in. Nath's muscles tightened between his shoulders. Something was wrong, more wrong than what was seen. He couldn't put his finger on it.

Tobias approached the orc, stopping as their horses stood nose to nose. With beady eyes, the orc glowered down at the smaller man. Tobias spoke quietly.

"Why is he talking so low?" Nath said, leaning over his saddle horn. He wasn't certain, but it sounded as if Tobias was speaking in orcen. "I find that strange."

"Be silent, Nath. He's bartering for our safe passage." Nina grabbed his sword arm. "Let go of your weapon and relax. Tobias is a polished communicator. We just want to move through here without any blood spilled."

"But these men are thieves. They should be jailed if not killed," Nath retorted. He found the slender-bearded brigand holding a crossbow staring right at him with a knowing look. He winked at Nath. "Something is not right."

Nina took a quick glance over her shoulder at Cullon and gave him a quick nod. The dwarf's crossbow was in his lap. With two strong fingers, he locked back the string and loaded a bolt. Nina eased her sword a little further from her sheath. Virgo's hands and fingers made very subtle motions in the open air by her sides. Worm sank into his saddle with his hands hidden in his clothing. The drizzling rain came down harder. Virgo sighed.

The orc looked past Tobias, right at Nath. The look sent a chill through Nath. He scanned the faces of the brigands. In almost every case, they were looking right at him. He swallowed. Under some strange compulsion, he grabbed Nina's hand that held his horse's reins and tried to peel her iron-strong fingers free. The fingers did not give. "Let go, Nina."

"Nath, what are you doing? Be still," Nina demanded. "This is almost over with. Trust me. Just look." She tipped her chin at two more riders coming out of the passage. A man on one horse led out a young woman with long, wavy, honey-colored hair on another. Her eyes, ears, and mouth were bound by cloth. Her elegant robes were torn and tattered. Dirt smudged her face and hands. "Janna," Nina said, acting a little too surprised.

"I don't understand," Nath said under his breath. "What is she doing here? It doesn't make any sense."

"Perhaps you are good fortune, Nath Dragon," Virgo said, giving him a quick smile. "The kidnappers are moving her, and now they have run right into us. Our timing couldn't have been better."

On the back of one of the horses, Nath caught a red-haired halfling peeking out from behind the rider he'd doubled up with. At first, Nath wondered if it was the halfling who shot him in the back of the leg. He wasn't sure, but he remembered there were two. Searching faces, he noticed that there were three halflings in all, each sitting behind a different rider. All three had rooster-red hair. His stomach twisted into a knot. Perspiration broke out on his forehead then was quickly washed away by the rain. Every halfling face became crystal clear. They were the trio sitting on the tall stools, singing songs, the first time he set foot in the Oxen Inn. He swallowed. "Nina, let go of my horse."

"Nath, what is wrong with you?" she said. "You look like you have seen an apparition. Just be still a few moments longer. You have to trust me. Let this play out. The Black Hand knows what it is doing."

He shook his head. With every fiber of his being on pins and needles combined with a sinking feeling of the walls closing in, he ripped her fingers free from the reins. "You've lied to me!"

Nina's aghast expression turned calm, cruel, and collected. "Of course I did. We are the Black Hand. Lying is our business." She glanced at his chest. "And yes, that is a target."

CHAPTER 54

NATH WENT FOR HIS SWORD.

Thwack!

A crossbow bolt fired by Cullon lodged itself in the hindquarters of Nath's horse. The beast reared up, throwing Nath to the ground. Landing flat on his belly, he rolled to one knee and started to draw his sword. Nina thundered into his path. She kicked him in the side of the face. Nath kissed mud again. Something heavy landed on his back. Boots stomped him into the ground.

"Get down and stay down!" Cullon said, locking a thick arm around his neck. "Worm, get that sword off him!"

In a blink, Worm disappeared from his horse and appeared over Nath. Nath thrashed against Cullon while Worm slit the straps for Nath's pack and slung it aside. "What's yours is mine as always," the rogue said with a bubbly cackle. He fastened his fingers around the pommel of Fang and slid it out. "What a pretty, pretty sword. Certainly worth a fortune. What did you name it? Fang?" Holding it up before his eyes, Worm said, "I think I'll rename it Money. Gah!" Worm dropped the great blade. His face turned ashen. "The cursed thing burned me!"

"Good!" Nath pushed his face up out of the mud, his temper

surging. Dragon heart pumping, he pushed against Cullon's dwarven strength. "Let go of me, you bearded bird's nest!"

"Hah!" Cullon shoved him down. "You're strong, boy, but you ain't that strong!"

A wellspring of endless strength flowed through Nath's left arm. The mud-covered Gauntlet of Goam's gem burned with the fire of starlight. Jaws clenched, Nath broke free of Cullon's grip.

Cullon's jaw hung. His dark eyes widened. "Impossible! How did you do—"

Nath punched Cullon in the chest. The burly dwarf flew backward, knocking Nina out of her saddle. His eyes slid over to Worm, who stood wide eyed over top of Nath's sword.

With a nervous smile, Worm said, "It's a pretty sword. You can have it."

Nath stormed the little man. Worm blinked out of sight. Nath snatched up his blade. Filled with boundless strength, he faced off his circling enemies. "Liars and thieves! Now you will face the wrath of Nath!"

From behind, lightning erupted from Virgo's fingertips. The streaks of white-hot light blasted into Nath's body.

"Gaaaaaaaaah!" Nath screamed, jaws wide as pain lanced through his body. His limbs juddered, and his teeth clacked together. Fang fell from his fingertips. His knees splashed into the mud. He stood on his knees, shaking and wooden, as Virgo, on horseback, came into view.

"Sorry, Nath," Virgo said with wisps of lightning still glowing on her fingertips. "But that painting on your chest is a target indeed." She tossed her head back and laughed.

Nath's vision blurred. The words she spoke became garbled. Light-headed and full of blinding pain, he tipped forward, splashing face-first in the mud.

CHAPTER 55

NATH PUSHED HIS FACE OUT of the sloppy clay and rolled to his side, groaning. With one eye cracked open, he watched Cullon come to his feet. A beet-red face glowed behind his beard. Holding his ribs in one hand, he helped Nina to her knees with the other. Dashed with mud, she glowered at Nath. Cullon stormed right at him. "He broke my ribs! He'll pay for that!" Cullon launched a kick into Nath's armor-covered gut. "Get that breastplate off him so I can crush him!" Furious, he started kicking Nath again and again.

Tobias cut in with a sharp voice. "That's enough!" Still mounted, he said, "He's not to be damaged, Cullon. If he is, there's no deal, so back yourself off!"

"I don't care!" Cullon gave Nath one more stiff kick. "I'm going to bust him!"

Even though Nath wore the armor, he could still feel some of the sting from the blows. The strength behind them rattled his aching bones, shooting more pain through his body. He made a left-handed gauntlet-covered fist with the gauntlet still glowing.

"No, you don't," Worm said, appearing beside him and slipping the gauntlet from Nath's fingers. "It's a bit big and clumsy for the likes of me, but I know who it would be perfect for." He tossed it over to Nina, who plucked it out of the air. "Enjoy."

Nina slipped it on with a broad smile.

"Put that sword in its scabbard too, Worm," Tobias said.

"But it burned me," Worm said, rubbing his hands. "My precious fingers still ring like a bell." Tobias's hard stare changed the rogue's mind. "I'm on it then." Worm cut away Nath's scabbard and managed to push the sword back in place from the ground. He picked it up and handed it to Tobias. "All yours."

"Why me?" Nath groaned. His body spasmed. "Why, Nina, Virgo? Why?"

"He still speaks," Virgo said with a raised eyebrow. "Such remarkable constitution. I have to admit, Nath, I am very impressed."

"Yes, he is full of surprises," Nina quipped. She dismounted, marched over, squatted down, and pulled his face up by the hair on his head. "But as for why, well, Nath, this is what the Black Hand does. We are a guild of slavers, liars, thieves, and cheats, operating in a veil of good intentions. And our influence is very deep. For example, Lord Jander, a good man, believes we are helping him, when really we're going to trade you for his daughter in order to get the reward. Isn't that something? We have so many fooled, including the soldiers who you met on your way in. They sent you right to us."

"I trusted you," he said with another fierce shiver. The feeling began to return to his hands. The pain was subsiding. As his strength built, Nath chose to keep her talking while he searched for an exit plan. "Why me? I was just passing through."

"Look at you. You're practically a walking sunflower. And that sword, it's worth a fortune. I'm just glad none of our rivals got to you first," Nina continued. "But when you walked into my inn, I was thrilled. I gained your confidence, told you a story about a kidnapped princess, which, by the way, though true, wasn't anything we wanted you involved in. It was just some frosting for the cake when we needed to seduce you. So I took you to those statues in hopes of robbing you of your belongings quietly. These brigands, you see..." She twisted his head to face the brood. "Often work with the Black Hand. But you beat them. You beat us all with that sword of yours." She rubbed her left ear. "My ears are still ringing. It created quite a dilemma. All we wanted were your goods, and we would have sent you away, but you made it more complicated, didn't you?"

Nath shrugged as it all came together. "I think you are the one that made it complicated."

Nina continued. "As it turns out, we have discovered there is a desire in the slave markets for one such as you. Of course, it should have been obvious at first, but I must have been blinded by the sight of you. Look at you, a young man without scar or blemish, with rich red hair as if it was spun from silk. And those eyes... I don't believe there is another pair like them in all of the world. You alone are worth a fortune. The only thing I can imagine being of greater desire would be an actual dragon. So we hatched another plan by inviting—well, maybe lured is a better way of putting it—you into the Whistler, another home of the Black Hand, much like the Oxen. It was there we got a better understanding of your strengths and weaknesses and hatched another plan to bring you here. We get your goods and the girl, and they get a valuable slave."

"You could have just killed me," Nath managed to say.

"True, but we aren't murderers. We are slavers and thieves," Nina said as if it made her a better person, "and we like to execute our plans with style. We enjoy practicing deceit, and you made for excellent practice. It will serve us well in the coming days." She pushed Nath down and rose to full height. "It's been nice knowing you, Nath. But now it's time to turn you over to Prawl the slaver."

The rain came down harder. Thunder cracked. Water poured down in streams from the upper rim of the Channel.

"Wait." Nath tried to get up on his hands and knees. Cullon

shoved him down again. "So you're taking the princess back to Riegelwood?"

"No, she'll stay with us at another location," Nina said, stuffing her boot into the stirrup of her horse and climbing into the saddle. "We will bleed the city lord's vaults and increase his concerns better that way. When the time comes, the Black Hand, as heroes, will return her home to her father safely. But this isn't something that you need to think on, Nath. Think to your future, for I am certain our paths will never cross again."

We'll see about that.

"Nina." Tobias gave a chin nod to the orc who approached. "We are ready to make the exchange. One person for another, Prawl."

"One person, yes," Prawl said in a gravelly voice, "and one gauntlet."

"What?" Nina said, pulling the gauntlet to her chest. "We already agreed that the mark's treasure would be ours, Prawl."

Prawl looked at her with fire in his beady eyes. "Tobias, do you let your mouthy woman speak for you?"

"You dare!" Nina pulled her sword free.

"Don't start it, orc." Tobias's hand fell to his pommel. "Nina, control yourself. Listen, Prawl, I don't know what game you are playing, but an agreement is an agreement. You will be paid when we receive the ransom. You'll be paid again when you deliver this man, Nath. In the meantime, the exchange is for the princess, and we'll handle it from there." He leaned over his saddle. "Give us your word, Prawl."

Prawl lifted his big face and grunted. "You voided the agreement when you deceived me. I will have the gauntlet and the man, or you won't have a princess."

"Only a fool would cross the Black Hand," Nina said, shooting daggers from her eyes. "Don't listen to him, Tobias."

"I'm not." Tobias moved his horse closer to Prawl and offered his hand. "The Black Hand will double your share of the ransom."

"What?" Nina, as well as the other members of the Black Hand, exclaimed. "Don't you dare agree to one coin more. These brigands failed us once already!"

Prawl showed a mouth full of ugly teeth and extended his hand. "Body for body, double the ransom and the gauntlet."

Tobias's expression darkened. "Now you're just insulting us, Prawl."

Prawl looked Tobias dead in the eye. "You insulted me first." He grabbed Tobias's arms, jerked him forward like a child, and popped him in the face with his fist. Tobias crashed to the ground. Prawl turned on Nina. "I'll have that gauntlet now!"

CHAPTER 56

NINA JUMPED OFF HER HORSE and collided with Prawl. Prawl, the taller of the two, tried to wrap his big hands around her. Nina, the quicker of the two brutes, slipped behind him, picked him up, and body-slammed him into the mud.

The brigands erupted in a chorus of cheers as the big orc and brawny woman wrestled in a tangle of limbs all over the muddy ground. The gemstone of the Gauntlet of Goam glowed brightly as Nina let loose a punch at Prawl. The orc took it in the shoulder, let out a roar, and stuffed his boot in her gut. Nina skidded over the rugged ground. She came at him in a fury.

Nath gathered his senses as the two titans clashed and thrashed on the ground. At the passage's exit, the princess sat in the saddle, slumped over and abandoned. Taking advantage of all the attention Nina and Prawl were getting, Nath summoned his reserves, reaching deep, with a single-minded focus.

Rescue the princess. Escape.

On stiff legs, he ambled as fast as he could toward the princess. A lone brigand stood watching the fight, holding the horse by the bridle. The brigand turned just quickly enough to catch a hard fist in his face. The man sagged to the ground. Nath took the man's dagger, slit the ropes from the woman's wrists, and climbed into the saddle.

The princess pushed and slapped against him. Sitting in the front, he wrapped her arms around his waist and shouted in her covered ear, "Hold on, princess. I'm here to rescue you!" She wrapped her arms tightly around his body and held on for dear life. Taking ahold of the reins, Nath dug in his heels. "Eeyah!"

The horse lunged forward, galloping into the passage at full speed. Nath rode on, turning and weaving through the rocks with the wind and rain in his face. Water cascaded from the rocks above, filling the Channel.

"Who are you?" the princess shouted in his ear.

Nath took a quick glance back. Janna had removed the cloth that bound her eyes, ears, and mouth. "Hello," he said, "I'm Nath."

She shouted over the wind and rain, "I take it my father sent you?"

"Yes, you could say that, in a roundabout way!" The horse leapt a tree that had fallen across the path. Janna bounced out of the saddle and landed hard on the path. "Princess!"

"Break it up! Break it up!" Tobias yelled at Prawl and Nina. He managed to hook Nina's arms from behind and pull her away. The brigands made a wall between Prawl, Nina, Tobias, and the rest of the Black Hand. "Listen to me, idiots!"

"Mind who you are talking to," the tall, slender brigand leader said. He pointed his crossbow at Tobias's head. "She started this, not us!"

"Shut it, Andee!" Tobias said. "Look at what you fools have done. Have you not noticed the princess and Nath are gone?"

All eyes moved to the spot where the knocked-out brigand lay flattened on the ground.

Prawl pointed at Nina. "We'll settle this later. But that gauntlet will be mine. You are not worthy of it, woman!"

Wiping blood from her mouth, Nina said, "You'll sleep in the grave long before you'll have this, Prawl."

"We'll see who sleeps forever first." He climbed onto his horse. The huge beast reared up. "Men of Whispers! Let us ride!"

Led by Prawn, the band of brigands thundered into the passage after Nath and the princess.

Getting back on his horse, Tobias shouted at Nina, "Well done, hothead!"

Mounting her horse, Nina fired back, "Me! You are the one that caved into that belligerent orc's ego! If I didn't intervene, you would have given him all of our horses and the rest of Nath's treasure."

"I had it under control. He just has to be worn down! You played right into his hands." Tobias slung his muddy hair out of his eyes. "Let's get after them then, before he winds up with Nath and the princess too."

"Shall we stay back," Worm suggested, "in case either one doubles back?"

"Fool, it's impossible to double back in this Channel," Cullon said.

"Oh, is that so? Perhaps it's impossible for you, but not the likes of me. I can slip by anything, and he's proven to be slippery before."

"He's not getting away," Tobias said. "He doesn't know the land or the terrain. He'll be caught soon enough, and we need to be there. Agreed?" The small group nodded. With water running over the horses' hooves, he added, "Then let's ride before we all get washed out of this place."

CHAPTER 57

THE RAIN CAME DOWN HARDER. Nath dismounted and rushed to Janna. She was lying on her side, holding her ankle. "Are you hurt?" he said.

Anguished, she said, "Yes, no thanks to you! Why did you have to ride so fast?"

"Because we are being chased. Here, let me help you up." He took her hand and pulled her up.

"Ah!" she said. "My ankle. I can't put any weight on it." She sat back down. "I'm not going anywhere!"

"You just have to be able to hang on. Come now, please, we need to get out of here."

She pulled away from him. "I'm not riding with you! You're dangerous."

Nath stepped back. The princess sat in the soaking rain with her bottom lip stuck out, rubbing her ankle. It reminded him of a defiant child. He squatted down in front of her. "Janna—"

"It's Princess Janna to you, servant."

The sudden shift in her disposition tempted Nath to leave her right where she was. After all, he didn't owe her anything, and eventually, the Black Hand would return her for ransom. But he couldn't do that. "Listen, *Janna*, if we don't get moving, you will be captured again. You don't want that, do you?"

With her face turned away, she said, "No."

"Please, trust me, once again, and I promise to ride slower." Horse hooves thundered up the Channel toward them. "But we really, really need to get moving. It's imperative."

She looked at him with her gorgeous, spacy eyes. "Do you think I'm pretty?"

"Huh?"

"I said, do you think I'm pretty?" she said, blinking her long lashes.

"What? Uh, you are beyond compare!" he said, looking back over his shoulder. The thundering horse hooves were getting closer. Princess Janna's personality was shifting like the wind. Instead of acting like she was being chased, she was acting like she was in another world. *They have done something to her.*

"That's what I thought." She held out her arms. "You may carry me then. But ride slowly. My rump and hip are sore from the fall you already caused."

He picked her up in his cradling arms and hurried to his horse.

Looking him in the face, she gave a glowing smile. "Tell me more about me. I like hearing how pretty I am."

Helping her into the saddle, he said, "You have a smile beyond compare and a wealth of golden hair."

"Ooh, I like that."

Nath climbed in the saddle. He wrapped her hands around him and clamped them together. "Hang on!" The horse lurched forward, taking the next turn in the Channel just as the brigands came up behind him.

Prawl, the orcen leader, shouted out, "There he is!"

Nath dug his heels into his horse. The horse bolted forward. With his free hand, he held fast to the princess's hands, which were gripped tight around his waist.

Shouting in his ear, she said, "You promised you would go slower!"

"It's either this or get caught! You don't want to get caught, do you?"

"I don't know!"

Nath spurred the horse forward. Hard rain smacked his face, and thunder roared overhead. "Just hang on!" he shouted back to her. "You're getting rescued whether you like it or not!"

The Channel broadened and narrowed, twisted and turned as it filled with rushing water that rose up to the horse's ankles. Waterfalls gushed off the higher ledges. They rode underneath one that was entirely unavoidable, giving them an unwanted bath.

Janna let out a bone-chilling scream. "What did you do that for? Isn't it bad enough that I'm soaked already?"

Nath ignored her continuous complaints. He wanted out of the Channel. Even though he didn't know the terrain or where he was, he was certain he could find help on the other side. He just needed to keep riding and hope he made it somewhere before they caught up with him.

"What did you say your name was?" she asked.

"Nath!"

"Gnat?"

"No, Nath. N-A-T-H!"

"Oh," she said. "Nath, they are gaining on us. Go faster!"

"I am. Hang on, we have a jump!" He gripped her hands. The horse jumped a fallen pine, landed hard, and kept on running. The princess was still with him. "Whew!"

They angled out of a narrow passage into a widening area of the ravine. The watery Channel split into two separate paths.

"Go left!" the princess said.

"Why?" Nath said.

"Just trust me!" she said.

Not wanting to slow, Nath veered left, into another narrow passage that sloped upward. It was like crossing a downhill stream as the horse labored against the torrential ankle-deep current. Nath had a good feeling that they were heading up onto the mountain. It would get them out of the rushing rain waters, but he wasn't so sure about the change in terrain. He needed help. He needed to find people. He found neither as he charged toward the huge mouth of a cave dripping water. "Gads!"

CHAPTER 58

"WE AREN'T GOING IN THERE, are we?" Janna said. Nath rode toward the vast cave mouth, which opened up fifty feet high and was just as wide. Stalactites hung down from the upper rim of the cave like teeth. "You said to go left."

"What do I know? It was just a suggestion. You should have gone right."

"Then you shouldn't have said left." Nath passed through the sheets of water as he entered the cave. "We don't have a choice now."

"Nath, we need to turn back. I don't like this place. It's chilly," she said with a shiver. "Not to mention as black as a witch's heart."

"So you've met a few witches before, have you?" he said, easing them deeper into the blackness.

"I have sisters. Ew, what is that smell? It's rank." She coughed and cleared her throat. "Nath, we have to go back. We can't stay here. It's pitch black." She seemed to be coming out of the strange lull she was in.

Nath's nose crinkled. Goose bumps popped up all over his soaking-wet arms. He led the horse deeper into the cavern. "Trust me, I know a few things about caves."

Deeper inside the cavern, his keen eyes made out the straight edges of rectangular columns chiseled out of the rock, giving it the face of an entrance to a building.

"Nath, I can't see anything," Janna said, looking behind her, "except a way out. Take me back, please. Just let them have me, and I'll wait to have my ransom paid. This place scares me."

"There's nothing to be afraid of," he said, moving closer to the wall inside the cave. It was a huge flat front, thirty feet high, with a stone archway entrance.

"If there is nothing to be afraid of, then why aren't our pursuers chasing after us?" she said.

Nath glanced back. "They just haven't caught up with us yet. Come on, now, we don't have a choice. Besides, every entrance must have an exit."

"My father's dungeons don't."

Something slithered beneath the horse's feet. A stone rattler struck, sinking its venomous fangs into the horse's leg. The horse bucked, took several steps, and collapsed. Nath and Janna tumbled off, landing side by side. She let out a scream. The stone rattler slithered right at her.

Nath snatched the snake by the neck before it could sink its fangs in her. Its body coiled around his arm and constricted. His fingers started to turn purple.

"Kill it!" she said, wide eyed and scooting back. "Kill it, Nath!"

Tilting his head, Nath stared at the evil creature with his golden eyes. "You're a wicked little serpent, aren't you?" He crushed its neck and flung it aside. "You're safe now."

"Maybe from the snake, but what about them?" She pointed to the cave entrance.

Led by the orc, the brigands passed through the sheets of water into the cave. Prawl said, "Surrender. There is certain death beyond the Wall of Hozam. None escape from there."

Nath picked up Janna and headed for the entrance.

"What are you doing?" she said, pushing against him. "Didn't you hear him? Nath, it's certain death. Release me!"

Nath passed through the entrance and into the chilly pitch blackness.

CHAPTER 59

INSIDE THE CAVE, THE BLACK Hand was in a heated exchange with Prawl. Sword in hand, spit came from the angry orc's teeth. "This is your doing! Not mine! I should split your skulls for it! And I will have my ransom!"

"You are the fool who got greedy, Prawl," Tobias fired back. He had his sword, Splitter, in hand. The even-tempered swordsman was red-faced now. "Had you stuck with our original arrangement, all of this could have been avoided, and we would be eating, drinking, and making merry right now. You are a fool of an orc! Now, take your men inside that hole," he said, pointing to the Wall of Hozam's entrance, "and bring back our ransom!"

"Hah! They are dead already! And you owe me that gauntlet and my share of the ransom, Tobias. It will be that, or the Men of Whispers will be at war with the Black Hand."

"That is outrageous!" Nina said, whisking her sword from her scabbard. Veins bulged in her neck. Her sinewy arms flexed as she squeezed her sword in a death grip. "You owe us! We don't owe you!"

"Huh-huh-huh," Prawl laughed. "We shall see."

"I'm going to kill you," Nina said. The gemstone in her gauntlet burned bright. "I challenge you to a fight."

"No!" Tobias said, wedging himself between Nina and Prawl once again. "No more distractions. For now, I say we wait. There is always a chance that they will be back out shortly. Everyone, catch your breath. An even-keeled mindset will serve our needs better." He sheathed his sword. "Nina?"

She stuffed her blade back in her sheath.

Prawl rested his sword on his shoulder. "None come back from behind the Wall of Hozam. None. You are welcome to find them if you will." He tipped his chin at the brigands. "I suggest you make good on this loss, Tobias. Now we depart from you." He eyed Nina. "And I will have that gauntlet. Men of Whispers, let's ride." Prawl led all of his men out of the cave, leaving the Black Hand all alone.

"Good riddance!" Cullon shouted after them. "I can't stand the stench of the orc anyway. I warned you."

"Not now, Cullon," Nina said. "I'm in no mood for your complaints."

"I say get in the mood then, Nina. Because they are coming. I warned you about aligning with the Men of Whispers. I said we need to keep our operations small, like we used to. But you got greedy."

"Oh, stop it!" Nina said. "We are thieves. We are all greedy! Especially you!"

"Har! You are the master planner of this caper, not me." Cullon shook the rain from his bushy beard like a dog. "You and your grand schemes. We should have just robbed Nath, like I said, and left him for dead."

Raising his hand, Worm said, "If I could say something, I would like to go on the record and say that I am the greediest, and I like Nina's devious plotting and planning. They are vastly more fashionable than the dwarven style of clubbing someone over the head and running. But I am the greediest. I just want to make that clear."

Virgo rolled her eyes. "Tobias, what are we going to do now? I'm drenched and freezing. I say we cut our losses and go home, where the wine flows from the presses and the fires warm cheeks. We have Nath's items. They alone are worth a fortune."

"And his purse," Nina said, looking at Worm. "Take it out, rogue, and don't open it. I'm watching your slippery hands."

Worm held up Nath's purse and gave a crooked smile. "I would never steal from my mates." He tossed it to Tobias.

Tobias's eyes grew big when he opened the sack, spilling part of the contents into his hands. Pieces of gold were mixed with emeralds, rubies, and diamonds. "Zanthar's toes! We wouldn't get this much for the princess! Who is this Nath Dragon that carries a hoard in his pocket?"

"He's from the south is all that I know." Nina eyed the entrance to the Wall of Hozam. "I think we should go after him."

"Are you mad?" Cullon said. "They are dead already."

"You are taking the orc's word now, Cullon." Nina shook her head. "You don't know what lies in there. You've never been. All any of us know are rumors and legends. For all we know, there might not be anything in there but spiders and cobwebs."

"And snakes," Worm said. He'd dismounted and wandered near the entrance. The stone rattler hung limp in his hands. "This skin and venom will fetch another small fortune," he said, stuffing it into a sack. "I say we take a vote, Tobias."

"I second the motion," Virgo added.

With eyes locked on the treasure in his hand, Tobias said, "All right, all in favor of pursuing Nath and Janna, say *aye*."

"Aye," Nina said with a frown.

Worm cackled.

"Sorry, Nina," Tobias said, putting away the purse of treasure, "but we go where the wine and warmth awaits."

With a lasting look at the entrance, she said, "So be it."

The Black Hand rode out of the cave, through the Channel, and never looked back.

Chapter 60

S TANDING JUST OUTSIDE OF THE cornfields near a small
rural town, Lord Darkken and Maefon watched it blaze. The
straw roofs of the stone cottages burned. The people of Tilly
scrambled back and forth, carrying buckets of water from the creek.
The effort did little to no good. The stiff night winds carried the
scorching flames from one haven to another, consuming all with fire.

With the fires reflecting in her eyes, Maefon said, "Did I do well,
Lord Darken?"

"It burns. That's what I expected." He put his arm over her
shoulder. "Though your execution could have been better. I would
have preferred that you waited a little longer into the night, to catch
more of them sleeping."

"You wanted them to die?" she said, keeping her glassy stare on
the growing inferno. "I thought the goal was simple discourse that
would spread like fire."

"True, but the death of the innocent will brew bad blood for
generations. And I like to hear the lamentations of the women. Their
woe-filled cries are song to me. Besides, it's important that I see you
have such killer instinct in you, Maefon." He hugged her with an
iron grip. "The Caligin must be ruthless. When the time comes to

kill, you must do so without remorse. It's our icy hearts that allow us to move forward and conquer."

"If I had known, I would have done more to please you," she said, trying not to wince under the pressure of his arm. "I killed the fledglings. Is that not enough?"

"I wasn't there, Maefon. I can only believe what I have seen for myself. After all, how fully can I trust a Caligin when I've trained them all to be excellent liars?"

She smirked. "Understood. But if you require fresh blood spilled—"

"Nay, you have proven much to me." He let go of her and gently caressed her back. "I just wanted to get you out, abroad, so you can experience how I prefer for the Caligin to operate. After all, you have been closed in on a single mission for a long time. Now that you are out, I want you to be fresh. Besides, I want you to focus on growing your magic skills. They will serve a greater purpose down the road."

"Again, I am glad to execute any order that you command, Lord Darkken." She took his hand and kissed his copper rings. "Any."

He shrugged his brows. "We'll see, eh…"

There was a jangle of armor and the clopping of hooves coming at them. Three riders rode up to Lord Darkken and Maefon. The riders wore faceless helmets, with one rider having a cross and eagle fashioned on the top. Soldiers. Wearing full suits of shining armor, breastplate with chainmail underneath, and a tunic over top embroidered in sky-blue and gold colors, they stopped several feet from Lord Darkken and encircled them.

"Good evening, Knight Commander," Lord Darkken said with a slight dip of his chin. "What brings the legionnaires of Quintuklen outside of the small town of Tilly?"

In a serious tone, the commander leaned forward in the saddle.

"I'm curious as to why you are standing in this field while a village burns."

"I could ask the same of you," Lord Darkken said. "Aren't the knights of Quintuklen sworn to protect and serve their interests in the lesser lands?"

"You speak with a sharp tongue, stranger," the commander said as he dismounted. He approached with his hand on his sword handle. "As a matter of fact, I am serving these smaller establishments. It is my charge to protect them, as you say. Currently, I am investigating some bizarre troubles that have overcome many of the small towns under my watch."

Lord Darkken nodded. "I'm sorry to hear this news. Maefon, are you aware of any troubles?"

"No, none, aside from Tilly collapsing to the ground." With her fingers locked together, she pled, "Knight Commander, we weren't meaning to stand here stupefied. By the time we arrived, we knew our efforts were too late." She grabbed Lord Darkken's hand. "We were on a stroll, alone, the two of us, celebrating our renewed devotion to one another."

"Yes, of course, a man and an elf. How delightful for the two of you. I'm sure your family in Elome will be thrilled by your decisions." He twisted off the lid of his canteen and drank deeply. Putting the cap back on, he said, "Ah!" He combed his long moustache with his fingers. "A funny coincidence, though, now that you mention it. You see, my investigation has revealed at every tragic event, there was a man"—he looked at Lord Darkken—"and an elf"—he glanced at Maefon—"that perfectly fit your description. I just can't rule out the likes of the two of you and these tragic occurrences as coincidental. And they say that the elf called herself Maefon. Isn't that your name, young lady?"

Lord Darkken stepped in front of Maefon. "Commander, are you accusing us of something?"

"I've been doing this a long time, and I know when something's awry. You two might look like roses, but you stink of trouble." He drew his sword. "I'm going to need you to come along with me, back to the outpost, for some questions. A lot of them."

"And if we refuse?" Lord Darkken said.

"It is within my purview to bring you in dead or alive if I have to. I trust my instincts. I know the fire starters and murderers are you two," the commander said. "I've been privy to these secret dealings for a long time. I suspected it was elves, but it was hard to explain because people would think I'm mad. But now, I've caught you red handed."

Lord Darkken's copper-colored eyes became slits like a serpent's. "You couldn't be more right, Commander. Please, try and take us in."

"Demon spawn!" The knight commander rushed Lord Darkken and delivered an overhanded chop. The bright steel came downward in a flashing arc of steel.

Lord Darkken caught the sword blade with his molten red hands. His fingers melted grooves in the metal. His snake eyes were fire. "I'm impressed. You have strong powers of deduction, or should I say had?" He grabbed the knight by the back of the neck and hoisted him high in the air. The man's body shriveled to char and ash. His armor became molten and dripped sizzling to the ground.

One of the other knights rammed a lance in Darkken's back. It quivered in his grasp, not penetrating even half an inch, and snapped halfway down the shaft. Dropping out of the sky, Galtur the two-headed vulture snatched the man out of the saddle. Wings beating, Galtur hauled the man into the sky, over the fires in the village, and dropped the legionnaire in the flames. As it all went down, Maefon climbed up behind the last knight, slipped a dagger between his ribs, and pushed his dying body out of the saddle.

Lord Darkken's glowing snake eyes cooled. A smile crossed his face. "It's been quite some time since that has happened. It seems some of my Caligin need to be more careful." He stared at the pile of molten metal and human ash. "Oh, how I enjoy letting loose my powers. Come, Maefon, it's time to return to Stonewater. We've been found out." He reached up and took her hand, and they both vanished.

CHAPTER 61

WITH JANNA CRADLED IN HIS arms, Nath eased inside the Wall of Hozam. Air, like a stale, cold breath, tickled his neck. A few feet inside, he stopped and turned. The exit back into the cave was gone. "Not good," he whispered.

"What's not good?" Janna clung to him as if her life depended on it. Her fingernails dug into his skin. "Where's the door? Nath? Where did the door go?"

"Ssssh, keep your voice down. We don't know what's in here."

"Don't say that!" Her voiced echoed.

"Will you be quiet? Just give me a moment while my eyes adjust."

Her warm body shivered. A very faint enticing fragrance still lingered in her damp locks of hair. Her breath was on his neck.

"We will be fine, I promise. Are you feeling better?" he asked, seeing how she seemed more alert.

"Those kidnappers poisoned me with a strange water to keep me calm, I believe. The truth is, I wish I had more of it now." Her big eyes swept the area. "I don't like this place. It stinks."

Even inside Dragon Home, in the darkest places that Nath explored, there'd been more light. The great mountain always had warmth on account of the fiery streams of lava that flowed through it. This place was cold and deathly, like some sort of void with a foul, stagnant stench. Nath crept forward, sliding on his feet an inch at a time. Even his own keen sight couldn't make out the outline of the walls. Left, right, up, or down, he didn't see anything.

"I don't like this, Nath. I want to go back," Janna said with her face buried in his neck. "Please take me back. I can't see anything. Even when I was blindfolded, I could at least feel the sun and rain. Here, I feel as if I'm in nothing. Are we dead?"

"You are warm as a morning biscuit, so I'd say not."

"A biscuit? Really, is that what I feel like to you? A lumpy, clumpy hunk of baked dough?"

"You are a little lumpy," he said, smiling in the dark. She pinched him. "Ow!"

"I'm not lumpy."

"It was intended to be a compliment," he said, sidestepping as he tried to feel the ground along the darkness.

"I don't see how. You don't have much experience with women, do you?" she said.

"More so of late," Nath said, still searching through the dark. He felt like he was standing on the ledge of an overlook. He made sure as he moved that he kept his feet in touch with the ground.

"Have you ever rescued a woman before?"

"Actually, I tried once, but it turned out she didn't want to be rescued. She wanted to rob me."

"That's no surprise these days. It seems everyone is robbing everybody. Was she pretty?"

Nath shrugged. Pretty was an understatement when it came to Calypsa. She carried an enchanting beauty that could make an elf jealous. "Fetching would be a more apt description."

"More fetching than me?"

Nath rolled his eyes. "It's hard to say. I haven't gotten a full look at you. Once we find a source of light, I'll render my comparison."

"You know, at times like this, the smart thing to say would be no. Goodness, were you raised in a cave?"

"Sort of. It's a long story." The ground beneath his feet shifted. "Did you feel that?"

"The only thing I feel is you."

The faint sound of stone rubbing against stone caught his ear. It happened every time he moved. Something weird was going on right beneath him. Nath felt something rub him beside his breastplate and chest. "Zophar's candles," he exclaimed in a whisper.

"Who is Zophar?" she asked.

"A wizard from the ages." Nath fished out a candle—four-sided in shape and little bigger than his finger, he'd tucked them inside his trousers. "This was a gift from my father. Its flame will not go out."

"How will you light it?"

"Hah," he said in the darkness, "the same way you extinguish it. I just put my lips together and blow." With the candle before him, he put his lips together and let out a huff of air. The candle wick ignited with a bright-orange flame.

With her eyes squeezed half shut, Janna let out a sigh. "That's much better." The little candle created a large radius of light. "Can I hold it, Nath, while you carry me?"

"Uh, sure," he said, absentmindedly handing her the candle. "Just don't drop it."

Eyeing the flame, she said, "I feel better already. Don't you?" Her comment was met with silence.

Nath's jaw hung. His eyes were fixed on the moving parts of the floor. He stood on a slab of rock, suspended over a bottomless chasm of blackness. He had no idea how it had gotten there. Other slabs of stone floated quickly by, like logs floating on a black river. They moved about like stone tiles, quickly rushing by one block at a time and bumping lightly into each other before gliding away. It reminded him of when he was trying to cross the moat of lava outside of Dragon

Home, but this seemed worse. "Princess, whatever you do, don't drop the candle. And please, keep your eyes on the flame."

"Why?" she said, peeling her eyes away from the candle. She stared right down into the abyss. She flinched. The candle fell from her fingers, bounced on the stone, and teetered on the edge. "Oh my!"

"Don't move a muscle," Nath said, bending at the knees. He reached for the candle. It fell into the chasm and vanished, leaving them enveloped in blackness again. "Gads!"

CHAPTER 62

NATH TOOK OUT ONE OF the remaining two candles. With a huff of breath on the wick, the candle ignited.

"Oh, thank goodness," Janna said, reaching for the candle.

"You can't drop this one," he said. "Do you understand?"

"I'm sorry, but the shock got to me. I swear I won't drop it again." She studied the rocks that swirled around them. "How are we going to cross this? I can barely walk, so I can't jump."

"I know, but I guess I'll have to make like a frog and jump from lily pad to lily pad."

"You can't jump with me."

"You aren't very heavy. I can do it. Just whatever you do, don't drop the candle again."

"I won't." She kissed his cheek. "Good luck."

Nath couldn't even see to the other side of the abyss. He didn't even know if there was one. All there was were random rocks floating around the one where he stood, which remained solid beneath his feet. The question was, how did he know if the rocks that he jumped on would hold him, let alone her and him? There was only one way. Forward. Like the lava moat around Dragon Home, he would have to go at it quickly. "Here goes everything." He jumped to the next passing rock. To his surprise, it was solid as the earth beneath him, though it moved quickly among the others of the expanse. He smiled at her.

"Well done. Keep going. I want to get out of this plaayyaace!"

The stone platform wobbled. It started to sink.

Propelled by very strong legs, Nath jumped to the next rock he could find. The stone he just came from dropped out of sight in the abyss. His eyes swept the chamber. None of the rocks that floated by came close. The slab he stood on began to wobble.

"Na-ath! Do something!"

"There's nowhere to jump," he said. Finally, a rock, a bit small, zoomed by. Timing it, he leapt. He landed on the ledge of the moving slab with his toes hanging over the edge. He bent back and forth and shuffled back, regaining his balance. He wasn't on the slab for two seconds when it started to sink. Nath made a quick calculation. As the stones glided by, he saw what he thought was a pattern and leapt. Without stopping, he jumped from one slab to the other, planning three jumps ahead as he passed.

"I can't watch! I can't watch!" Janna squeezed her eyes shut. "Please don't get me killed!"

He didn't stop. A ledge revealed itself on the other side. He made three more leaps, and his feet landed on the ledge. Panting and sweating, he backed to the wall. Only a handful of stones still floated above the abyss. All of the slab tiles he touched had dropped from sight. "You can open your eyes now, Janna. We are safe," he said.

She cracked an eye open. "Oh, thank goodness. I think you can put me down now. I want to walk on my own two feet."

He let her down. She put some weight on her leg and winced.

"I can still carry you."

"No, no, I can manage. Most of the sting is gone." Her knuckles were white around the candle. Her hand still shook like a leaf. "Where do we go now?"

"There's only two ways to go," he said, pointing over her shoulder. "Through that tunnel." He hitched his thumb over his shoulder. "Or that one."

"I think we'll go that way," she said, eyeing the exit behind Nath.

"No, you picked the last time. This time, we go my way." He grabbed her by the wrist and dragged her along behind him. She limped, so he didn't move too fast. The arch in the rock let them into a dry and musty corridor. The tunnels split off in many directions. Nath stayed on the path that angled upward.

"I heard stories from my father, but I never imagined there really were places such as this," Janna said. Her eyes were big as a moon. "And why does it smell so bad? Nothing could possibly live in here, could it?"

"It's a cave. Many creatures dwell in the earth. Like dragons." Nath led the way, moving from tunnel to tunnel, passing cove after cove. There were corpses, skeletons lying dead in their armor, and ragged clothing covering others. One skeleton's legs had been bitten clean through.

Shielding her mouth and nose with her hand, Janna said, "That is dreadful. What happened to them?"

Nath picked up a dragon tooth lying on the dusty ground, and one of the torches that lay nearby. "I'd say they ran out of light, couldn't find their way out, and then a monster came and got them. Either that, or they died first. I can't tell. Let's keep moving."

For hours they walked, winding through tunnel after tunnel. The light flickered, revealing the same bodies and broken bones as when they'd begun. Nath scowled. They were right where they'd started. Janna sat down. "I can't walk anymore. My feet are burning, and my ankle and hip are sore. What kind of madness is this? Will we ever get out of here?"

"We will," he said, putting his arm over her shoulder. "Just rest while I think about this." Nath wished he had his pack. It was times like this when he could use Winzee's Lantern of Revealing. He was certain there was something he was missing. Additionally, he could feel the walls closing in like a steel trap. He figured out why the other adventurers died. Wandering and lost, eventually, they ran out of flame. If it weren't for Zothar's candles, Nath and Janna would be doomed. Its flames would not extinguish, not by water, not by wind. The wick burned everlasting. He stroked her hair. "Don't worry. I'll find a way out of here."

Princess Janna gently snored.

A rumbling roar echoed through tunnels, stirring the cobwebs.

Janna's bleary eyes snapped open. She sat upright. "What was that?"

"I'm not sure," he said, coming to his feet, "but it sounded hungry."

CHAPTER 63

R UMMAGING THROUGH THE ROTTING CORPSES, Nath searched for a weapon. He pulled a longsword out of a deteriorating sheath. The blade was coated with dirt, webbing, and grit. He banged the steel on the hard rocks, knocking the ancient debris free, and thumbed the keen edge. He turned it over in his hand a few times. "This will do." With a sword to match the dagger he'd taken earlier from the brigand, he said to Janna, "We need to move."

"What was that thing I heard? Tell me I was dreaming. Sometimes sounds in dreams are louder than they really are."

"I don't know what it was," he said. Nath suspected it was a dragon, but even dragons had different kinds of roars. It could have been a bear or a lion. There was no telling with the way sound traveled in the tunnels. One thing he did know was that whatever made that sound came from somewhere else, meaning there must have been another path he'd missed. "We just need to keep moving."

Janna clung to his elbow with her hand. She kept the candle before her. Hard creases appeared in her forehead. "This is going to give me wrinkles. I don't want to die."

"You won't." He moved down the same path he'd crossed a dozen times. It broadened into wide caverns only to narrow back down again. The walls were slick with bright deposits of mineral specks, making a smooth and glistening surface. There were flecks of gold and silver within, mixed with copper, brass, and other bright flecks made from rocks and minerals.

The strange roar thundered throughout the chamber, sending a chill down his spine.

"Nath," Janna said with a shaking voice, "I can't move. My knees are frozen."

"I'm with you. Whatever that is, it won't find us if we find a way out first." Nath tried to pull her along, but she hunkered down. "Come on, Janna, we must keep moving."

"I can't!"

With his sword and dagger in hand, Nath managed to scoop her up in his arms. "I can move for the both of us." He moved on, using the light of the candle that quavered in her trembling hand. Poor Janna shook like a leaf. Her delicate body quaked in his arms. He picked up the pace as he entered a cavern covered in broken stone. He weaved through the rocks. A stir caught his ears. Ahead, at the far end of the cavern, Nath caught a glimpse of small men scurrying into the field of stones.

Nath tensed. He started backward, not stopping until he stood underneath a rocky canopy of mineral stone. He set Janna down. "Stay here."

"Where are you going? What is out there?"

"I'll be right here," he said, looking from side to side. He made out hairy men dashing from rock to rock, coming toward him. Covered in black fur, they had big bulging eyes that were illuminated like the hot coals of a fire. Some crept forward on all fours. Others jumped silently from rock to rock. The bestial men skulked only a few yards away. Gooey spittle dripped from their lantern-shaped jaws, revealing large carnivorous teeth. Nath cut his sword through the air. "Stay back."

The bestial men slid from the rocks and crouched to the ground, creeping closer like prowling animals. Their long toe- and fingernails made scratching and clicking noises on the floor.

Cowering behind Nath, Janna said, "I'm frightened, Nath. Don't leave me!"

"I promise I won't. Just stay right where you are." Nath swung his sword through the air. If he ever missed Fang, he missed his magnificent blade the most right now. His dragon blood rushed like whitewater rapids. His heart pounded. "Back off, you hairy demons. I'll use this sword and dagger to put an end to you."

The smallish bestial men crept right at him with wide jaws that clacked and bit. One of them rushed Nath from the right.

Nath charged.

CHAPTER 64

NATH TURNED HIS HIPS INTO his swing. The longsword whistled through the air, delivering a fatal chop that took the beastman's head from its shoulders. A guttural howl erupted from the surrounding orange-eyed savages. All at once, they came at Nath in a wild frenzy. Sword in hand, he recollected Dragon Master Elween's endless lessons. Nath lashed out. His sword seemed to move with a life of its own.

A beastman howled when the sword sank into its chest. A second savage fell to a quick strike from Nath's dagger. Fingers were severed from hands. The beastmen came at him in a savage knot of brute strength, long, clawlike fingernails reaching out and teeth gnashing. The undisciplined lot's efforts were spoiled by the sting of Nath's longsword.

Slice! Chop!

The beastmen fell beneath the skill of Nath's singing blade. The battle raged. The sword flickered like the tongue of a striking snake. "Back off, monsters!" Nath shouted as he plunged his dagger in the heart of a beastman swatting at him from behind. Woozy, it staggered away, clutching its chest before falling to the ground.

Nath didn't let up. The beastmen didn't either. Howling like ravenous wolves, they came at him in desperation. Quick and powerful, they charged him as one. Nath cut and stabbed. The hairy brutes rushed forward, maimed and bleeding, and overpowered Nath. Their sheer weight and numbers knocked him from his feet and drove him to the ground.

"Get off me!" Nath cried out. Thrashing and kicking for his life, he cracked them in the face with the butt of his sword. Bone gave way, but their flesh did not. Teeth sank into Nath's arms. Claws scraped his face. Strong, thick hands clamped under his chin, squeezing his neck. "Now!"

The beastmen, though smaller, worked like a relentless hive of bees. They clubbed Nath with the hard knuckles of their fists. Howling and grunting, they beat on Nath's breastplate, trying to crack him open like some kind of egg. Teeth bit into Nath's ankle. He let out a scream. "Aaaaaaah!"

The beastmen wrapped him up in a coarse, hairy blanket made of constricting muscles. His arms and legs were seized, his weapons torn from his grip.

"Nath!" Janna called out in a high-pitched voice. "Help me, Nath! Help meeeeee!" Her voice trailed off.

Nath caught a glimpse through the brawny builds of the wiry men. Another group hauled Janna off by her wrists and ankles as they skittered away. "Janna! Janna! I'm coming! Let go of me, demons!" He broke their grip with one hand and landed a solid punch on a beastman's nose. It let out a howl, drew back its fist, and walloped Nath in the jaw. Somehow, Nath got hold of it by the chest hair. He ripped a fistful out and screamed, "Jaaanna!"

A beastman clocked Nath in the head with a stone.

"Guh!" Nath's taut muscles loosened. Blurry purple spots appeared in his eyes. He flexed against the rank horde again. Stone still in hand, the little brute struck him a second and third time. The lone light from the Zothar's candle went dim. Nath's thoughts for survival swam. The beastmen hauled him away with soft steps and heavy breathing. Nath hung suspended in their grip, fighting the darkness that crept over his consciousness.

CHAPTER 65

N ATH WOKE WITH A THROBBING headache. His blood had begun to dry and cake on his face. His eyelids hurt. He rubbed his swollen forehead and jaw. Lying flat on his back, he grunted and turned on his side.

"Trespasser. Thief. Arise," said a voice that was as ancient and cold as the winter wind.

Racked with pain from toe to forehead, Nath made it to his knees. He felt his heart beating in his tongue. His blurry vision cleared. Warm light illuminated the room like the sun from a hazy day. Small urns with green-blue flames burned around the outer edges of a chamber made from chiseled-out stone. The beastmen squatted by the urns, one on each side with their knuckles on the ground.

"Who are you?" the cold voice said.

Nath twisted his head around and realized he was facing the wrong direction. The person who spoke sat behind him in a throne chiseled from a black block of solid marble. The man was covered in loose cloth wrappings that wound around his limbs and body. Stringy strands of dry hair hung down past his shoulders. Ancient and dry skin covered the few spots able to be seen, and his eyes burned like the rising sun. He wore a crown made from entwined silver serpents on his head. He held Zothar's candles in a very bony hand covered with age spots and deep wrinkles.

Janna lay on the ground between them, passed out on the stone floor. A blue dome of mystic energy shielded her.

On impulse, Nath moved to the dome. "Janna! You better not have hurt her!" He attacked the dome with his fist. A jolt coursed through his body, standing his hairs on end and throwing him backward.

"Ah-hah-hah," the venerable man sitting on the throne said. "It's been quite some time since I've had a laugh." He coughed. Dust and moths came out of his mouth. "Pardon me." He waved his hand. A female beastman wearing a tattered blue dress brought over a tray with a golden goblet. The ancient man took the goblet with a steady hand and drank. He flicked his wrist at the female beastman, and she hurried away, disappearing into the darkness behind him. "I am Hozam, thief. Who are you?"

Nath stood. "I'm no thief, and you better not have hurt my friend. Let her go."

"Heh. She is quite safe, and you test my patience." Hozam set his goblet on the arm of the chair and waved the candle before his eyes. "This is a very valuable acquisition. This candle got you this far, but now your journey of robbing and stealing has come to an end. Now, tell me who you are."

"I am no thief," Nath replied, shaking out his fingertips. "My name is Nath."

"Nath." Hozam leaned back. With his free hand, he rubbed his chin. "A lousy name for a thief. Tell me, why did you dare seek out the treasure of the great Hozam? Is there not enough elsewhere in Nalzambor?"

"We didn't come to rob you. We came seeking refuge." Nath eased closer. "We were chased inside this... tomb."

Hozam's neck popped and cracked as he moved it from side to side, his eyes boring into Nath. His voice rose like thunder. "Hah-

hah-hah... I have heard every lie from those that venture within. They all stretch wild tales as they plead for their lives. At least have the courtesy to tell me something original. I become quite bored down here."

"It is the truth. I was chased within by the Black Hand and the Men of Whispers. They sought to ransom this princess to her father and make a slave of me. I didn't come here by choice."

Hozam scratched the scabbing skin from his cheek. "Not very colorful or rich. It almost sounds believable. But you and this woman will die, unless you would prefer to be converted into one of my children—my precious beastmen, many of which you have slaughtered. Trying to steal my treasure is one transgression, but slaughtering my family is another."

"I didn't mean to kill them. But they attacked me—"

"Silence!"

Nath's hair bristled.

Hozam continued, "You are the trespasser. The thief. The liar. But a clever one, I must say. Not many make it as far as you did. Most perish in the abyss of slabs that you traversed. Others fall prey to the darkness, unless they have magical light, of course." He held up the candle. "Like this. That is when I send the beastmen. Most don't make it farther than that, but a few have. They face the great beast that lies within. You heard him, didn't you... Nath?"

"I heard a growl, yes."

"Yesss, that is my precious pet, the devourer of the dark. It can smell your fear. It feeds on it. It is the guardian of my treasure." Hozam placed the candle in his mouth and swallowed it. "Mmmm... delicious. I feed on magic." He coughed out yellow smoke.

"It looks more to me like you waste it," Nath commented.

"Heh." Hozam pushed out of his chair and started to stand. He became tall as a tower. At full height, he stood eight feet tall. Standing at the top of the steps, he glowered down at Nath.

Nath felt like he was shrinking under the withered wizard's white-hot stare. He leaned backward as Hozam approached. The great wizard stood over the mystic dome of energy that surrounded Janna. "I don't mean to show disrespect, Hozam, but are you dead or alive?"

"Behind the wall of Hozam, I live. Beyond, I die. That is the price for my omnipotent power and immortality." He put his huge bony bare foot on the dome over Janna. "I am the last of my kind from long, long ago. Yet I still thrive, as ruler, in my city in the darkness. It's not often that I have guests. I relish in it." He took a deep breath. "You have an odd smell about you for a man. What race are you?"

"I'm not sure what you mean. I am what you see." Nath said, holding back the full truth while at the same time not lying.

"No, you are more. But we shall see." Hozam lowered his gaze to Janna. "I think this one is ready to transform. She is soft. She is weak. I shall make her stronger than ever before and make her life everlasting." The dome over the young woman swirled with scarlet. Janna bucked. Gasping, she came out of her sleep. Her little fists beat against the energy field. She screamed, but her voice was not heard. The hair on her head, arms, and face started to grow and thicken.

"What are you doing to her?" Nath charged Hozam. Hozam shot a bolt of energy out of his palm. The bright blast knocked Nath from his feet. His chest armor smoked. He stood up.

Janna's face was in agony. She stared wide-eyed at her hairy hands. "Stop it!"

"No. I won't stop it, but you can, trespasser." Hozam pointed to an opening that appeared on the chamber wall. "Kill the devourer in the dark that guards my treasure, and you shall find a cure for her there. Then you and she can leave." The roaring sound of a beast came out of the opened portal. "I'll be waiting."

CHAPTER 66

"Y OU ARE SENDING ME TO my death!" Nath's temper flared. His voice rose. "You expect me to fight a monster, and I don't even have a weapon. You play games, Hozam!"

"It's what I do. It's very boring down here. Of course, you are always welcome to stay if you willingly give yourself over to me." Hozam patted the dome of energy. "It isn't as painful when you don't resist. Your fellow thief resists. The more you resist, the more you suffer. But she will break, and when she does, there is only one way to save her. But you still have time. In the treasure chamber is a potion. Only one. Fetch it, before the devourer of the dark fetches you. He hungers. It's been a long time since he's fed, and he's tired of beastmen."

"This is a rotten game. You send me to a certain death. I need something to fight it with, at least."

"You cannot kill what you cannot see, but you can run from it, quickly. Now, stop wasting time. Your comrade needs you."

Nath hustled over to Janna. He put his hands on the dome. She put her hands to his. Her face had begun to change toward the likeness of the beastmen. Hair had sprouted on her face and chin.

Her eyes bulged. Her frightened gaze was wet with tears. "I'll be back for you!"

He could read her lips as she said, "Help me, Nath! Help me!"

Hozam shoved Nath away with an ice-cold hand. "Stop wasting time, fool! My mercy will quickly end!"

"This better not be a lie, Hozam! If it is, I'll finish you!" He ran for the portal in the wall. He could hear Hozam's icy words as he crossed the threshold.

"Not when the devourer finishes you first."

The portal plunged Nath back into the pitch blackness. His fingertips grazed the wall. He crept forward, slowly at first, heart racing until his dragon senses homed in on the new environment. The walls were solid, made from rough stone. Tunnels spread out around him. It wasn't long before he had the distinct feeling that he was inside a city built inside of the mountain. He sniffed the stale air. His eyes searched for warmth and light. The only thing he heard were bugs that crawled on the walls and floor. As his eyes adjusted, he saw small centipedes and other bugs that glowed. Their small crawling bodies outlined the walls and floor.

"That's helpful."

A hungry roar shattered the silence, surrounding him.

Nath froze. It sounded close. "And that's not helpful."

Using the glowing centipedes as guides, Nath picked up his pace, hoping that he was moving in a direction opposite of whatever prowled the caverns with him. He came to a landing with a broad stone staircase that spiraled downward. Taking two steps at a time, he moved downward, quiet as a cat, hoping that somehow, some way, he was heading toward the treasure room. Of course, there was no way of knowing if there was even any sort of treasure at all. Hozam was an evil thing, and evil was prone to lying. Most likely, all the ancient wizard had done was send him to a certain death in the jaws of the devourer.

Nath tried to stay focused. His head hurt. The jolt Hozam sent through him still stung. Fists and jaws clenched, he fought through his pain and frustration with determination coursing through him. *I must do this!* The Black Hand duped him. They made him look like a fool. At the same time, he was mad at himself for letting it happen. Since he'd left Dragon Home, he hadn't done one single thing right. He'd been robbed twice, but the second robbery was sticking. To make matters worse, doubt crawled in his belly. Perhaps he made the wrong decision by crossing through the Wall of Hozam. The princess would have been better off in the hands of the kidnappers. At least they wouldn't have gotten her killed. They would have just turned her over for ransom. Nath could have dealt with that later.

I'm such a fool!

Step after step, he moved on, determined to make it right. He had to save Janna. He couldn't shake the horror of her beauty being slowly turned into an abomination. Even if Hozam had lied about a potion, he had to take a chance that he didn't. He had to move on with hope.

Suddenly, the glowing bugs spotted on the walls and floors went black. The air turned icy cold and felt like a fetid breath on his neck. Something made a distinctive *sssszz* sound. Nath's flesh crawled. He spread out his arms and reached out. A presence was there, filling the gap behind him. Then it was gone. The bugs illuminated again. Nath could breathe again.

What in the world was that?

A few steps up, a centipede crawled over a scorched and smoking spot on the stone. As the bug crawled over the surface, it coiled up like it just passed through fire. Its inner light dimmed forever. Something had just been there, right behind Nath, that could have gobbled him up, but didn't. He had no doubt that it was the devourer, and it was toying with him. He took a deep breath and started back down the steps. His aching body throbbed, and his senses were on edge.

Onward, Nath, onward.

CHAPTER 67

AT THE BOTTOM OF THE steps, Nath heard water trickling down and splashing into a pool. The floor was wet and slick beneath him. The light from the bugs on the walls and floor had gone cold. Nath stood in the pitch blackness again, but this time there was a cool, damp mist on his face. The splashing and dripping water he heard gave him a little hope. Perhaps it was from the rainfall seeping through the mountain and it would provide another way out if he could just find its source.

He felt something digging into his ribs under his armor. He fished it out. "I'm such a fool!" he uttered. He held the last of Zothar's candles in his hand. He intentionally didn't tell Janna, since she'd dropped the first one. So much had been happening that he'd forgotten all about the last one. He blew on the wick. The flame flickered on. The warm candlelight might as well have been a sunray. Nath couldn't contain his jubilation. "Ha-hah!"

A huge reservoir of water filled the chamber. On the far side was a broad row of steps. Above, water dripped from a chasm in the ceiling. Standing at the edge of the pool, Nath put his fingers in the water. Small, white, glowing fish scattered. As far as he could see, there wasn't a way around the pool, but the water smelled as fresh as rainwater. Nath climbed over the rim of the stone basin and lowered himself into the water. Thigh deep in the waters, he began to cross. The waves he created sloshed over the edge of the pool, splashing loudly on the floor. He moved more quickly toward the steps on the other side. The pool became deeper the farther he went. Something snaked around his ankles. "Gah!"

He plunged the candle into the water. The wick of the magic candle still burned brightly, but nothing was there. Moving onward, Nath found himself neck deep in the waters and started to paddle over. His breastplate dragged him down to where his feet touched bottom. He walked across the soft mud that clung to his feet. The fully submerged glowing fish started to circle. Baring sharp teeth, they darted in and bit him. Nath screamed underwater. Covered in biting fish, he climbed over the bottom, pulling himself toward the other side, hand over hand. His lungs burned. He needed air. When the pool became shallow enough, he burst out of the water and raced toward the steps on the other side. He flung the fish clamped onto his body aside as he did so. "Get off me!" The fish were still snapping once he made his way onto the steps. He picked them off and slung them across the pool. "What kind of fish eats you?"

He sat on the steps, panting and bleeding from a dozen small wounds. The fish remained in a frenzy where the steps and water met. Nath climbed up farther. He combed his hair out of his eyes and noticed a small skiff tied up at the end of the steps. "I'll use you next time."

Slowly, he traversed the steps to the top. He stood underneath another archway. On the left and right of the entrance were two stone statues of knights in full suits of armor. Beyond them, the floor to the room sloped downward. A crevice of golden light showed the way. Nath ventured past the knights and down the slope. Something moved out of the corner of his eye. The knights jumped down from their pedestals and attacked. One drew a sword, and another jabbed with a spear. They moved quickly for men made from granite.

Nath slipped to the side of a jabbing spear. He ducked underneath a sword swing and let out a savage war cry. "EEEEEE-YAAAAAAH!" Shoulders down, he plowed into the spear-wielding guardian and lifted the one-ton monster onto his shoulders. With a tremendous heave, he slammed it down on the ground. The stone knight burst into several large pieces. Nath rolled aside, dodging a deadly chop from the sword-wielding knight. He scrambled back to his feet.

The stone knight came at him on wooden limbs but stabbed at Nath with swift, powerful cuts that would split a man in two. Nath backpedaled toward the steps of the pool. He took a few steps down, standing out of the stone fighter's range. "Come on, what are you waiting for?"

The mindless automaton chopped at him, but the edge of the sword was nowhere close. It looked down and came forward.

Fast as a big cat, Nath raced up the steps, slipped behind the stone knight, and shoved it forward. Unable to keep its balance, the stone knight hit the steps with a resounding crack. Its stone sword snapped. One arm and leg broke off, and it lay still.

"Whew," Nath said, backing away from the scene. "I guess it's true. The bigger you are, the harder you fall."

Sssszz...

Nath spun around. He found himself face to face with a dark-scaled dragon with a bat-like face. Its ruby-red eyes bored into him. Its scales were hard as stone. It had no horns but was as big as a horse. It opened its jaws wide. Saliva dripped from its razor-sharp rows of teeth and sizzled on the floor. Its rancid breath was cold as death. Unlike other dragons, it didn't have any front arms, but small hands on the ends of its black wings like a bat. On reflex, Nath punched it in the nose. It didn't flinch. "Uh-oh."

CHAPTER 68

WIN SCALED PREHENSILE TAILS COILED around Nath's ankles and yanked him from his feet. The dragon's small hands clamped around Nath's neck. Its saliva dripped on Nath's breastplate in white-hot globs. His candle fell from his fingers. Nath had seen hundreds of dragons in his time, but never a shadow dragon. He'd only read about them. They were known to be one of the most vicious and deadliest dragons of all.

Nath grabbed the dragon's hands at the wrists and twisted with all his might. The dragon slung him aside and pounced on his back. It kicked him all over the floor. Swatting and slapping him, it beat Nath senseless. Nath crawled out of its grip only to be dragged back by its tails. It slapped his face, roared, and burned his arms and legs with its saliva.

Nath pushed himself up from lying on his belly. He'd studied all of the dragons and remembered most of what he learned. All dragons had a weakness. Sometimes, it was something as simple as pollen from a flower, or a soft spot not protected by their scales. With the shadow dragon, he wasn't certain, but he kept trying, kicking and swinging back, aiming for another spot every time he punched.

The dragon just kicked him around like some sort of toy. Nath skidded over stone and slammed into support columns. When Nath's weary limbs reached their limits, he finally shouted out in dragonese, "Will you quit playing around and just kill me!"

The shadow dragon pounced. Pinning Nath down, it glared into his eyes.

Nath tried to worm free, but his own strength finally faded. Spittle from the dragon's maw dripped and sizzled on his armor. The scales on the dragon's chest were a creamy white, unlike the hard, granite-colored scales covering the body. There were long eyelashes over its burning red eyes.

"Go ahead, sister, kill me."

The dragon put its snout in Nath's face and breathed deeply. Speaking mind to mind, in a harsh female voice, it said, "*You leak the blood of a dragon. You are no man. What are you?*"

"*I'm a dragon, born a man. I'm Nath, the son of Balzurth.*"

"*Balzurth!*" the dragon hissed in his mind. "*You speak lies!*" The dragon pushed down harder on Nath's shoulders. "*Who are you?*"

Nath was shocked that she was speaking to him, but he fired back. "*I told you, I am Balzurth's son! I come from Dragon Home! Search your own heart—you know it is true. No man can speak dragonese, especially mind to mind like me and you.*"

The dragon eased back. Head tilting from side to side, she said, "*I don't understand, but I know you speak truth, for the dragon blood runs through you.*" The dragon sat back. "*Why have you left Dragon Home to come here? And be specific. Very specific.*"

Fighting his way to his knees with a groan, out loud Nath quickly recounted everything that had happened since he left Dragon Home. If there was one thing he knew about dragons, it was that they enjoyed a good story. "And that's why I am here, trying to save Princess Janna from becoming one of the Hozam's cursed beastmen, as well as myself."

The shadow dragon stretched out her wings and folded them

behind her back. "*It is a wondrous story thus far, and the ring of truth is with it. It's been a very long time since I've spoken to my brethren. I've been alone since Hozam made me his prisoner.*"

Rubbing his stiff neck, Nath asked, "I would be honored to help you, uh..."

"*You may call me Obsidian, little brother. Come.*" She turned her back and headed down the slope that led toward the glare of golden light.

With a wooden effort, Nath followed behind her. When she called him little brother, it put his mind at ease. It gave him comfort that he didn't have with the other dragons who'd ignored him. She didn't pass judgment on him like the rest of his brethren did.

At the bottom of the slope, lit by torches of endless fire, were a vaulted room and an open dungeon door. Inside was a small kingdom's treasure, not anything like Balzurth's throne room, but very ample for a city. There were golden plates, chalices, and silverware. Small chests full of coins and precious gems. Marvelous paintings were stacked against the walls, and the floor was covered with rare pelts and furs. In the rear of the vault, a jade decanter sat on a marble pedestal.

"*That is the potion you seek,*" Obsidian said. Nath advanced. She blocked his passage with her arm. "*Do not be so hasty. This does not work as you believe it does. Hozam has lied to you.*"

"What do you mean?" Nath said, trying to push by. Obsidian shoved him back. "Let me pass!"

"*Don't be a fool!*" Obsidian spoke from her lips now. "The potion will work, but you must understand the proper application." She stuck her head in his face. "*And do you really think that Hozam is going to let you use it to serve your own purpose? I would laugh if I still remembered how.*"

"He gave me his word," Nath said, "and we do not have a quarrel with him. It's a chance I have to take."

"*This place where you now dwell once thrived with life with a small race of renowned men who kept to themselves. Hozam killed them all in his quest for immortality. He only achieved it in part. He lives, but he cannot leave. He still searches for more power, that I fear your own blood could provide.*"

"What will my blood do?"

"*Feed him. Make him stronger. He will leave and take more lives— the more he takes, the more power he has. He will not only be a threat to man, but to dragons. He will figure out what you are soon enough, Nath. That is why we must act quickly.*"

"Let me take the potion then."

"*No.*" She fully blocked his path. Her tone darkened. "*I did not bring you here to help you. I brought you here to help me. I long for my wings to caress the open sky once more. You are my only hope since I was captured. I will not pass up on this chance. Look upon my neck. There is an entanglement of serpents. It is how Hozam controls me.*"

For the first time, Nath noticed the silver collar fashioned like entwined snakes on Obsidian's neck. Her scales grew over it in part as it bit into her skin and appeared uncomfortable, if not painful. It was the same craft as Hozam's crown. "I can try to remove it."

"*No. There is only one way. You must take the crown from Hozam's head and destroy it. That will free me and weaken him enough to kill. Once we have done that, I will show you how to heal your friend and let you out of this hole.*"

Nath shook his head. "I don't know that I can trust you."

"*You don't have a choice.*"

CHAPTER 69

O BSIDIAN CARRIED NATH IN HER jaws. It wasn't what Nath had in mind when he agreed to help the dragon, but it made sense. He couldn't waltz back into Hozam's chamber and hope to negotiate. It would end in failure. No, his best chance was to put his trust in Obsidian and hope that they could fool the ancient wizard. Soon, Hozam would see them. As the dragon crept up the steps and slunk toward the wizard's throne room, Nath lay limp. The dragon dragged him by the arm with sharp teeth that almost broke the skin. He did his best to stay loose and play along.

Using thought, Obsidian said to him one last time, "*Trust me and don't move. I will handle this. Strike when I say strike.*"

Nath felt the light on his eyelids the moment they entered the chamber. He could smell the rank dander of the beastmen and hear their grunting and scratching.

"What is this that my pet brings me?" Hozam's hollowed-out voice said. "Why did you not eat him? Are you not hungry, my pet?"

Obsidian dropped Nath on the floor. "This one is not edible," she said out loud. "He has a very unique blood that runs through his veins. It is the kind of blood that you require to achieve the immortality you desire."

"Do not toy with me, Obsidian. Explain."

The dragon picked Nath up by the armpits and held him in a standing position. She coiled one of her prehensile tails around his neck. "Can you not smell his blood? It's all over him. That is not man's blood—that is the immortal blood of a dragon."

Nath could hear Hozam's crusty robes dragging over the ground. The wizard stopped short. His foul and icy breath hit Nath's face. Nath remained limp, fighting the urge to strike. A finger cold as an icicle swiped over Nath's bloody skin. It sounded like Hozam was tasting it.

"Mmmm, this blood is strong, Obsidian. You have done well," Hozam said.

"Anything for my master." Obsidian pulled Nath closer to her body. "But I require a favor before I give this jewel into your hands. I want my freedom in exchange, or I will kill him where he stands. He will be no good to you dead, Hozam. The bargain is freedom for freedom."

A sliver of doubt suddenly crawled into Nath's belly. If Hozam gave Obsidian what she wanted, she wouldn't need Nath at all. Once the dragon had freedom, she would be gone. Shadow dragons weren't noble creatures. They marched to their own drum. And how good could a dragon be with the word *shadow* in it? If anything, they would be the perfect vessels of evil.

"Certainly, Obsidian," Hozam said, "whatever you wish. But I cannot release you until I have taken possession of his life force, for there is no guarantee that it will work, and where would I be here, without you, for all eternity?"

Obsidian's tail constricted more tightly on Nath's neck. "He is barely alive now. Don't tempt me to finish it. Remove this collar from my neck, for I have nothing else to live for."

"Heh, neither do I. It seems that we are at a standstill. No freedom for me, and no freedom for you. I think I can wait longer. Can you?"

To Nath, it sounded as if Hozam was turning away and moving on. *No, this can't be happening!*

"No, wait," Obsidian said. "Give me your word, and you can do what you do while I hold him still. Is it a deal, Hozam?"

Obsidian, you lying traitor!

"We agree. Now hold him higher. I need eye-to-eye contact to drain him." The wizard put his icy-cold fingers on Nath's shoulders. "Let's wake him up, shall we?"

"Yes," the shadow dragon said. "Let's wake him." She lifted Nath's toes from the ground. "Have at him. I want my freedom." Then with thought, Obsidian said to Nath, "The moment he speaks again, strike with all of your heart."

Hozam's cold, dead hands clasped Nath's face. His thumbs pushed his eyelids open. "Yes, yes," he said with hungry vigor. "I can feel the power of his blood within him. It will be mine."

Nath snapped his eyes open fully. "Surprise!" With a closed fist, he hammered Hozam underneath the jaw. The giant wizard's teeth clacked together. The serpent crown popped off the top of his head.

As Obsidian released Nath, she said, "The crown!" She pounced on Hozam. "Destroy the crown!"

"What is this? You dare betray me!" Hozam shouted with rage. "You will suffer for all eternity, lying dragon!" Bolts of energy fired out of the wizard's hands and into the dragon's body. Her scales smoked, but she clung to the wizard.

The crown rolled away from Nath with a life of its own. He chased it down and snatched it up with one hand. The ring came to life. The silver snakes bit his hands and fingers. "Argh! I've had enough of this!" Squeezing the snakes that coiled around his hands, Nath stretched them out to full length. They were one body with three heads on each end. Hissing and snapping, they writhed in his grip. Nath tried to pull them apart. It was like stretching steel. He put every ounce of strength he had into it. "Hurk!"

"Nooooo!" Hozam screamed. He punched Obsidian in the jaw with a flaming fist. The dragon fought to hang on.

The snake stretched in his hands, getting longer and longer. Its scales spread out, revealing flesh underneath, but it wasn't dying. It was growing.

"You fool! The crown lives. You cannot kill it. You cannot!" Hozam shouted as he pounded Obsidian's face harder and harder. "You will fail!"

"No! I won't!" On impulse, Nath bit down on the snake's body. It snapped into two pieces as it tore clear apart. An energy wave blasted across the room. Nath found himself on the other side of the room, head ringing, searching out Obsidian and Hozam.

The shadow dragon had the rotting wizard pinned down once more. The dragon's chest expanded. A geyser of flame erupted from the dragon's mouth, engulfing Hozam. His flaming arms flailed and burning legs kicked. He let out a scream that shook the room. "I will have vengeance!" he shouted. There was a loud pop, and his ashes filled the room.

Obsidian swiped her tails through the smoking ashes. "No, you won't. Great Guzan, that felt good. I haven't been able to use my flame in over a millennium because of that collar. I am in your debt, Nath. I won't forget this."

"What about the potion, and how do we get out of here?" he said.

"Pour the potion in the pool below. It will cure them all. The way out is the way you came in. With Hozam gone, the path will be revealed now. Goodbye, Nath." She slapped him on the back with her tails. "You did well. Balzurth would be proud." Obsidian spread her wings and rose into the cavern, fading from sight.

Nath rushed over to Janna and scooped her up in his arms. She had transformed in part to a beast. Her delicate features now bulged with ugliness. Hair covered most of her body like a coat of fur. He raced out of the room, through the portal, and down the steps. The night bugs lit up the corridor, scurrying away from his feet as he passed. The beastmen chased after him, but they did not attack. They moved about, hooting and grunting like frightened animals.

Outside of the pool, the jade decanter waited, alongside the still-burning candle. Obsidian had set it aside there when they hatched their plan to take down Hozam. She told Nath it would be ready when it was over. Now it was. Nath picked up the decanter and poured it into the pool. The water bubbled and foamed. As the surface cleared, a soft light shone through the blue waters. Nath carried Janna into the waters and submerged her fully. With a shimmer, her face and body transformed back into the radiant woman she was before. Her eyes fluttered open as he brought her out again.

"Janna," he said, "how do you feel?"

Her stare was blank and glassy. As he held her, the other beastmen climbed into the pool's waters. One by one, dozens of men and women of all races transformed back into their natural forms. Before Nath could bat an eye, a fight broke out among them. They fought and clawed their way toward the treasure.

"Are you mad?" Nath shouted. The greedy fools didn't even stop to thank him. After centuries of captivity, their greedy nature chose treasure over freedom. Nath carried Janna away in his arms and shouted back as he ascended the steps, "Have at it then! Fools!"

CHAPTER 70

E XHAUSTED AND ON STIFF LEGS, Nath carried Princess Janna in his arms through the Channel. The rain had stopped, but the ground was thick with sloppy mud. Water still poured from the mountain's ledges above. He stumbled, fought for footing, and splashed through the mud. Still standing, he rested his back against the canyon's wall. His back and shoulders burned. Janna wasn't heavy, but Nath was tired. Plus, nightfall had started to descend, turning the already-darkening chasm black.

"Can't stop now," he said, half talking to himself and half talking to Janna. She hadn't said a word, but her hands were locked tight around his neck. She kept her face buried in his chest and her eyes squeezed shut. She shivered the entire time as if she was trapped in a nightmare. Nath felt bad for her. She'd been through too much. The transformation into a beastman must have shocked her. "I'll get you home, Janna. I promise."

With his jaw set, he limped on, forcing himself forward one heavy step at a time. His boots stuck in the mud, making a sucking sound every time he pulled them out. Finally, covered in mud, he exited the mouth of the Channel. The road stretched before him, surrounded by green trees and thick in brush.

"Thank goodness."

Night had fallen. The air was damp and cool. Owls hooted from the trees as Nath continued down the road. On foot, it would probably take until morning to make it back to Riegelwood. Determined not to stop, Nath kept going forward, aching all over with his body burning. His belly moaned. He could eat a cow if he had one.

Two things kept him going: getting Princess Janna home and finding the Black Hand. They embarrassed Nath, and worst of all, they had Fang and the rest of his belongings. He would get them back, expose the Black Hand to City Lord Jander, and move on to his quest to find the Trahaydeen and Maefon. It seemed like an age had passed since he began his quest. So much had happened. Rogue Trahaydeen killed fledgling dragons. Nath had been exiled from his home to avenge them, and he couldn't return for a hundred years. It was all sinking in at once. For the first time, he truly missed home and his life among the dragons. The world outside had so far been inexplicably worse than he imagined.

I will see this through even if it kills me.

Fields of farmland appeared on the horizon, spreading out for miles outside of Riegelwood. Nath passed by barns where roosters crowed. Men and women stirred, hustling out of their cottages and tending to the livestock and the fields. They paid Nath no mind as he moved along the road, not stopping until he made it to the city's cobblestone streets just as dawn broke over the hillside horizon. Just outside of the city lord's gates, he dropped to his knees. "Help," he said.

Two soldiers approached. "What seems to be the problem, son?"

Nath barely managed to look up. It was the two soldiers he met when he came into the city—Hartson, black bearded, and Kevan, clean shaven. They were the ones who sent him to the Oxen Inn where he met Nina. He shook his head. "Nothing. We just got caught in the storm. We'll be fine. Just tired. It was a very long night."

"You're all muddy and covered in blood. It looks like you've been in more than just a storm. More like an awful fight." Hartson's hand went to his sword. "Say, you're that fella who came through a few days ago. Who's this woman with you?"

"A friend." Nath forced himself up to one knee. "I'll be taking her home now."

Kevan whispered in Hartson's ear. Hartson's eyes grew big. He took a hard look at the woman in Nath's arms. "That's Princess Janna," Hartson said. "Isn't it?"

"Yes," Nath said, "but you—"

"Kidnapper!" Hartson roared. He drew his sword while his son blew a whistle.

"I didn't kidnap her. I rescued her from the Black Hand!" Nath said, coming to his feet.

Hartson put his sword to Nath's neck. Kevan held a spear at his back. "Don't you dare move," Hartson said.

"You must listen to me, Hartson. I need to take the princess back to City Lord Jander. I have to explain all about the kidnappers, the Black Hand. I must warn him about them."

"Stop with your gibberish, man! I'm just doing my job." Hartson's eyes narrowed on Nath. "If you were wise, you never would have come back, stranger. The city lord doesn't like troublemakers."

The castle's barbicans opened up. More soldiers ran from within the castle archways. A commotion of people chattering started in the streets. Within seconds, Nath was surrounded by hard-eyed soldiers brandishing their weapons. As they took Princess Janna from his arms, her fingers brushed his cheek. Looking him in the eyes, she said, "Thank you, stranger." She vanished behind a wall of armored soldiers.

"Stranger?" Nath said to himself. Scanning the faces of the soldiers, he said to them as they crowded around him with numbers and sharp weapons, "I'm not the kidnapper! I saved her!"

"Take him to the dungeon." Hartson glowered at Nath. "Don't fight, or you'll die."

Nath didn't have the strength to fight anything. They shackled him and hauled him away as the third rooster crowed that day.

CHAPTER 71

FOR THREE DAYS, NATH SAT in a dingy dungeon cell on a bed of rotting hay, mulling over how the Black Hand betrayed him. The guards brought him food once a day. Outside of the cell were a wooden ladle and a bucket of water that he could drink from. With his back to the stone wall, he looked through the bars. He gently beat his head against the wall, saying, "I'm stupid, stupid, stupid."

The most disturbing part of the entire predicament was Princess Janna. When she was torn from his arms, she didn't recognize him. She called him stranger. He worried that part of her was lost. So far, he hadn't been accused of anything, but the guards wouldn't say a word to him. It was possible that he might be left to rot forever.

The main door to the dungeon opened. A lone set of hard-soled footsteps approached. It wasn't the same soft scuffle that the guards made. This was someone different. Nath rose to his feet as the door closed the newcomer inside.

Nina stood right in front of him. She was nicely dressed, wearing new gold and jewels on her arms, wrists, and neck, with a pelt of wolf hair over her shoulders. Her hair was in braids on the top of her head, and her bare muscular arms had a silky sheen to them. The tall woman never looked better. "Hello, Nath. You look horrible."

"You!" He thrust his arms through the bars, fingers clutching, but she stood too far away.

She let out a delightful little laugh. "Settle yourself. You have a long journey ahead, and you will need your energy."

Hands on the bars, he yanked on them. Arms shaking, he sighed. "What are you talking about now?"

"First, let me catch you up on your present situation. Currently, you are accused of kidnapping Princess Janna."

"That's a lie, and you know it! The Black Hand did it. You did it!"

She held out her hand. "Compose yourself, please. Or I will leave." She looked at her black-painted nails. "Do we have an understanding?"

"Yes."

She approached the bars and smiled. "You never fail to surprise me. I told Tobias when we left you behind the Wall of Hozam not to be surprised if we saw you again. He laughed. Anyway, we returned to the city with news that we believed Princess Janna had perished and we couldn't recover the body. I have City Lord Jander's ear, so he bought into the story where we chased you into the Channel and lost you and her behind the Wall of Hozam. But we did pin it all on you, Nath. And I put the word out that you might return with her and try to dupe City Lord Jander. He bought it all."

"Then you actually did show up," she said, incredulous. "And with the princess in your arms. You could have very well exposed us if she were able to tell the truth. As it turns out, to your misfortune, and our good fortune, she struggles to even remember who she is. I would love to know what happened behind that wall, but now I'm filthy rich, and I don't really care."

"You have one thing right," Nath said with a snarl.

"Oh really? What is that?"

"You're filthy."

"Hmph." She stroked the wolf pelt. "Listen to me, Nath. You would do well to not agitate me. Frankly, it is disappointing that you didn't join with us. But we all agreed that there was too much good in you to do the dirty deeds that need to be done, and it has cost you. However, I want to thank you. Since you did return the princess, we were able to convince Lord Jander of our efforts and collect her ransom. He trusts us deeply. We will use that to get back in the good graces of Prawl and the Men of Whispers. You're a part of that too."

"You collected the reward for someone that you kidnapped?" He kicked the bars. "That is madness."

"No, that is good business. And you should be thankful for us as well. Kidnapping the city lord's daughter is punishable by death," she said. "But because we need you alive, I talked City Lord Jander out of it. Plus, there really wasn't much evidence that you did it."

"Because I didn't do it," he said, hanging his head.

"That hardly matters. Only what the city lord and the people of this blinded city believe matters. Anyway, today, you will ride out of here and be delivered to Prawl as part of our original agreement. His needs will be satisfied, and so will ours. We can go back to business as usual."

"As kidnappers and slavers," he said, shaking his head. "Don't you have enough money now?"

"One can never have enough money or power, Nath. It's how we control people." She touched his hand. "It's been nice knowing you. I wish your circumstances could have been a little better, but not at the cost of mine. I'd wish you well, but I really don't want that to happen."

As she walked away, Nath said, "Can you tell me one thing?"

She turned on her heel. "Perhaps."

"Who has my sword, Fang?"

"Tobias. I'm certain that he plans to sell it for a fortune."

CHAPTER 72

ATER THAT DAY, NATH WAS led out of the city lord's castle in a prison wagon. His wrists and ankles were in irons and chains. A metal collar bit into his neck. The citizens of Riegelwood lined up along the streets, booing and cursing him as they hurled rotten food at him. Nath sat inside the bars, swaying as the wagon rattled down the cobblestone streets. A squad of twelve soldiers accompanied him out of the city. Half of them were on horseback and the other half on foot. Nath knew their faces. They were the Men of Whispers. They stared at him with gloating faces.

How big of a fool can City Lord Jander be?

He felt worse for Janna as he watched the castle banners fade in the distance. She would be blinded, too. The entire city, it seemed, was secretly controlled by the Black Hand.

Finally, the wagon came to a stop several miles out of the city. The transport cell was opened, and Nath was led out. Farther up the hill stood six more horses and riders. One of them was Prawl. The other five were the Black Hand. Tobias, Nina, Virgo, Worm, and Cullon all sat tall in their saddles, smirking at Nath as he was pushed toward them. Nath didn't see Fang or any of his other items. As he walked by the group toward Prawl, he said, "This isn't over."

The Black Hand chuckled. Tobias spoke. "It was over the moment you walked in the Oxen Inn, son." He had a leather bag that appeared heavy with gold. He held it out to Prawl. "Your full share of the reward, or ransom, whatever you want to call it."

"Give it to Andeen. He'll cut out my share." Prawl nodded to the slender brigand leader among the Men of Whispers. Prawl dismounted, grabbed a coil of rawhide rope, and approached Nath.

"Iron cord, eh," Tobias said of the rope. "Good stuff."

Prawl bound up the irons on Nath's wrists and tethered Nath to his huge horse. "This is the one that I want. You made good, Black Hand. It's a good thing that you did." He glared at Nina. "I will have that gauntlet one day, woman, one way or another."

"We'll see," Nina said.

Tobias leaned over his saddle. "The slate is clean, then?"

Prawl and Andeen nodded.

"Until next time we do business." Tobias turned his horse away and looked at Nath. "Except for you, obviously. May you never show up again."

One at a time, following Tobias, all of the members of the Black Hand rode by Nath. Cullon spat on his feet. Worm cackled as he went. Virgo gave him a flirty wink, but Nina didn't even glance at him. Slowly, they shrank into the countryside. Andeen, dressed as a soldier of Riegelwood, led the other disguised brigands manning the cell cart after them. That left Nath and Prawl all alone. Prawl's horse let out a nasty nicker. Dark clouds blotted out the sunlight overhead.

Nath looked at Prawl. "Where are you taking me?"

The big orc didn't reply. Loaded down with weapons and gear, Prawl urged his horse forward. The big beast chugged along, pulling Nath behind them. Nath hustled, trying to keep pace with the horse's big stride. He took a long, lasting look over his shoulder. His enemies were gone.

CHAPTER 73

THE STORMY SKIES BROUGHT A hard and steady rain. The cloud cover was a blanket of darkness that turned the day to night. Raindrops splattered on the muddy road. Nath's worn leather boots sank beneath the mud with every step. The strapping young man had reached his limits. His strong frame, bruised and scabbed, was broken down. The fire in his tireless eyes barely flickered. With his wrists and ankles in irons, he trudged along, chin down and shoulders slumped. He clinked with every step.

Ahead, a big horse, dark as coal, with muddy ankle hair that covered its hooves, let out a monstrous snort. Nath's arms were yanked forward. He stumbled forward, fighting for his footing. A length of durable rope called iron cord tethered him to the saddle. The horse moved on, pushing through the rain, a juggernaut not affected by the stiff winds or the storm's fury.

With his voice cracking, Nath said, "Do you think we could rest for a spell?" He brushed his soaked red hair out of his eyes. "My feet are aching, not to mention my wrists, neck, and ankles. And this collar on my neck is chafing my skin. Especially right underneath my chin." His grubby fingers dug at it. "I'm not sure who designed this contraption, but if it were a little leaner, it would still have the desired imprisoning effect. Unless, of course, discomfort is part of the design. In that case, it's fairly well done."

Prawl didn't reply. The horse snorted, however. The rugged mount's snorts, whinnies, neighs, and disruptive nickering were the only communication Nath had had with anyone in over a day.

Nath summoned the reserves of his aching limbs and sped up his pace. The heavy weight of the chain and short length between his ankles cut his lengthy stride in half. He shuffled up alongside his captor and looked up to him as rain pelted his swollen face. "Please, I beg of you, Prawl. I am exhausted. Can we rest, just a short span? And eat. I'd really like to eat."

The orc's beady yellow eyes remained set on the road ahead. His head was thick with matted black hair, and he had a broad face lumpy with scars, and flaring nostrils like tunnels. The hood of his worn traveling cloak was down over his broad shoulders. Chain-mail armor covered his barrel chest, tight, like it was part of his body. A broadsword hung from the belt on his hip. Another pair of swords was strapped to the saddle. There were hand axes, rope, saddle bags. A bedroll was tied down on the back of the saddle. He smelled... bad, as if he hadn't bathed in over a year and had spent most of that time sweating.

"At least tell me how far we're going?" Nath pleaded. If he'd asked once, he'd asked a dozen times. He wasn't trying to be weak. All he wanted was to know something new about his situation. He understood well enough how he got here. He'd been betrayed, igniting a chronic anger burning inside of him, giving him the strength to go on. "Can you hear me?" Nath yelled at the top of his lungs. His voice rose higher. "Where exactly in Nalzambor are you taking me?"

Prawl turned in his saddle and glowered down at Nath with beady eyes like simmering coals. He showed a twisted smile of broken teeth. He dug his heels into the horse. The horse reared up on two legs and bolted forward.

"No! No! Nooooooo!" Nath cried out. He ran as the horse took off in a full gallop. He kept up for a few seconds before he was yanked off his feet. He hit the ground chest first, slipping and sliding down the muddy road. Mud filled his mouth. His eyes were covered in wet slop. Spitting mud out of his mouth, he rolled to his back. The gravel road ripped at his back. It burned. He tucked his chin into his chest and flipped back over. The breastplate he wore saved his skin. "Stop! Please stop!" he shouted.

The horse continued its gallop down the mud-soaked road. It went on minute after agonizing minute. Nath's arms were stretched out to their full length. His shoulders burned. He locked his fingers on the iron cord. Straining, he pulled, somewhat righting himself. It was all he could do to keep his arms from popping out of their sockets. His strength faded. Finally, when his arms were about to give, the horse came to a stop.

"Oh, Great Guzan, thank you." Nath rolled to his back. Rain pelted his muddy face. His chest heaved beneath his breastplate. He used his numb fingers to wipe more mud from his eyes. "That was awful."

The orc dismounted. His huge boots splashed through the puddles. He strolled over to Nath and stood over top of him for moments. He took a knee and said in a very gravelly voice that was difficult to understand, "Still hungry?"

Nath knew what he should say, but instead he said, "Very much so. Thanks for asking. A couple of roasted quail would be delightful. And some milk. The long journey's made my tummy queasy and—"

The orc slugged him in the face. He grabbed Nath by the back of the hair, pulled it back, and looked him in the eye. "How about some mud stew instead?" He stuffed Nath's face into the muddy road and held him down.

Nath kicked and squirmed. The orc's powerful hand pushed his face deeper into the road, grinding his face into the mud.

The orc pulled Nath up.

Nath gulped in a lungful of air.

"Still hungry?" the orc said.

"Yes!" Nath tried to pull away after he said it.

With bearish strength, the orc shoved his face back into the mud.

Nath pushed up on his arms. Straining with all he had left, he couldn't get his face out of the mud. *Gads, he's strong!* He pushed until he couldn't push anymore. He kicked out to no avail. The husky orc felt like he was an ogre.

The orc pulled him out of the mud again. "Still hungry?"

"Yes…" Nath managed to say, spitting out dirt at the same time.

The orc plunged his face into the sopping sludge again and again. Nath replied yes, every time, until he didn't have the energy to reply anymore. The orc shoved his head down, one last time, then stood.

Nath looked at him.

The orc busted him in the jaw with the boot of his toe. The world spun once before it went black.

CHAPTER 74

PINE NEEDLES PRICKED NATH'S FACE, his head pounding as he woke. He caught the sound of a crackling campfire and, groaning, turned in its direction. There it was. The warming flames of a fire roasted two hunks of meat on the spit. His mouth watered. His stomach moaned. Sitting up, he rubbed his sore jaw. At least, that was the sorest part of his busted-up body at the moment. His legs were scraped up and his trousers torn through. The toe of one of his boots was missing. He crawled toward the flame.

"Urk!" He gasped.

The metal collar on his neck snagged. He looked back to see that he was tethered to a pine tree by the iron cord. He reached around, grabbed it, and gave it a fierce yank. He was strong, but the iron cord was much stronger.

Nearby, the black horse stood on the other side of the fire, chewing on a bush in the glade. It was night, and the rain had come to a stop, but the ground was still soft and muddy beneath Nath. He turned back, faced the fire, crossed his legs, and licked his dirty, busted lips. The hunger pangs were the worst he'd ever had. Never in his life had he been at the brink of starvation. Not to mention thirst. His parched lips were cracking. The tongue he'd already bitten more than once was swollen. Yet there was nothing he could do about it. He was a prisoner.

How did I not see this coming? I'm so stupid! I could kick myself!

The scrunch of footsteps caught his ear. Prawl emerged from the darkness of the forest. Large, dark, and dusky, he stood with four dead rabbits clasped by the ears in one hand. Nath had only encountered a few orcs before, at a distance, but none like this one. He was bigger, and even uglier with his misshapen face shadowed in the fire's light. Not only that, but the way the orc carried himself was formidable. A snarl remained fixed on his face. The seasoned orc carried many weapons. The handles were polished and the blades oiled. The orc pulled out a knife with a handle made from elk horn and a keen curved blade. He began skinning the rabbits.

"I suppose one of those rabbits is for me?" Nath said politely. "I'd be more than happy to prepare one for myself, even yours, if you like. It's the least I can do since you fetched it."

The big orc kept skinning.

"That dagger you have has a very clever design. I'm curious. Did you make it yourself? I'm a bit of a blacksmith myself."

Prawl tore the skin off the rabbit. "I made it to silence things that annoy me, such as you."

"So rabbits annoy you? Interesting. I'd probably be a lot more content to be quiet if I had some food and maybe a little more information." Nath combed his hair out of his eyes. "You aren't going to kill me, it seems. We both know this, so at least give me a hint as to what is in store for me. Who wants to buy me, or do you know?"

Prawl finished skinning the other rabbits and placed them on the same spit where the other two rabbits had finished cooking. He tore off a leg, stuffed it in his mouth—bone and all—and started chewing.

Nath grimaced. The crunching of bone gnawed at his ears. "I promise I'll save you my bones when I'm finished eating."

Looking Nath in the eye, the orc ate the entire rabbit. A few moments later, he belched. "South," Prawl said.

"What's that?" Nath leaned forward.

"You asked where. I gave it." The orc tore into the other hunk of cooked meat. "South, very south. That's where I take you."

"Ah, Prawl, thank you. As if the sun didn't tell me that already." Nath offered a smile. "And please, call me Nath."

"I don't care what your name is."

"Of course you don't. I was just offering a proper introduction." Nath moved his hands back and forth. "Now that we are formally acquainted, we can dine together."

Prawl continued to chew with his pronounced lower jaw jutting out. Rabbit flesh hung from tusk-like teeth on his bottom jaw.

"You say we are going south, very south. Is there a name for it? Perhaps I'm acquainted with it? Cherlon maybe? I heard that is one of the fairest cities on the inland sea. They say the castle spires are gilded in gold and decorated in abalone."

"The more you talk, the less you eat," Prawl said. He waggled a rabbit leg at Nath. "Less."

Nath's mouth started open. Prawl pulled back the leg. Nath sealed his lips.

The orc tossed the leg over.

After snatching the meat out of the air, Nath quickly ate. There was little meat, but it tasted wonderful—so good, in fact, he considered eating the bone. Instead, he snapped the bone and sucked on the juicy marrow. "More, please."

"Hah," Prawl said. "I shouldn't have fed you at all. Slaves are troublesome with a full belly. It gives them strength to escape, and I have to track them down again. I'd rather not."

Sucking his fingers, Nath said, "Just a little more, please. I'm no good to you if I'm so weak that I can't walk."

"You'll manage. You don't look it, but you're tougher than ogre's hide. You'll do well, heh-heh."

"Do well at what?"

The orc stuffed the rest of the meat in his mouth, crunched it up, swallowed it, and washed it down with water from a skin. He wiped his hands on the dirt. His expression darkened as he picked up the knife in his hand. "Stop talking. I won't say it again."

Nath pulled his knees to his chest. He looked away and stared into the campfire, where the broken limbs were turning to ash. Small blue flames burned in the middle. Even though he knew that Prawl wouldn't kill him, he'd learned firsthand that Prawl wasn't one to be trifled with.

Hang on, Nath, hang on.

As the rabbit meat sizzled on the spit and grease dripped into the fire, Nath, still starving, focused on something else. The gloating faces of his betrayers burned forever in his mind. They tricked him, lied to him, stole every precious thing from him, and sold him to a slaver. His gold eyes glowed as hot as the flames.

I will survive this! I will hunt my enemies down and make them pay.

CHAPTER 75

NATH'S VENGEFUL THOUGHTS WERE INTERRUPTED by
Prawl crunching on rabbit bones. The orc sucked his dirty,
greasy fingers clean. There was one last rabbit burning on
the spit. Nath's mouth watered. One rabbit leg wasn't enough. He
needed more.

"Go ahead, take it," Prawl said, tossing the last bit of meat on the
ground before Nath.

Nath walked on his knees as far as the length of rope would
take him. Collared and tied to a tree like a dog by the iron cord, he
stretched out his fingers. He grabbed the meat with his fingertips.
Steaming-hot rabbit meat stung his bound hands. He juggled the
meat between his fingers the best he could.

"What is the matter? Don't you like my hot food?" Prawl growled.
Up on his feet, moving with alarming speed, he crossed over the
campfire in a single stride and tried to snag the rabbit from Nath's
fingers. Nath bit down hard on a rabbit leg just as Prawl ripped the
creature from his grasp. The orc swatted Nath hard in the face.

Nath ate hungrily every bit he had, licking it clean to the bone.
Prawl kicked him as he stuffed the entire rabbit in his mouth,
crunched it up, and swallowed.

"You weren't really going to give me that entire thing anyway. You just play games."

"I like games." Prawl crossed back over to the other side and sat down. He propped himself up on his elbow and stared at the fire. "I like torture better. It's like games, but deadlier."

Savagely, Nath licked his own fingers clean. "You've certainly had your fair share of games recently. I can't help but wonder why you let the Black Hand take you like they did. They took a fortune in coins and gems from me that made that reward money look like a widow's purse. I'd be very angry if I were you. How much could I be worth, anyway?"

Prawl narrowed an eye on him. "More than that."

"That doesn't make any sense," Nath said.

"Some things are worth more than precious pieces. That's the Black Hand's loss and my gain. Now, shut your mouth and rest. The journey is many days, and I will ride in silence, unless you don't want to be fed."

"If I'm to be sold, I'm certain my buyer doesn't want me hungry and bruised." Nath swatted at a mosquito that buzzed in his face. "He or she would be angry."

"You're to be delivered alive and fully limbed. That's what the slave lords expect. That's what I deliver." Prawl closed his eyes.

Nath worked at the ropes on his wrists. The more he fidgeted, the more the coarse bindings bit into his wrists. He considered running, but Prawl secured his legs with more iron cord the moment they camped. He wasn't running anywhere if he didn't want to cut off the blood supply that fed his extremities. He closed his eyes for a moment, and before he realized what happened, he was fast asleep, dreaming of all the horrors of Nalzambor that he'd already faced.

Prawl woke him with a stiff kick. The early glow of dawn showed on the leaves of the trees. The orc undid the rope that tangled Nath's legs. He didn't understand how Prawl could tie it and untie it, but he could. It was as if the iron cord had one lock on it that only orcs had the key to. With Nath tethered again to the horse, they moved on. Every time Nath spoke, the orc would spur his horse into a gallop and drag Nath a half mile over the rugged plains. Tired of eating dirt and grass, he gave up speaking entirely. He hated Prawl. He hated all obnoxious orcs. He hated the Black Hand too. He kept his burning legs churning.

Judging by the sun, they moved southeast at a brisk pace, taking paths almost overcome with vegetation. There was a moment as they crossed the plains when Nath could see the very tip of Dragon Home in the far distance. His heart ached to be home again. He never imagined that he would miss it so much. With a long and suffering heart, he had to look away.

Five days later, beyond broken from travel, they ventured down a road deep into the lush southern hemisphere. Ahead, a city-like establishment sat on a hill behind walls made out of wood. Prawl and Nath weren't the only ones on the busy road. Merchants were coming and going. Like Nath, there were people bound by rope or chains on their hands, feet, and neck, bringing up the rear behind horse and wagon. Nath walked by at least a dozen slaves with their heads down. Grubby and scrawny, they walked on rickety limbs with blank stares on their faces. He stopped. A hard tug of his rope towed him forward.

There was a sign written in common mounted in rocks just outside the city's wooden gates. "Slaver Town: You bring the gold, we bring the slaves."

Nath ground his teeth. His fists balled up as he was led inside the gates. Lavishly clad men and women haggled over an assortment of people of all races and creeds, standing up on auction blocks. There were at least a dozen going on all at once. *What is wrong with this world?*

Prawl dismounted. He untethered Nath from the saddle, found a young boy, and had him stable his horse. The orc led Nath through the filthy streets into a huge barn-like structure made of stone. Inside the barn were rows of stables that had been converted into prisoner cells. People were stuffed inside the cells in twos, threes, and fours. Judging by appearances, the slaves were fed like animals. Many desperate stares hung on Nath. Others looked down and away.

A human jailer with bulging and sweaty rolls of fat on his neck and wrists sauntered over to Prawl. "This is a fine one. You continue to impress as always, Prawl. Our purchasers will be pleased." He smacked his lips. "Very pleased."

"He gets his own cell. No one touches him until the buyer who contracted me to get him comes," Prawl warned.

"No, of course not. This one will be well provided for in his own cell." The jailer reached for Nath's hair. Nath flinched away. "That hair will make the wig weavers sing."

Prawl poked the jailer in his flabby chest. "Don't touch him."

"Yes-yes," the man said nervously. "Come, come." He led them to the very back of the barn, separated from the rest of the barn by heavy curtains. It was a dark, dank room busted out of the rocks with metal bars walling off the front. Prawl untied Nath and shoved him inside. The jailer closed the door. He extended his hand. "All is in order."

Prawl nodded.

"Then I shall send word out to your buyer. Come with me, Prawl. We'll go over the papers and get your payment prepared." The jailer looked at Nath. "I'll have food sent."

"No," Prawl said, glowering at Nath. "Not until after I leave. The journey has been long. I plan on enjoying myself for a bit."

"As you wish," the jailer said. He pushed the curtains aside, and they left.

Ravenous, Nath gripped the bars of his new home and screamed, "Praaaaawlll!"

EPILOGUE

ONTHS LATER, BACK AT STONEWATER Keep, the home of the Caligin, Lord Darkken and Maefon stared into the Pool of Eversight. The waters swirled with a phantasmagoria of colors, but there was no image. Maefon had a film of sweat on her forehead. Her eyebrows were knit together.

Dressed in all-black clothes that enhanced Lord Darkken's domineering demeanor, he said to her, "You've been training very hard, Maefon. You should have mastered the pools by now."

"I know." She waved her hands over the waters. She'd been at it all morning, trying to link to the pool's mighty powers, but her extensive training left her exhausted. She did not dare disappoint Lord Darkken. Failure was the equivalent of death. "I will make it happen. I swear it." The waters heaved for a moment then calmed. The prism of swirling colors cleared. She immediately took a knee and bowed. "Apologies, Lord of the Dark in the Day. I've failed you."

"No," he said with the soothing voice of an all-knowing father, "you have only failed yourself. You can learn from that, Maefon." He took her hands. "Rise." She did. "Look at me, Maefon. Your hard work has not gone without notice, and I admit, I have neglected you over the last several weeks. But now, I am here to guide you through this. Tell me, what image were you trying to summon from the pool?"

"The town, Tilly, that I burned. I was curious to see how it fared since the disaster."

"Do you feel connected to those people that suffered at your hand?"

"No, I swear it. I was more curious than anything."

Lord Darkken put his arms over her shoulders and turned her toward the pool. "Easy, Maefon. I have more faith in you than you realize. My point is that because you don't have a strong connection, for you it will be difficult to summon the power of the waters. That comes later. For now, you need to think of something or someone that you are strongly connected with. The Pool of Eversight can relate to that. Open yourself to it, and it will open itself to you." He spoke right in her ear with his hand on the small of her back. "Who do you care for most, aside from me, of course? Who comes to your mind first?"

Nath came to mind the moment Lord Darkken asked the question. She didn't want to say it—it seemed like the wrong answer—but Lord Darkken would know she was lying if she claimed any other. "Nath."

"Let it all out, Maefon. Trust the pool, and the pool will trust you. Besides, I am very curious to observe his condition. You should be too. After all, he is looking for you."

She took a deep breath and gazed into the waters. With her fingers tapping over the pool, she let her own mystic energy out. At the same time, she recalled her times with Nath. There was a lot of laughter with Nath, and his share of frowns too when he didn't get what he wanted. It all flowed out of her, as if she were feeding the pool what it wanted. In an instant, she felt herself being rocketed over Nalzambor. She soared over the trees and hilltops and flew by flocks of birds. She slowed in the southern lands where the forests were thick with vines and leaves. A city in the hills, defended by wooden walls and battlements, was nestled on the rocks.

"Ah, how refreshing. Slavertown," Lord Darkken said, as if he was surprised, but it came across as if he already knew it.

The pool showed the city from a bird's point of view. It hovered by droves of depraved people. There was a crowd gathered around muddy fields, hooting and cheering with vigor. Their hungry eyes were in the field where the action was. Men pulled sleds with rocks piled on top across the muddy field. Halflings sat on the rocks, cracking whips at the men's backs. Like beasts of burden, the men's hands clawed at the mud as they pulled with all of their might. Covered in mud up to his elbows, the sled puller in the lead was Nath.

Maefon let out a little gasp. The image in the pool quavered.

"Concentrate, Maefon," Lord Darkken said, hugging her tightly around the waist. "I want to see who wins this."

Nath's golden eyes were full of anger and anguish. She had never seen him in such condition. It was a shock to see him, once so perfect, now sticky in mud and blood from superficial wounds. He surged ahead of the other men with the whip cracking on his back, pumping his knees with all of his might.

"As I recall, the winner of this type of event gets to eat while the others starve. It looks as if Nath is very, very hungry." Lord Darkken passed his hand over the image in the pool. Ripples took the image away, and the waters cleared.

Maefon fell back into Lord Darkken's arms, panting.

"That is enough. Your first connection will drain you. You'll be stronger after that. You did well. A good thing… for you."

Straightening up, she faced him. "What is Nath doing there of all places? Is he enslaved?"

"Of course he is. I had him enslaved."

"But why? I don't mean any disrespect by asking, but I can't help but be curious." She closed her eyes and rubbed her temples. A nagging headache had come on. "I'm having trouble understanding the end game."

"Certainly, you've earned the answer." Lord Darkken put his hands on the rim of the basin and stared into the waters. "I'm making him tougher. I want him to hate this land and hate its people. It is the only way to break the good that is in him."

"Wouldn't killing him do the trick?"

He showed a clever smile. "Of course, but he is of no use to me dead. I need him alive. I will be vastly more powerful with my brother by my side than with him dead."

Maefon paled. "Brother?"

"Yes. You see, I am Balzurth's other son, a dragon born a man. But I despised the dragons from the start." The Pool of Eversight came to life. A new image started to form. "Like you, I slaughtered the fledglings, my own kind." He shrugged. "For sport. But in Balzurth's heart of hearts, he could not kill me. He banished me instead, to walk along in the dust of men forever. I'll never fly, but I'll never die so long as I can turn Nath to my side."

"So you are the one the dragons would not speak about."

"Yes."

It all came together for her. "And that's why they despised him so?"

"That's how I planned it all along. My little brother was doomed from the start, and thanks to you, Maefon, and your work among the Trahaydeen, my master scheme is set into motion. I will turn Nath, or he will die."

A new image formed in the pool. It was the same field of mud in Slaver Town. Nath's sled was stuck in the mud. He hadn't finished. The others did. People were booing and throwing stones at him.

"It looks like he lost. Tsk. Tsk. What a shame."

"Can't he die?"

"Of course, but he's a lot tougher than even he can imagine. Trust me when I say that, Maefon." He passed his hand over the pool. The waters cleared again. "I'm hungry. How about you?"

"Famished, actually." She put her hands around his waiting elbow. "So how much stronger would the two of you be together?"

"Powerful enough to rule the world and ruin the dragons forever."

Next Book Enslaved And More

Thanks for reading, Exiled: The Odyssey of Nath Dragon. Book 2, Enslaved, is available for sale. Also, I really hope you will take time to leave a review. They are a huge help for me. In case you are new to Nath Dragon and his adventures, this is a prequel series, hence, his very first adventures. If you want to jump forward and read about his escapades when he was 200 years old, I'll leave information for you below.

Do me a favor and join my newsletter. I'll send you FOUR FREE BOOKS. I run all kinds of specials all of the time too! Also, I love to hear from you. You can find me at these websites too. That would be great!

Bookbub – Craig Halloran
Facebook – The Darkslayer Report by Craig
Twitter – Craig Halloran
www.craighalloran.com

OTHER BOOKS AND AUTHOR INFO

Craig Halloran resides with his family outside his hometown of Charleston, West Virginia. When he isn't entertaining mankind, he is seeking adventure, working out, or watching sports. To learn more about him, go to: www.CRAIGHALLORAN.com.

Check out all of my great stories …

Clash Of Heroes
Nath Dragon Meets The Darkslayer

THE CHRONICLES OF DRAGON SERIES 1
The Hero, the Sword and the Dragons (Book 1)
Dragon Bones and Tombstones (Book 2)
Terror at the Temple (Book 3)
Clutch of the Cleric (Book 4)
Hunt for the Hero (Book 5)
Siege at the Settlements (Book 6)
Strife in the Sky (Book 7)
Fight and the Fury (Book 8)

War in the Winds (Book 9)

Finale (Book 10)

Slaughter in the Streets (Book 8)

Hunt of the Beat (Book 9)

The Battle for Bone (Book 10)

THE SUPERNATURAL BOUNTY HUNTER FILES

Smoke Rising (2015)

I Smell Smoke (2015)

Where There's Smoke (2015)

Smoke on the Water (2015)

Smoke and Mirrors (2015)

Up in Smoke

Smoke Signals

Holy Smoke

Smoke Happens

Smoke Out

THE DOMINION SERIES

THE GAMMA EARTH CYCLE

Escape from the Dominion

Flight from the Dominion

Prison of the Dominion

ZOMBIE IMPACT SERIES

Zombie Day Care: Book 1

Zombie Rehab: Book 2

Zombie Warfare: Book 3

The Savage and the Sorcerer Series

The Scarab's Curse

The Scarab's Power

The Scarab's Command

You can learn more about the Darkslayer and
my other books' deals and specials at:
Facebook – The Darkslayer Report by Craig
Twitter – Craig Halloran
www.craighalloran.com

Made in the USA
Monee, IL
20 December 2019